Home is the Sailor

Home is the Sailor

Lee Rowan

Cheyenne Publishing
Camas, Washington
www.cheyennepublishing.com

ISBN: 978-0-9828267-0-6

Edited by Leslie H. Nicoll & P.T. Smith
Cover art by Alex Beecroft

An eBook version of this work is published by Bristlecone Pine Press (ISBN 978-1-60722-022-0) www.bcpinepress.com

Published by Cheyenne Publishing
Camas, Washington
Mailing Address:
    P. O. Box 872412 Vancouver, WA 98687-2412
Website: www.cheyennepublishing.com

Other titles from Cheyenne Publishing

Frost Fair by Erastes
Speak Its Name: A Trilogy by various
Hidden Conflict: Tales from Lost Voices in Battle by various
Normal Miguel by Erik Orrantia
L. A. Mischief by P.A. Brown
Prove a Villain by K.C. Warwick
A Dangerous Man by Anne Brooke
The Glass Minstrel by Hayden Thorne
The Filly by Mark R. Probst

and by Lee Rowan:
The Royal Navy Series Book 1: Ransom
The Royal Navy Series Book 2: Winds of Change
The Royal Navy Series Book 3: Eye of the Storm
Walking Wounded
Sail Away

Dedication

To PS: As always, forever

Acknowledgments

Thanks to Ann, Marnie, and JD for Brit-picking,
Marian for cheering-on,
& Dr. S. Watson for medical review!

Chapter 1

No one saw it coming. The only warning of attack was the shrill whistle of a cannonball, a second before the schooner *Mermaid* shuddered under its impact. Splinters flew from the starboard bow as a puff of smoke on a high bluff they were passing betrayed the attacker's position.

"Hard a-port!" shouted the *Mermaid's* captain, William Marshall, running back to take the wheel from his bosun, Barrow. "All hands!"

"Aye, sir!"

"All hands" was a pitiful fighting force; the *Mermaid* was a private vessel, and had only four small guns—swivel guns, at that. They could not defend themselves against a land-based cannon, and in fact they had nothing aboard that could reach their attackers. But his men—twenty of them, barely enough to work the vessel while their mates sprang to the guns—responded as though they were still on the frigate where he'd first commanded them as a midshipman—his crew, men with whom he'd survived five years of war.

Marshall had not expected anything like this. They'd been sailing on a quick and supposedly routine mission to pick up an agent of His Majesty's secret service from the coast of Spain, and the rendezvous had been uneventful. A lone fisherman in a rowboat had caught no one's attention, and had been brought aboard with no fuss. All had seemed well—until now.

Marshall pulled the wheel with all his strength, dragging the *Mermaid* as close to the cold, powerful wind as he dared, ticking off the seconds in his mind. He held the schooner on the new course, fighting the wheel, watching over his shoulder until he saw the puff of smoke that signaled the next shot fired.

He let the wheel run through his hands, freeing the rudder to bring her sharply about, bracing himself as the sloop wheeled over and her sails filled once again. The second cannonball splashed harmlessly a few yards off the port bow. He brought her back into a steady run, still counting off the seconds. The trick had worked—but it would not work a second time.

It wouldn't have to, though. By the time the crew could reload, the swift-running *Mermaid* would be out of range. If he could get beyond the fishing vessel that lay between them and the open sea, a weathered schooner not much larger than the *Mermaid* herself, they'd be too poor a target to even attempt. "Damage?" he called to Barrow.

"Rail's clean off, sir, and we took on some water when she went over, but she's got at least a foot clear of the waterline for now."

"Will we need to fother—Damn!"

The apparently harmless craft, which they had passed on their way into shore, was now bristling with guns; passing close to it would be too risky. As the *Mermaid* came into small-arms range, the enemy began to fire.

At least this was a target their little guns could reach. "Fire as you bear," Marshall shouted.

He could have sworn he heard a similar order from the other ship, and the pop-pop of the small arms was punctuated by the boom of an undersized cannon, most likely a swivel gun like their own. One lucky shot was all either of them would require, and the fight would be over. On his present course, he would be past them in only a few minutes. But with the wind as it was, he could not veer too far away, without risking that damaged section of bow. If the *Mermaid* dipped enough that the hole in her bow scooped up water, not only would she be impossible to steer, they might well founder, and if any of his men went into this cold January sea...

He put that fear out of his mind, concentrating instead on holding her steady in the strong current, hearing a yelp as one of his men at the starboard gun caught a flying projectile. His gun crews were at work, though, even with their pitiful popguns, and he grinned as the enemy snipers ducked down below their own railing. Just like old times. A pity they weren't actually supposed to engage the enemy...

Then, amid the uproar of conflict, he caught a glimpse of a familiar figure running about in the smoke and flying lead, and his heart stopped within him. "Davy, to me!"

David Archer ran up, carrying a rifle. "Thought we'd need this. Orders?"

Marshall's hands stayed steady on the wheel, but his mind was gibbering, flooded with memories of Davy lying near death, struck down during the last battle they'd fought together, carried below with blood staining his white uniform waistcoat. His throat was so tight he could hardly speak. "Get below."

Davy frowned. "Sorry, what?"

A spent bullet ricocheted off the binnacle, and Marshall's whole body jerked in reaction. *"Get below. Now,* Davy. Go! I can't—"

Davy glanced about the deck, bit his lip, and nodded. As he disappeared down the stair to the captain's cabin, Marshall's attention returned to the matter at hand. The fishing boat—Frenchman, Spaniard, it made no difference, really, that neutral Portuguese flag they flew was a joke—was coming about, making ready to pursue them.

"Aim for her sails!" he shouted. But the words were barely out when he felt a ball slam into their own hull, and the wheel shuddered in his hands. The *Mermaid* kept moving, though, gallant little craft that she was. He prayed the damage was above the waterline, that it was something they could repair, and then they shot past the other boat and were out into open water.

He whirled at the sound of a shot just behind him, so close his ears rang. Davy stood there, his face grim. "You didn't see the sniper in their chains, did you? He had you dead in his sights."

Their stern-chaser boomed as if in emphasis, and the fishing boat faltered as the ball went home, carrying away their bowsprit and staysail.

"Thank you," Marshall managed. They were out of range now, and so long as they could keep moving, they would have their passenger back to the *Endymion* within a few hours, and make at least part of the trip back to England under her protection. Though why anyone would bother to attack them, and under a neutral flag, was the real question. He could think of only one possible answer, and he didn't like it at all, but he had no time to spare for speculation now.

"Take the wheel," he told Davy, and hurried over to see about the damage to his ship and crew. The puzzle of why they had been attacked was secondary to another, far more critical matter. In the midst of a battle, he had been completely distracted from the matter at hand—life and death, his ship and all who sailed aboard her. That was unconscionable.

Marshall had suspected that this would happen, when the treaty was broken and war resumed. He had feared it would happen; worse than that, he had known it would. And it left him with an insoluble dilemma.

William Marshall was a Commander in His Majesty's Navy. He was also, against all laws of God and man, David Archer's lover. As his own behavior had just proven beyond all doubt, he cared more for Davy than for any living soul or even for the ship under his command.

With Davy aboard, Marshall could not command a ship of war. And he knew how to do nothing else.

He did know enough to stand back and let Barrow direct the immediate repairs, and to wait until his bosun stepped back with a nod of approval to ask whether the damage could be mended.

"Aye, we can fix her, sir, well enough for a few days, but we haven't materials enough to do a proper job. Another close call like that, or a bad storm, and we might lose her."

He had to believe Barrow. The son of a carpenter himself, Barrow had gone to sea as a carpenter's mate and eventually wound up as bosun aboard the *Valiant,* a two-deck man o'war that was the last ship on which Marshall and Davy had served together. Barrow had forgotten more about the structure of sailing vessels than Marshall had ever learned; if he said the *Mermaid* was safe for now, that was a load off her captain's mind. The damage would slow their arrival at the rendezvous, but the weather looked to hold fair enough, and they had allowed time for such delays. They could not afford another close call. He would just have to hope that whoever had attacked them had expected to succeed, and not made plans for a second attempt.

Two of his men were wounded, as well—neither fatally, though he'd lose both the Owen twins if Joey Owen's broken arm required he be set ashore. They'd no other family, and Jules would not leave his brother in such a pinch. If the *Mermaid* were a frigate, with a full complement of crew, that would be no problem; Joey could be put on light duty until he healed. The other seaman, Thorne, had a nasty cut across his side, but the oaken splinter had not gone deep, thank God. Marshall wished he had a surgeon aboard, and was grateful that the *Endymion* was waiting for them.

Once the damage to ship and crew was seen to, Marshall's thoughts returned to his more serious concern. He was almost grateful for their passenger, who had been stowed in a hastily-slung hammock in the cabin that Marshall generally shared only with his lover. The man had appeared exhausted when he'd come aboard, and his presence in their sanctuary meant there was no place that would afford even a minimum of privacy, for conversation or anything else.

What are we going to do? He saw that question in Davy's eyes, too, when he returned to take the helm. "She's all right for now," he said. "We should rendezvous with *Endymion* by tomorrow evening, and beg help to fix ourselves up as best we can. Any sign of more trouble?"

"Clear as far as the eye can see," Davy replied, waving a hand at a horizon occupied by nothing save a few seagulls. "Do you have any idea what all that was about?"

"Our passenger must not have been as clever or careful as he thought he was." Will shrugged. "If this is peace, then give me a nice, simple war. At least when a Frenchman honors you with a broadside, there's no question of his motives."

His lover smiled wryly. "I suppose I ought to apologize for coming back up against your orders," he said. "But honestly, I cannot be sorry."

"I'd have done the same," Marshall said. "It's of no consequence."

Davy gave him a sharp look. "We both know it is," he said, "but there's nothing to be done about it now. I'll stay below if the situation arises again."

Marshall nodded. "It had better not," he said.

⚓ ⚓ ⚓

Their luck held good in making their rendezvous with *Endymion*, and Marshall's poor *Mermaid,* and her crew, were sufficiently patched up to make the trip back to Portsmouth. The frigate escorted them a good part of the way home, and while the weather displayed all the usual charm of the season—grey, cold, and damp—they were spared any dangerous storms.

David Archer was glad of it. His mind was still in a turmoil, as he knew Will's must also be, at the truth revealed to both of them in that brief skirmish in the Bay of Biscay. He had always thought Will was exaggerating his concern about their serving together—after all the battles they had been through, David had expected a return to the old habits of brothers-in-arms. But he had been mistaken. Will, once fearless in battle, seemed unable to detach himself from an anxious worry over his lover's safety. Whatever might happen once they reached land, David knew one thing was certain: he would be leaving the ship. Leaving Will.

The very thought made him feel hollow inside. Granted, there had never been a guarantee that they would stay together—or live very long if they did—but once Will had attained the rank of Commander, he would have the right to choose his own Ship's Master, and Archer was a qualified navigator. They *should* have been able to stay together, even though they might rarely have the chance to share their love in a physical way. At least they could be together...

No more.

The presence of their passenger was a trial. Mr. George (why could these cloak-and-dagger gentlemen not find less obvious pseudonyms?) kept mostly to himself, though during the meals he shared with Captain Marshall and Mr. St. John—David's *nom de* temporarily suspended *guerre*—he was quite willing to share information about those parts of Spain through which he had traveled. George was pleasant enough, in an undistinguished way that probably served him well in his occupation. His discourse was interesting and potentially useful, but Archer found himself not infrequently wishing Mr. George to the devil. These last few precious days together, and their tiny refuge was crowded by that third hammock, slung between them like the cocoon of some invasive moth.

They stole a few kisses when George was on deck and they chanced to be in their cabin together. That was all they dared attempt. But they did not talk about the decision looming in their future, or much of anything else.

When at last Portsmouth came into view on the horizon, Archer felt able to breathe again. Since their roles of yacht-owner and hired captain were not official Royal Navy ranks, Will was not required to sleep aboard. They would be able to get a room somewhere together, if only for a night. And, like as not, spend it trying to decide how to explain to Sir Percy, the man who had recruited them into England's secret service and who gave them their assignments, why it was that one of them, at least, would have to resign.

One of us...me, of course. It has to be.

As he had told Will months ago, David Archer felt no regret at the idea of leaving the Navy. The choice had been forced on him by circumstances; he had not yet attained his majority when his father had decided to buy him a commission in his brother's regiment, and he'd had no other way to support himself. At the time, the Navy had seemed his only alternative, very much the lesser of two evils.

He knew that Will felt otherwise. Small wonder; Will was an orphan, with no family in England—no family at all, really. He had some cousins off in America, but the war of rebellion had apparently strained those family ties to the breaking point before Will was even born. The only connections he had ashore were intimately related to the service. For all practical purposes, the Royal Navy was Will's family as well as his career.

David himself had family in abundance. With two elder brothers and four sisters, plus a growing number of nieces and nephews, he could hardly call himself solitary. And yet...apart from his mother and his sister Amelia, the only person who really mattered to him was Will. They had come so close to being parted last year, when Will's fear and guilt had driven him away. Had Will been right? Was he only drawing out the inevitable ending?

The wind was blowing them inexorably home. Ships moored in Portsmouth Harbor were visible now, the buildings on shore growing larger, the antlike creatures scurrying about becoming visibly human as the *Mermaid* drew near. The signal crew was sending up flags, firing a salute...All the usual rituals of coming into port at the conclusion of a successful cruise were drained of meaning by his apprehension. He had never known so bleak a homecoming.

The hope of some time alone with Will was dashed as soon as they set foot on shore, where a messenger met them with a courteous but mandatory invitation to meet Sir Percy at the earliest possible moment.

⚓ ⚓ ⚓

It was a pity, it really was. If only the old fellow had not made the fatal mistake of being the firstborn son, this would not have been necessary. He could have played the squire dawn till dusk, and tended to all the tedious chores about the place. But the poor devil had been born first, so there was nothing to do but clear him out of the way.

And it was so simple, easier than he'd expected. That Frog Lepage knew what he was about when he designed the silex carbine. Beautifully accurate, a gentleman's weapon. Merci, monsieur, and thanks to the luck of the battlefield in turning up such a prize. Now to trust to luck once more, and finish the job...

Chapter 2

"You gentlemen have made some enemies in high places," Sir Percy said, once the landlord had shown the three of them to a private dining room and closed the door behind him. "Careless of you!"

He said it as though they'd tracked mud onto someone's Aubusson, but Will knew that the frivolity was just a cover for a razor-sharp mind. "It was not as though we had much choice," he replied. "The Beauchenes might have been arrested for treason if we had not brought them out of France with us."

Sir Percy flipped open an elegant enameled snuffbox and offered it to his guests; both declined. After going through the sniff-and-sneeze ritual, he said, "Since Madame B means to marry one of our agents—*retired* agents, I should say—she would have had to depart in any case. And with his eyesight so poor, her son could hardly stay on alone. But you brought out a plum in his research. Of course that's what has brought you such ill repute in Boney's circles, and apparently even earned a price on your heads."

"Are the Beauchenes safe, sir?" Will asked. He had inadvertently entangled the French civilians, mother and son, when he had gone ashore in France to meet what he had believed to be another innocent civilian, Davy's uncle by marriage. But just as Étienne Beauchene had proven to be more than a nearsighted gentleman with a hobby of mathematics, Dr. Colbert had turned out to be far more than a strayed tourist, and they'd all had a narrow escape from Bonaparte's secret police.

"As safe as we can make them," Sir Percy assured him. "Monsieur Beauchene has declined to work for the British government against his own country, but we have offered him asylum as a way of preventing him from working *for* them. The Colbert home is under guard as well, so if Bonaparte's agents investigate, it will appear that Beauchene is a very highly regarded prisoner."

At this point two servants came in bearing their dinner, and they changed the topic of conversation to inconsequential matters until they were left alone once more with no other company than a decanter of brandy.

"What do you have in mind for us to do now, sir?" Davy asked. "It's clear the *Mermaid* will need repair, but what then?"

"She needs more than repair," Sir Percy said. "She's going to have her rigging altered and her topsail removed. At present there aren't more than half a dozen of those topsail schooners anywhere, and you can hardly undertake secret missions in a vessel that any landlubber could identify. As for the two of you—there ain't a French agent anywhere this side of the Atlantic who would be fooled by your cover story."

Will hated to ask. He'd only had command for about two months. On the other hand, he was not quite ready to say goodbye to Davy, either, and did not believe he ever would be. "Are we to be set ashore, then?"

"Not precisely. Your cover will be overhauled as well, and I've no notion what your new identities may be, assuming you're not called back to duty. But while the Admiralty would spend your lives without a qualm, they have no reason to waste them, and Those Above have decided that you should play least-in-sight for a month or two and let our enemy squander their time looking for you. You'll stay in Portsmouth tonight, certainly. But in the morning…the sooner you disappear, the better. It would be best if you could take your holiday away from Portsmouth. Do you not have family who would welcome a visit?"

"I'm sorry," said Will. "There's no one."

"Of course we do," said Davy. "Captain Marshall is welcome at my home, at any time—on my mother's orders. But we'd have been better off putting in at Plymouth, as the family seat's in Devon."

Sir Percy's brows drew together. "That should not be a problem. I took the liberty of holding a room for you here, and had your sea-chests brought from the *Mermaid*. I believe I'll be able to arrange something in the way of transportation for you, come morning, and muddle your trail a bit in the process. Is there any other business here that requires your attention?"

Will glanced at Davy, who shook his head. "No, sir. Except to see to our crew. We had two men wounded."

"I've sent a doctor to take care of them. The rest of your crew will be given a month's wages, and I shall keep an eye on your bosun in case we need to find reliable men in a hurry. Is that satisfactory, Captain?"

Will breathed easier at the lifting of a load he had not realized he was carrying. "Better than I could have done myself, sir. Thank you."

"That's enough of business, then. Let us enjoy this brandy!" Sir Percy passed around the bottle with a smile. "I brought it over myself, but please do not ask me *precisely* how I got it out of France!"

⚓ ⚓ ⚓

The door was shut, bolted, and locked, a coat hung on the knob to block the keyhole. Even in his distracted state, Will observed the precautions necessary to protect them from the laws of the land they risked their lives for—laws that would see them hanged for loving one another.

That done, he met Davy's eyes and, without a word, took him in his arms, gratefully breathing in the scent of his hair, allowing the weight of command to slip from his shoulders. For a little while they simply held one another, the sound of their breathing lost in the crackle of the fire and the wind nagging outside the shutters.

What are we going to do? Neither said it. There was no need, and he was glad of it, for he had no answers.

The warmth of Davy's body against his gradually thawed Marshall's frozen soul, and life—sensation—began to return. Then, suddenly, like an ice-pack breaking on a frozen river, desire surged through him. His hands slipped down to Davy's arse, and his lover's hands on his own body mirrored his action. Their first real kiss in uncounted days left him breathless and hungry for more.

Davy pulled back a bit and started to loosen his neckcloth. "Let me," Will said. With clumsy fingers he undid the knot and nuzzled Davy's neck, savoring the scent that was uniquely Davy's own.

Davy sighed and let his head drop back. "You're growing bolder, sir." He tugged at the laces at the back of Will's breeches. "Shall we dispense with these?"

Touching, kissing, never quite letting go of each other, they managed to shed their clothing and leave it draped over the chair beside the table near the window.

They didn't often have a room to themselves; he didn't often get the chance to just look at Davy. Will held him at arms' length and took advantage of the opportunity. He'd never get used to the short-cropped hair, even though Davy had assured him it was the fashion now. But that didn't matter. Here he was, still a little too thin but golden and beautiful and his own dear love.

But for how much longer?

The fear made him desperate. He stepped back to the bed, pulling Davy down on top of him, his own body aching with desire. Davy responded eagerly, as he always did, and before very long Will was able to silence all the questions in his mind with the simple certainty of passion. They rocked together, their sweat and the pressure of skin on skin supplying all that was necessary. At some point Davy rolled onto his back and Will drove against him, feeling his lover rise to meet him. Honor, duty...what did any of it mean without this?

Davy gasped and dug his fingers into Will's arse, and the warm surge of his release triggered Will's own. He relaxed afterward, in the warm afterglow, rolling to one side so Davy would be able to move.

"Lovely," Davy said. "Here, let me tidy us up." He slid out of bed and Will, his eyes still closed, heard water pour into the washbasin.

"It's cold," Davy warned, before wiping off Will's belly. And it was, too, but no more than he expected. Another precaution; they made it a habit to leave no evidence of their lovemaking. "Here's your nightshirt."

Will groaned and sat up, pulling the unwanted garment on before he flopped back down on the mattress. "Are you certain your family won't be put out?" he asked, dog-tired and ready for sleep.

"Certain sure. It's a big house. There's room for you. Move over."

He did, unconvinced. "Davy—"

"No, Will, honestly. When we first went aboard the *Mermaid,* I wrote my mother that I was back in England but might not have time to visit. When she wrote back—remember the hamper of food she sent for Christmas?—she said to come straight home if I got the chance, and bring you with me if I could. She'll be thrilled, and so will my sisters."

That sounded ominous, but Will could not keep his eyes open a moment longer. He curled himself against Davy's warm back and took advantage of oblivion.

⚓ ⚓ ⚓

They spent most of the next two days aboard a small private vessel belonging to one of Sir Percy's friends. Its owner was not aboard, but the first mate, Abernathy, made them welcome and gave them the liberty of the captain's cabin, where their dunnage had been placed below the stern windows. "Be best if you stay belowdecks, I'm told," Abernathy said cryptically, "even at night."

"Very well," Will said, "but if we're to spend all our time

here, might we have a couple of hammocks? That berth seems a bit small for the two of us."

The first mate chuckled. "Yes, sir, we'll have 'em brought in right away. A bit small—indeed it is!"

He left, still full of mirth, and David scowled. "It *is* too small, more's the pity. I'd hoped for a bit of luck in that direction."

"No, hammocks are better," Will said. "Why tempt fate? Anyone might walk in at any time."

"It wasn't fate I was hoping to tempt, but I suppose you're right." He sat on his sea-chest, as the ship's movement and the faint sounds from the deck above told them they were getting under way. "Will, what do you propose to tell Sir Percy about our plans, once the *Mermaid* is seaworthy? If I'm to stay ashore I must resign, and I'd rather have some excuse other than having developed a sudden aversion to gunfire."

"There's no guarantee I'll get command of her when she is repaired," Will said. "And in any case, I think we'd better not discuss that here, either, with no hope of privacy—"

His point was demonstrated by a sailor bringing in the requested hammocks and hanging them on beams near the stern, one on either side of the cabin.

"That's all very well," David said, after the sailor had departed. "How do you propose we spend our time, then? I have a book or two, of course, but that doesn't do you much good."

Will looked around the cabin—pleasant enough, but no more than ten feet square—and smiled apologetically. "Sir Percy did say there were cards and a chess set in the drawer under the Captain's berth."

⚓ ⚓ ⚓

Their destination was Teignmouth; Abernathy brought them ashore, guided them to an inn, and gave them directions to the nearest livery stable, where they could hire transportation in the morning—before dawn, he advised.

And in all that time, Will uttered not one word about what was on both their minds. David had tried to bring it up once or twice, in the late watches when most of the ship was asleep, but Will only repeated his objections on the grounds of privacy. He did not want to risk doing anything else, either, which was prudent, if frustrating. Their lives were put in abeyance by circumstances beyond their control.

And those circumstances weren't likely to improve in the near future. If a well-connected spymaster like Sir Percy indicated that one was walking around with a target painted on one's back, only a fool would argue against evasive action. But if Will thought they were short of privacy here, he had no idea how restricted they would be at Grenbrook, with family everywhere and servants who might turn up around any corner.

What a relief that once they were in the small, sparsely-furnished room at the inn, Will's apparent indifference vanished. After securing the door, Will began pulling his clothing off and made fierce, tender love to David, in almost total silence. He responded with enthusiasm, but the intensity worried him a little. Will had been like that back in Jamaica last year, the night before he'd said a goodbye that they'd both feared would be forever. He had become more withdrawn, more private, even in intimacy, and David was uneasy about what that might mean.

⚓ ⚓ ⚓

They were up early the next morning, and Marshall was eager to get on the road as soon as possible. Sir Percy had provided them with traveling expenses, sufficient funds to hire a post-chaise that would carry them directly to their destination. Grenbrook was somewhere north of Plymouth, in the general direction of Tavistock. Davy gave the post-boys very specific directions, but Marshall was as imprecise about directions on land as he was clear about nautical navigation. Davy knew where they were going, and that was sufficient. Marshall felt adrift, without ship or purpose, and he was content to let his lover take command.

But locked in a chaise, without another soul around to hear them, he could not avoid Davy's questions—questions for which he had no answers. Not that Davy expected him to solve everything; that almost made it worse. Marshall felt that, since it was his failure of nerve that created their problem, he ought to have a solution, especially if he could not reconcile himself to the one his lover advocated.

Sitting opposite him in the chaise, Davy persisted. "It seems reasonable to me, Will. Much as I love my family—some of them, anyway—my father and I do not get on comfortably. I've money enough to live quietly in London, and even a place to live—the house my grandmother left me. It's rented now, but there if I should need it. And if the Peace holds, so much the better—we could both live there, or use that rent to hire ourselves a snug little cottage nearer the sea."

"It will never hold."

Davy sighed patiently. "Then you will have to choose. If you go back to sea, I shall live alone, and haunt Portsmouth when your ship is expected back. I own it will be strange to know you are out there somewhere, in mortal danger, without me around to keep you out of trouble. I had hoped—" He caught himself, and there was an apology in his smile. "I should have believed you, Will. You did warn me."

Will almost wished Davy would rail at him for his cowardice. "I am sorrier than I possibly express," he said finally. "I know I should be more resolute. God knows we've seen enough carnage that I ought to be inured to it." He turned away to watch the landscape rolling by outside the coach window. "I fear I've lost my nerve."

"Oh, Will." Davy shifted over to sit beside him, and took his hand. "I watched you. You were having a fine time, until I showed up. And truly, if I had seen you as thoroughly perforated as I was, I know I would feel the same. I do, in fact. The thought of you sailing off alone does not please me." He reached over to close the shade at Will's window and leaned in for a kiss as he did.

Will gave it gladly. They'd have no chance for this at Grenbrook. "Do you think we have time for..?"

"Oh, yes. Hours. I like closed coaches," Davy said, his lips brushing against Will's while his fingers unbuttoned Will's waistcoat. "Remember the first one?"

"How could I forget? You seduced me!" They had become lovers while they were prisoners aboard a renegade's ship; after their escape, they had attempted to go back to the warm but chaste friendship that they'd had for many years before that. Two days on the road, alone in a hired coach, had been more than their good intentions could withstand.

"*I?* Will, you're a terrible liar. I remember quite clearly, it was you who closed the curtains."

With a quick thrill of anticipation, Will did the same on the side that was still open. "Only because I knew you were about to do something rash," he said. "But we are older and calmer now, are we not?"

"Indeed." Even in the dimness, the mischief sparkled in Davy's blue eyes. "I would never be so bold as I was then. I might muss my uniform." He picked up one of the carriage blankets thoughtfully provided by the liveryman, for a fee, and placed it solemnly upon the floor. "There. My knees are safe. And now, Captain Marshall..." He knelt upon the blanket and surrendered to Will's embrace.

Three years of loving David Archer had done nothing to damp the fire Will felt every time their bodies came together. That first time had been in late summer, this was in late winter; it made no difference. If anything, the lightning rushing through him was more intense because he knew the ecstasy that lay in store. Davy's hands were on his back as their lips met, but they moved, down to the small of his back, sliding him forward on the seat so his cock pressed against Davy's belly through the layers of their clothing. He arched forward at the contact, and Davy pulled back, laughing in the gloom. "Shall I seduce you again, Captain?" He brought his hands around beneath Will's arms, thumbs brushing against his nipples.

"I—*oh!*—I don't see how I can prevent you."

"I'm very pleased to hear it." Davy mouthed the tingling nubs through Will's shirt as he unbuttoned his commander's breeches. By the time he'd worked his cock free of the underclothes, Will was beyond rational thought. His fingers tangled in Davy's hair as he let the rocking of the coach move him with the rhythm of his lover's mouth. He gave up trying to think and simply let himself feel. The heat of Davy's mouth, the cool rush of air, the building urgency—

He gasped as his body reached its release. Limp and satiated, he could do little more than shift to one side and pull Davy up to sit beside him. "Give me a moment," he begged.

"Certainly." Davy rested his head against Will's. "I wish there were some way we could be more...athletic," he said. "I'd love to feel you inside me. But I fear it's not possible."

"Certainly *not,*" Will said. "We'd tip the coach over. Besides, you've wrung me out." But he was beginning to recover himself, and a quick caress showed that Davy was more than ready for action himself. Will tugged his lover's shirt up out of his breeches, and slid his hands up under Davy's clothing, stroking his flat, warm belly with the left while he attacked the fly buttons with the right. "We might have tried if you hadn't been so hasty."

"No." Davy leaned against Will's chest, his head tilted back in pleasure. "Wouldn't dare. My uniform...We've only one quick stop to change horses before we—*Will!*" Will's hand closed around him, and he twisted around to meet Will's lips with his own. The conversation evaporated; Davy's state of excitement required very little encouragement, and when Will reached one hand around to slide a finger inside at a critical moment, he lost composure altogether. Things might have been quite raucous if he had shouted into the air instead of Will's mouth.

"Thank God for road noise," he said fervently, when his quivering stopped. Will wondered how he managed to put two thoughts together under the circumstances, but Davy had always been better with words. They were becoming disgracefully adept at dalliance in a coach. The circumstances were ideal: curtains that could be closed, a gentle rocking motion ideally suited for close contact...not as comfortable as a room, perhaps, but in its own way even better. The post-boy was riding the lead horse; they ran absolutely no risk of being disturbed without warning.

Will tried to ignore the small voice in the back of his mind that warned this might have been their last opportunity, and brought up something that had been nagging at him since Davy blithely announced their destination. "Before we get to your home, Davy, would you please do me one favor?"

Busy tidying himself with his handkerchief, Davy grinned. "Good heavens, Will, after all that? You must be indefatigable!"

"Not that!" he said, blushing despite himself. "It's your family. There are so many of them. I've met your mother, and your sister—Mary, was it? And I know your sister Amelia writes to you sometimes. Could you remind me once more of the rest of their names?"

"Of course, Will. I'm sorry, there's quite a crowd of Archers, isn't there? I have two brothers and four sisters: Mark, the eldest brother, is my father's heir. Then there's Mary, Ronald, Anne, Amelia, myself, and Genie. Amelia and Genie are still at home. Mark and his wife Virginia also live at Grenbrook with their three daughters when they are not in town, but the girls often spend the Christmas season with Virginia's mother. If we're lucky, she may keep them till Spring—they prefer the city in winter, and their Grandmama is very fond of them. Any of the others may be there, with or without their spouses—the last I heard, Anne's husband was away in the Army. And I believe we have a cousin staying at the place, and of course there are all manner of servants. I shall write up a list of *dramatis personae* when I can get hold of a pen and paper."

He was joking, of course, but Will was not when he said, "I may need it."

Chapter 3

"Good Lord." The words were spoken in reverence, not as an oath, when the post-chaise left the road and entered the tree-lined drive to Grenbrook Manor, which wound through a grove of young oaks, their bare branches making patterns against the sky. The house, dignified without being extravagant, lay some half a mile away, though the curving drive extended the distance. "Davy, when you said your family had a 'biggish country house' I thought you actually meant a fair-sized country house, not a half-grown castle. They won't be expecting you to bring home strays, I'm sure. You'd best have the driver let me off at the servants' entrance."

David chuckled as Will nervously adjusted the single epaulet that identified him as a Commander in His Majesty's Navy. The old place did look impressive, especially when the bare trees let it be seen from such a distance. Only the newer part of the house was visible from here, the stern brick walls brightened by evergreen shrubbery. He wished he might have brought Will to see it in the spring. "If you go in the servants' entrance, I'll have to, as well. Bear up, Will, once you've passed inspection we should be given at least some time to ourselves. I have always been so far down the chain of command in this place, I ought to salute the butler."

"Yes, but you're an Archer, a son of the house. You belong here. I'm—"

"I've told you this before, sir! You are an officer of His Majesty's Navy, you are in command of your own ship—or at least you were until a few days ago, and you still hold that rank, regardless—and you are my commanding officer. You are also my dearest friend, and if it weren't for you I wouldn't be here myself." Will still looked so serious he could not resist teasing, "By now Father must be desperate to find a husband for Amelia, and Genie's old enough to be considering the question, too."

Will's black eyebrows flew up in alarm. "Davy!"

"Gently, Will, gently. You're safe enough." He squeezed his lover's hand. "I wouldn't let Genie have you, even if she weren't far too young. She would drive you mad straight-away, and you would make her miserable. And from all I can determine, Amelia means to be a bluestocking spinster. She cares more for her books than any living man, though if you were in the market she might actually consider you, on my recommendation."

Will did not look consoled. "But your father—would he actually expect me to…?"

"Oh, good Lord, of course not! I'm sure he would be delighted if you took a fancy to each other, but you've not even met her yet, and I do have a certain prior claim!"

"Yes, but that's hardly something you could tell your family."

"I'm afraid not. Wouldn't if I could—it would make all my sisters jealous." Truth be known, if David were to compare his friend to his two brothers-in-law, the gentlemen married to his elder sisters would suffer by the comparison. "Even if we did not have ..." he stroked Will's palm with his thumb, "our own arrangement, you have done me service enough by coming with me into the lions' den."

Will gave him an odd look. "Is it so difficult to live in this grand style?"

David realized how foolish he must have sounded, and smiled apologetically. "It's not the place, as such. I love it, if you want to know the truth. And I can't deny its superiority to a midshipman's berth...But that's not what I meant, Will. It's not the place so much as the people—or, rather, my own place among them, as a disappointment of a youngest son."

"Disappointment?" Will snorted. "I'll not speak ill of your father, but if he is disappointed in you, his expectations must have been preposterous."

"They were stringent, at any rate. But I believe the new uniform will improve my standing." David looked down at his own extremely elegant Lieutenant's dress uniform, which he had barely had occasion to wear since he'd picked it up at a Portsmouth tailor's shop over a year ago. "It's been almost four years since I've been home, and I was only a midshipman then. The novelty ought to give me a bit of credit."

"If the prospect is so unpleasant, Davy, why on earth did you wish to come here? I'd have gone anywhere else with you, and gladly."

"Oh, you mustn't take my complaints too seriously." He wasn't entirely sure of his own reasons, though traveling elsewhere with Will did sound agreeable. "I thought Sir Percy's suggestion had the sound of an order about it, didn't you? Where else were we to go?"

"We'd have thought of something." Will hesitated. "But—surely your family will be glad to see you, and have you home for a little while? Especially after they came so close to losing you!"

David sometimes envied Will his freedom from the weight of family expectations. "Most of them will, yes. I do want to see my mother again, and my sisters." It would be good to be reunited with at least some of the family, especially after that time when he thought he might never see any of them again. "And my eldest brother."

Will nodded. "Will your other brother be here as well?"

"Ronald? I hope not. But I truly don't know. Amelia said he had planned to be home for Christmas, but for some reason could not get leave. With the Peace, I'd have expected his regiment to return to England. Or it may not have been brought home; I've no idea where he was last stationed."

With a slight frown, Will said, "Are you certain there'll be room for me?"

"Yes, of course. This is nothing unusual, really; the family often gathers here at Christmastime. If Anne's husband in still in India, she may well have come with the intention of staying until spring." He smiled once more at the look of worry on his lover's face. "Look at the bright side, Will. The house itself is bigger than a dreadnought, the entire crew is much smaller, and we can always go out for a stroll if the togetherness is more than we can bear."

"I'm sorry," Will said. "Of course you should visit your family—how often do you get the chance? And I do appreciate the hospitality. It has simply been so long since I've been ashore, in civilian company—what shall I do, with no one to salute?"

"Oh, if that's your only worry, rest assured. You'll know who's in command. My father is quite masterful." Although, he remembered, Mark was beginning to take the reins. It would be interesting to see how smoothly the Earl and his heir were dealing with the transfer of power; his father was proud of Mark, and getting on in years. It was none too soon to pass the torch. But would he be able, in fact, to relinquish his control over every last detail?

David bit his lip as the carriage swept around the last curve to slow before the pillared entryway. It felt as though returning to the family home was moving him back through time, turning him once again into the youngest brother, the least among them, always cautious, guarding his words.

No. He would not go back to that old role. Whatever the family might expect, he had outgrown it. He had a modest inheritance, the prize-money he'd won, the house in London. He was a man grown, in control of his own life. His father would simply have to accept that fact.

As the coach drew up under the porte-cochère, he acknowledged to himself where his true loyalties lay. "Will, I know I've spoken of him before, and it is vile of me to cast aspersions on my own flesh and blood—but if Ronald should be here, you must always be on your guard around him."

Will shot him a curious look, but said nothing. They had

been through enough together that Will knew he would not say such a thing without cause, and the few times he had mentioned Brother Ronald before, he'd never had anything good to say of him.

Then Will looked at the house, and caught his breath. "Davy, over the door…"

David looked, and felt his heart constrict at the sight of the black bunting. Mourning. A death in the family?

"I'm sorry," Will said quickly. "Do you have any idea who—?"

"None. But my father's not young." The Earl—strange, to think of one's father only by his title—was sixty-eight now, his wife seven years younger. "They were all in good health, the last I heard. Mark is nearing forty, and is almost never ill. But no, if it were Father there would be hatchments up as well—his coat of arms. Oh, God, I hope it's not my mother!"

After many years of walking about on a moving deck, David didn't wait for the carriage to stop, or worry about a dignified exit. Will was a few steps behind, having given the post-boys instructions, and then the door opened and Leland's honest face gaped at him in amazement. "Master David—I'm sorry, sir, Lieutenant Archer—we had no word you were coming."

How had his hair grown so grizzled in only four years? David took off his cloak and handed it over. "It's all right, Leland, the leave was unexpected. I saw the mourning outside. My father—?"

"He is as well as might be. It was your brother, sir. Lord Mark."

Mark? He swallowed, for a moment unable to speak. "But— When? How?"

"The funeral was three days ago, sir. You had no letter?"

"The letter's probably on the water hoy doing Channel duty," Will said, just behind him. He looked slightly startled to have his overclothes taken out of his hands; Leland disappeared with them through a nearby door. "We weren't expected in port, after all. I am sorry, Davy."

David nodded. "Leland, how is my mother?" The butler, returning empty-handed, smiled sadly.

"I'm sure your presence will be a great comfort, sir. She is in her rooms, and may be asleep. Shall I show you upstairs?"

"No—no, I can still find my way about. Is my father in his study?"

"I believe he is out riding, sir. Three of your sisters are at home, however; I shall see they are informed them of your arrival."

"Thank you." Slightly relieved that he was not required to face his father immediately, David turned. "Well, Will, it seems we're left to our own devices. I believe I can still find my way around the place, unless you would like some refreshment first?"

"Whatever suits you. I'm glad enough to just stand and walk about for a bit."

"Let me show you the old place, then—starting with the necessary facilities."

The necessary attended to, he was unsure where to begin. After living on a ship-of-war, the halls of Grenbrook seemed much larger than he remembered, their footfalls echoing hollowly on the polished floors. Mark dead! Mark, big, bluff, hearty, almost a living model of an English landed gentleman. Their mother would be devastated, and the Earl...it had only been a year or two since his eldest son had retired from his Army career to come home and run the estate, after his father had finally admitted that his age and health left him unequal to the task.

Then it struck him. *Ronald is heir, now. Oh, holy Jesus.* The thought halted David in his tracks; he felt as if the ground was falling away beneath him.

"What is it?" Will asked.

He shook his head, unable to explain it in any coherent way. As he hesitated, he realized that two very small, identical toddlers were peeking around the morning-room door, studying the strangers in their handsome blue and white uniforms. "Girls, come back here!" a woman's voice said from beyond the doorway. Then another familiar face appeared behind the children, foreign-looking in her somber black gown. "Davy!" his sister exclaimed, rushing toward them.

"Amelia!"

"When did you arrive? We've had no word, how long will you stay, oh, it's so good to see you!"

He was enveloped in a hearty squeeze, saluted with a kiss on the cheek. "My sister Amelia," he explained hastily, at Will's broad grin.

"Your twin, I would guess," Will said.

"Not quite." Conscious of the ambiguity due a lady's age, he added, "There's a year and a bit between us. Amelia, this is my friend and shipmate, Commander William Marshall."

"I am honored to meet you, Lady Amelia," Will bowed slightly, on his best behavior. "My condolences on your loss." He glanced at David, then said, "I did not mean to intrude on your grief; if you wish, I can remove to an inn—"

"Oh, no." She took his hand. "It was good of you to come. My brother has written of you so often, I feel I'm meeting an old friend."

Will smiled, a bit nervously, and looked around as if seeking distraction. He nodded toward the toddlers. "And who are these lovely young ladies?"

"My sister Anne's daughters, Catherine and Marianne, and you need *not* address them as 'my lady.' They are almost three. Come here, my dears." She knelt and held her arms out; the little ones giggled and ran off." They are contrary little things," Lady Amelia said, rising. "Nurse has the patience of a saint. The only one they obey without question is Father."

"Small wonder," David said. "Why should they rank above the rest of us?"

"Oh, Davy." She took his arm as though she needed an anchor. "You cannot imagine the change in him. Mark's death was such a blow, I fear for his health, as well as Mama's. The doctor has given her a cordial with valerian, to help her sleep."

"And Father?"

"Out riding now. He always seems to be out of doors, and spends most of the daylight hours riding or walking. So much has changed for him now; all the work he and Mark were doing together...." She gave herself a brisk shake. "But you've only just arrived. Come, let us have tea and biscuits, at least. You must be famished after your journey!" She took them each by an arm and led them down the hall.

"Amelia, what happened? Leland told me nothing."

"An accident, apparently. He was out hunting, with only his dog. Alone, as usual. You know how he likes—liked—"

"To bring something fresh for the pot," David finished. He had not expected Mark would ever change his habits. "Because Cook loves to improvise."

"Just so. When he had not returned by noontide, Cook spoke to Leland, and he sent a boy out. They found him near the stream, at the bottom of the embankment, with his dog sitting at the top, waiting for him and whimpering."

"By the fishing pool?"

"Yes. It appeared he had been on the edge, lost his balance, and fell. His fowling piece discharged—they would only let Father see him, of course, but they said he had a terrible wound in his chest. According to the doctor, it was instantly fatal."

"A small mercy." He meant it, too; after spending days hovering between life and death himself when he'd been wounded the year before, it was a bit of comfort to know his brother had not suffered.

"David, what are we going to do? Ronald—"

"I don't know," he said, further unsettled by her anxiety. "There's not much we can do, is there? I suppose he's been sent for—has he arrived?"

"No, but he might, at any time. He will be insufferable."

Of that, David had no doubt. "I'm sure Father will keep him in line."

She shook her head slightly. "I hope so, if he is able. But he—you have not seen him."

David could not bring himself to believe what she was suggesting. "Is he truly so different, then?"

"Yes. It is ...I expected to see him grow old—that is, I knew he would—but I never imagined this. He has aged twenty years in the past week. I cannot bear to see him so diminished." She squeezed his arm, and he returned the pressure.

He had come home with the expectation of everything as it had always been—much of it not to his liking, but solid and established. Now, nothing was the same. It was strange and unsettling to have Amelia looking up to him. In his childhood, she had been just enough older to stand as his champion against their bullying elder brother. To have her seeking his aid gave David an inkling of how badly the situation in their home had altered. As the eldest daughter still living at home, he guessed Amelia had been required to shoulder the burden of their aging parents' sorrow as well as her own.

The children reappeared suddenly, tugging at Amelia's skirts, and the two newcomers were swallowed up in a cluster of female relations. David could see the confusion on his friend's face; Will was ill at ease around women at the best of times, never good at remembering names until he had become acquainted with their owners. This little deficiency mattered not at all aboard ship, with its seldom-altered masculine society. An officer who did remember his men's names was a cut above most, and Will could give the name, function, and sometimes even length of service for all the 300-plus men who'd lived aboard the frigate *Calypso* on which they'd both served. But he'd had years to learn, and this was a very different situation.

David made the introductions as briefly as possible. Anne—Mrs. Clive Gilliam—mother of the twins and second of the family's four daughters, and Eugenie, the youngest of his sisters, looked as though they might be mother and daughter, both fair-haired and poised, with wide-set blue eyes. Though David was fond of them both, he was ten years Anne's junior and eight Eugenie's senior; the gap meant that he'd never had a friendship with either of them like the one he shared with Amelia. The one brunette among the ladies was his cousin, Jane Winston, daughter of his mother's elder brother, who had come to live at Grenbrook a year or two previously. Though Amelia had mentioned family troubles, she had not gone into detail in her letters. Jane was pleasant-looking rather than beautiful, with dark brown eyes that seemed to see everything in depth. She was also very quiet, unlike the cheerful, ebullient girl David remembered from his childhood. Her hair was dressed neatly, and she wore a simple grey gown, appropriate garb for mourning a cousin. Jane seemed happy to see him, though, and put in a word now and then—when his sisters were quiet long enough to give her a chance.

Anne had been married the year Eugenie was born, and her Army-Major husband was, as David had thought, presently stationed in India. A skilled hostess, she engaged Will with the sort of polite interrogation that ladies used to draw gentlemen out. For Commander Marshall, bold in battle but shy in social settings, this was a very good thing.

David noted with mild amusement that little Genie, though he would not be so unkind as to call her that to her face, was studying Will as though he'd been ordered up for her approval. Amelia had mentioned in her last letter that Eugenie, still the baby of the family at fifteen, was chafing at her schoolgirl status. But Will was surely safe from her feminine wiles; Amelia said that Genie had set her cap at a title. Since she was still too young to be brought out at the next Season, she would have plenty of time to decide how she might achieve that goal.

As he sat there, with baby Catherine on his knee and Marianne similarly situated on Will's, David considered one

of the things he had missed most about his home—the won-
derful food. Tea piping hot and fresh-brewed, served with
real Devon cream, the fresh bread—"soft-tack" was how he
thought of it, now—the thin tangy slices of ham cured in
their own smoke-house instead of salt pork of indeterminate
age, laden with brine.

He had been so long at sea that he had lost the habit of
ordinary meals until he had been wounded the previous year.
The months of convalescence at his cousin's home in Jamaica had ruined his appreciation for shipboard rations, and
even that had not been the food that said, "home." Even as
his mind continued to worry, his body relaxed in the familiar
atmosphere.

But the ladies' conversation reminded him of those
things he did not miss. Without being asked, Anne and
Amelia provided an exhaustive catalog of the disposition of
the rest of the family. No doubt it was meant to serve as a
sort of social briefing for Will; it was thoughtful of them to
consider that. And David needed to know such details as
well—at least some of them.

Lady Virginia, Mark's new-made widow, had suffered a
collapse and was keeping to her rooms. Her three daughters
were indeed staying in London with their maternal grandmother. There was some explanation of being fitted for
mourning dress, but David had the uncharitable suspicion
that Patience, Prudence, and Verity—ill-named, he had always thought—had been as happy to stay with their Stafford
relations as the Archers had been to surrender them. The
young ladies had always been keenly aware that their father
had wanted a son and got them instead, and the knowledge
had somehow spoiled their temperaments. It was unkind to
think such things of fatherless girls, but David was relieved
to know that the visit would be free of his nieces' airs and
pouts.

"Will we see Mary and her family?" he asked, when both
his sisters paused for refreshment.

"Not unless you have time to pay her a visit in London,"

Anne said. "She's gone to be with her eldest, Susannah, who has just given birth to a son. You are a great-uncle now, as well as an officer!"

David fell back in the chair, as much as he could with the child perched on his knee. "Why do I suddenly feel so ancient?"

Anne smiled, and even the somber black of deep mourning could not dampen her genuine pleasure. "You should have seen Mama when she heard the news. She has always been so happy to be a grandmother, and now she would not change places with the Queen!"

"Don't breathe a word to Mama," Amelia added quickly, "but Father has arranged to have a miniature painted of the first great-grandchild—and a grandson, at that! It was before the accident, of course, but he knew it would be some time before Susannah and the child could travel. I hope the artist works quickly. Nothing can console Mama over losing Mark, but a new baby brings such hope." She touched her elder sister's hand. "I am so glad you brought your little ones, Anne."

"As am I," said Lady Anne. "Nurse is a treasure, but I'll be pleased to see them coming to know their family...and friends." She turned to Will, who was absently feeding Marianne bits of a currant scone as though she were some sort of featherless parrot. "Are you certain she's not a bother, Commander?"

"Not in the least," Will said gamely, wiping small sticky fingers with his clean handkerchief. "As long as she prefers the refreshments to my buttons. It's kind of you take in a wanderer this way. If not for your hospitality, I'd have been cooling my heels in Portsmouth for at least a month. Thank you so much!" Will gave one of his rare smiles, and David could see his sister melt.

"It is our pleasure, Captain. From all my brother has said, we've you to thank that he's still among the living!"

"I can say the same of him, a dozen times over," Will

said. He looked embarrassed. "It's not the sort of thing one tallies at the end of the day."

"Not the done thing at all," David said, trying for levity. "Even if one were petty enough to keep count, judging the value of one thing versus another would be tedious. Say Captain Marshall put a Frenchie to the sword just as he was aiming for my brisket, and I pulled him out of the way of a falling bit of yardarm, that's one potentially serious wound balanced by one potential concussion or possibly cracked skull.... No. It would be too silly to keep score."

"And after a few years, pointless." Will added.

"My mind refuses to admit the hazards you gentlemen face," Lady Anne said. "War is dangerous, of course, but to dwell on the details is more than I could endure. Although my husband writes to me of his successes, I know there must be much he never sees fit to share...and I am grateful for his discretion. I am content not to know too much."

"But it must be so exciting!" Lady Eugenie leaned forward, fluttering her lashes at Will. "Did that really happen—the Frogs, the falling yardarm?"

"Any number of times, my child." David received the expected glare for the endearment. "And eventually it ceases to be exciting and becomes just a part of the job. May His Majesty's Navy be preserved from midshipmen who sign aboard for the excitement!"

"Indeed," said Will. "Though it's best that they come aboard with enthusiasm, for they have much to learn and they must learn quickly. But it's a gallon of drudgery to every pint of excitement. For some of our young gentlemen, the most terrifying battles are with chalk, slate, and navigational calculations."

Lady Eugenie frowned at that, and David grinned. "Not your sort of study, Genie. And you would not enjoy a battle. You would be tucked away belowdecks, as safe as might be, with naught to do but endure the cacophony above."

She frowned prettily. "Very well, then. I promise I'll not run away and join the Navy."

"I am sure His Majesty would be all gratitude if he but knew," he responded.

"His Majesty would not think well of a young lady who entertained such hoydenish aspirations," Lady Anne said with a quelling look at her youngest sister. "Really, Eugenie, such foolishness is unbecoming."

"I *think* the gentlemen knew that I was speaking in jest," the girl said with excessive dignity.

The situation was shaping in a direction David had seen a score of times before—Anne waxing heavy-handed in what she considered to be her duty in their mother's absence, Eugenie feeling obliged to point out that Anne was not, in fact, her mother, nor was her opinion required or desired. Amelia intervened before things came to that pass, as was her right since she was the one most often tasked to keep her younger sister in hand. "Well, *I* think our brother and Captain Marshall have their fill of tea and gossip, don't you? Your rooms will be prepared by now, gentlemen. Would you care for a bath and a rest before supper?"

"Yes, Lia, thank you," David said quickly, and transferred Catherine to Eugenie's lap, while Anne retrieved her other daughter from Will's. "Am I in my old room?"

"Yes, of course. Captain Marshall—it *is* Captain, is it not?" She looked to Will. "My brother said that when you have your own ship, you are addressed as Captain, not Commander. Which do you prefer, sir?"

Taken by surprise, Will actually blushed. "Oh...either will do, my lady."

"Call him Captain," David advised. "There's not a sailor afloat who doesn't wish to be called Captain, no matter what he may tell you to the contrary."

"Captain, then. Your room shares a dressing-room with my brother's, so you will not feel cast adrift in this strange backwater."

"Not strange, my lady," Will said. "Only unfamiliar. But I thank you. And I wish that I were not imposing on you at such a difficult time."

Amelia flicked a glance at her brother that spoke of approval as they took their leave of the other ladies and left the room. "Captain, I am sure that your presence, and my brother's, will make us all more comfortable. Tobias should be here to show you—yes, here he is. Please let him know if there is anything you require."

Tobias' face was not one David remembered, but some of the servants had been getting on in years when he'd last lived at home, and the younger ones often went off to work in London, so change was to be expected. So many changes.... He hardly needed a guide; the courtesy was mostly for Will's sake, so he followed the footman through the main hall and up the right-hand staircase, excusing himself at the door of his own room while Will was shown to the following one.

A fire had been lit, taking the chill off the air and inviting him to approach. A moment later, the connecting door to the dressing room swung open and Will poked his head through, tentatively. "That footman—Tobias, wasn't it?—has gone to order a bathtub."

"That should be pleasant. Not so fine as the one we shared on the way to London, though."

"Much finer, I imagine," Will said. He came the rest of the way into the room but stopped a foot or two away. "I don't suppose we shall have the privacy to enjoy it, and even if we did..."

"We shan't. I wish it were otherwise, but we dare not take the chance, here in my father's house." He studied Will's solemn features. "Are you sorry you came?"

"Oh, not at all. I've often wondered about your home, and your sisters have been very kind. Is everything as you remember it?"

"Nearly so," David said, moving about the room, exploring what had once been familiar. His books were still here, that was the main thing. He wasn't surprised to find his seachest unpacked—obviously, Tobias had been busy while they were visiting the ladies—but his toiletries were now set out upon a mahogany shaving-stand that had not been in the room when he'd left. He ran a finger along the smooth, polished wood. "This is new, or perhaps it was moved in from another room. When I last slept in this room, I was not quite old enough to shave."

Will was gazing around him, looking back at David from time to time. "Will, what is it?"

With a rueful smile, Will shook his head. "The middies' mess and a hammock must have come as a terrible shock to you, Davy. This is so...so very grand. So far above anything I would have expected. Though I suppose your cousin's estate in Jamaica should have given me a hint."

David looked around him, trying to imagine how the place must seem to his lover's eyes. The high, carved bed with its heavy curtains was certainly more elaborate than anything Will had likely ever slept in, but David rather wished they were still back at the coaching inn in Teignmouth.

And he suddenly realized why Will seemed so uncertain. "Yes, it is very nice," he agreed. "But it's not *mine*, Will, and I never expected it would be. This is all entailed...well, there's some property that isn't, and I know my mother would never let the Earl leave me out of the will completely—which he wouldn't do in any event, because it would cause talk, and neither of them would stand for that. But in this family, I'm insignificant. If Virginia bears a son to Mark, as I hope she does, the place will go to that child. If not, it goes to Ronald. Which, I admit, I should hate to see, because I don't think he will care for it as Mark would have."

"You could live here, though."

"Perhaps, if I had nowhere else to go. But really...oh, for heaven's sake, Will, let us sit down." He led his friend over to a set of chairs placed near the windows, and shifted one a little closer to the other. "You must stop worrying about where I shall live, and how. I've told you—I have the London house, or the rent from it, and that will be enough for us to keep a nice set of rooms. Sharing expenses on half-pay, we shall do very well. There's no sense in borrowing trouble." They'd have quite enough trouble as things stood, once Ronald showed up.

But for the moment, the only immediate question was where to put the bathtub, and Tobias answered that by having it brought into Will's room, since it was less drafty. A parade of maidservants brought in sufficient heated water, and then they were left alone, after assuring the footman that they were quite accustomed to bathing unaided. Tobias bowed and departed, but not before appropriating the coats of their dress uniforms so that any little evidence of their journey might be cleaned and pressed away.

"I should have remembered that this room was always warmer," David said, once their privacy was restored for at least a little while. Seeing Will hang back, he stripped off the rest of his clothes and stepped into the tub, a high-backed hip bath with room to sit comfortably. "This room was where my cousin Kit would sleep when his family came to visit. I think my mother put him here beside me so we would not disturb anyone else with our games."

"What sort of games?" Will asked.

"Oh, the usual sort of things boys play at." David soaped himself up quickly so Will would have at least some of the heat. "Adventures of one kind or another. Sometimes our toy soldiers were explorers, and one of the beds was Australia or India or the New World. Sometimes they were smugglers or pirates, and we'd pretend there were caves under the beds, and hide treasure there."

Will's dark eyes were on him. "I wish we could pretend we were at some little inn, Davy, where no one knew us and we could lock the door."

Even though he knew they could do nothing, David smiled back. "And no chance of a servant coming in unexpectedly? So do I. But for now—would you pour some water so I may wash my hair?"

"Of course." Will was a gentleman and did exactly as

asked, and if his free hand happened to rest briefly on his shipmate's shoulder, not even the most curious onlooker would have thought it was for any reason other than to steady his aim with the pitcher.

By the time Will had taken his own bath, the daylight had begun to fade outside the windows. When he had finished toweling himself dry, David handed him a dressing gown. He wrapped it around himself and frowned. "Davy, when will your footman bring our coats back?"

"Soon enough." He didn't want to patronize Will, who was wandering around the room with a puzzled look on his face. When they'd stayed at Kit's estate in Kingston, the circumstances had been far less formal, and David did not want his friend embarrassed by ignorance of family customs—or by calling in a valet to see that he came up to the mark. "We shall need to dress for dinner, of course, everything fresh from the skin outward. It takes a bit of getting used to, after shipboard life. A laundress in residence, no need to wash our linen in salt water and wear everything for days on end...I've extra shirts and neckcloths here in case you need to borrow any, but I expect yours have been unpacked and put away." He opened the armoire that Will seemed to be avoiding. "Ah, just as I thought—here they are."

Will looked a little lost as he walked over and collected his clothing. "So much space, Davy! This room alone is bigger than the Captain's cabin in the old *Calypso*. I almost feel I should sling a hammock here in this cupboard, instead of trying to sleep in that huge bed. And you could almost fit the house I grew up in inside the grand hall downstairs."

David smiled. "It seems strange to me, too, now, and I grew up in this house. You start your dressing, Will, while I go fetch my things. We might as well keep one another company. If you like, we could have my brother's valet assist us—"

"God, no!" Will blurted, and David laughed aloud.

"I feel the same," he said. "Thank God for uniforms, and ranking low enough to be allowed to dress ourselves! But I would not dare wear my second-best coat to the dinner table, so you must suffer as well—particularly since, while you're here as my friend, you are also my commanding officer."

Even after they were dressed as far as they were able they had a while yet to wait, sitting near the fire, each lost in his own thoughts. David wondered whether it would be worthwhile asking after his father. The Earl had no doubt returned by now, and he would certainly have been informed of their arrival. That he had not sent for his youngest son was no real surprise.

Perhaps Will had been right, after all. Why had he insisted they come home? It was not really his home. Not any longer.

Chapter 4

"Lieutenant Archer, your mother has requested the pleasure of your company."

Will started awake in the comfortable armchair, realizing belatedly that he had fallen into a doze. He allowed the servant who had brought their coats to help him into his—he attempted to demur, but the man seemed to think it necessary, giving far more attention to the precise position of the scraper on his left shoulder than Commander Marshall appreciated. Davy, on the other hand, had taken possession of his own coat and slipped it on without assistance.

"Did she mention Captain Marshall?" Davy asked.

"Yes, sir, she would like to welcome you both to Grenbrook." Tobias stepped back, frowned at the imbalance between Marshall's ornate epaulet and his unadorned right shoulder, but seemed to be aware that there was nothing to be done, since that second adornment could be worn only by a full Post Captain.

"Thank you, we will attend her immediately. Do you know whether my father has returned?"

"He has, sir. He is in his study, and said he will see you at dinner."

Davy smiled wryly. "Very good. Thank you, Tobias, that will be all." He waited long enough to be sure the man was out of earshot before saying, "Well, some things at least are as I expected. With luck, our presence here will go almost unnoticed. At worst, my father may find it necessary to explain my shortcomings to me, but he will probably refrain from doing so in your presence. And who knows, perhaps the prospect of having Ronald as his heir will make my inadequacy a little more bearable."

Will tugged at the scraper, which did not seem to be seated properly. "What of your mother?"

"I'll know better when I have seen her. Oh, for pity's sake, Will, hold still." He made some trifling adjustment and the epaulet settled into place. "I *think* Tobias was attempting to treat you with the respect due your position," he said, suppressing a grin. "You will just have to endure the pampering as best you can."

He glanced up. Will met his sparkling eyes, and wished again that they could be safely private. "If your mother is very unwell, I should hate to be a nuisance."

"It would trouble her more to know she had not made you welcome, after telling me so many times to bring you here. She may wish to speak to me alone—you'll know if that's the case, I think. I do hope..." He broke off with a sigh. "Well, let us go see for ourselves how things stand."

Will followed Davy along the open gallery that ran from one end of the open hall to the other, giving access to the floor below via a gracefully curving staircase on either side. They proceeded a short way down the opposite hall, where Davy tapped at the first door on their right; they were admitted to a sitting room by an angular, middle-aged maid who greeted "Master David" warmly. Lady Amelia stepped out of the door at the other end of the room, but before she could say a word a faint voice called "Come in, my dear," from behind her, and the two men followed Amelia back into the bedroom.

Will had met Lady Grenbrook when Davy stood as godfather to Kit's first child. They had only been able to stay for the christening ceremony and a bite to eat afterwards, so he had never exchanged more than a few words with Davy's mother or his eldest sister, Mary, Lady Crandall, who had also been at the service. Lady Grenbrook had seemed in the best of health and spirits at the time, and though her hair was faded blonde-grey beneath her fashionable bonnet, her eyes had been as bright and blue as Davy's own, her carriage strong and lively.

It was a much older woman who greeted them this time, aged in spirit if not in body. She lay as though thrown against a heap of pillows, and the only color in her face was in the purple shadows beneath her eyes. When Davy stepped forward to take her hand, she pulled him into an embrace as if she never meant to let him go. "Oh, my son," she said at last, releasing him. "What a man you've become! I am so proud of you!"

Davy looked abashed, but Will was happy for him. "As are all of us who've served with him, my lady," he said.

The weary eyes turned in his direction. "Captain Marshall," she said, as though just noticing him. "I wish...that I were better able to greet you as you deserve."

He bowed slightly and took the hand she extended, a brief touch of fingers rather than a handshake. "I wish that the circumstances were anything but what they are, my lady. May I express my deepest sympathy?"

"Thank you." Her eyes rested again upon her son, with a look of weary joy. "So good to see you both," she said with obvious effort. "We are...this has been…"

Will glanced at Davy, who nodded. "I shall let you and your son enjoy your reunion, my lady. Thank you again for the honor of your invitation to this lovely place."

She nodded absently, and Amelia followed Will out as Davy drew a chair up to his mother's bedside. Once in the hall she said, "Thank you so much for bringing my brother home. Having him here to comfort her will help, I think. I believe she has been fearful ever since he was wounded last year, afraid that she would never see him again."

"I feared that myself, for a time," Will admitted. "But your brother is a strong man, and very determined."

They had moved a few steps along the hall, into the open gallery. She turned to regard him steadily. "Is he really well, Captain? He seems thinner than I ever remember seeing him."

"Indeed he is, but his health is much improved. Perhaps it's as well that he did not return here immediately, because for a time he did look ..." *He looked white as a new sail, wasting away, he could barely keep food down....*Swamped by the memories, Will ran out of conversation. "I thought we had lost him," he said baldly. "Please forgive me, my lady, but your brother is my dearest friend and I wished—I still wish—that I had taken the bullet myself."

She put a hand on his arm. "I knew we should be friends," she said warmly. "Davy is the dearest of my brothers, and I am so glad he has you to look after him."

"You are too kind." Will felt the proverbial coals of fire on his head. He had not done a very good job thus far, and due to his own weakness he would not be able to do so in the future, whatever that might hold.

"May we hope your visit will be a long one?" she asked. "I know the treaty still endures, but my brother said you had found another ship. Was it a private commission?"

"Yes, we sailed for a friend of your cousin, Baron Guilford, doing messenger work for a few months." That was more or less true, to a point. "Our vessel was damaged—no fault of ours, I hasten to say—and is now undergoing repairs. Whether our service shall be required when she is once more whole, I cannot say. If and when the Peace is broken, I expect we shall be recalled to duty." Even if he could discuss such matters with a civilian, and a woman at that, he could not even bring himself to speculate about them to himself. He shrugged. "I know no more than you, my lady. I wish I did."

Lady Amelia seemed to sense his discomfort, and changed the subject. "You are both here for now, at least, and I am grateful for that. How may we entertain you, Captain? My sister Anne is in the drawing room doing some needlework, and Eugenie is suffering the same fate. Miss Winston is there as well. But I cannot think such things would interest you. Might I offer you a tour of the house?"

"Oh, I've mended my own shirts," he said. "Sewn on

buttons, too, and so has your brother, but only from necessity. If a tour would not keep you from your own diversions, I would enjoy that." It made little difference, really; he was equally uncomfortable with either prospect and hoped only to avoid sounding like a fool.

Her smile was very like Davy's. "I can bear the disappointment. If I had been reading a novel, that would be another matter altogether. Let us begin here, then. The hall below us is more modern than the bedrooms. The stairs and this gallery were added when my grandfather—"

The door to Lady Grenbrook's suite opened, and Davy slipped out, a thoughtful expression on his face. "She's asleep," he said. "Kirby gave her a dose of her cordial, and she just dropped off. I'm sure Kirby knows exactly what to do—she always has, as far back as I can remember. My mother's maid," he explained to Will, then added, "Has Mama been like this since the accident, Lia?"

"Not immediately. After the first shock had passed, Mama seemed very calm. She kept her composure until the funeral, but on the way home she fainted, woke up weeping, then took to her bed. Dr. Fiske says we must let her rest and regain her strength. I had hoped she would feel well enough to come down to dinner tonight."

"I asked her that myself. She said perhaps she will make the attempt tomorrow."

"That is more than she said this morning." She turned to Will, "He has always been the only one of us able to bring Mama around to his wishes."

"If that's so, then you are the only one who can win a concession from Father," Davy retorted. "Except for—" He caught himself. "The only one, now."

Lady Amelia nodded soberly. "I feel as though this is a nightmare, and I cannot wake up," she said. "I catch myself that same way, so very often. What will become of this family without Mark, when Father's gone?"

Will felt as though he was intruding on something that should have been private between the two of them. "I would rather not intrude—shall I excuse myself?"

Lady Amelia turned to Davy, who shrugged. "I think that whatever concerns my brother need not be hidden from you, Captain, but if you would rather—"

"I think he might rather," Davy said. "I shall ask his advice if that seems necessary, but I would not drag him into our troubles without need. This cannot be pleasant for you, Will."

"Nor for you," Will answered. "It is only that I would hate to intrude."

Davy's smile and a faint shake of the head said wordlessly that he was being foolish. "Well, then, as you choose."

"We were about to take a tour of the house," Amelia said. "Perhaps we might begin with the portrait gallery? Captain Marshall can walk a little behind us, if he likes, though that is truly unnecessary."

Despite himself, Will was impressed by the long, open hall that afforded the Grenbrook ladies a place to exercise when the weather was inclement. The portraits would have been easier to see when there was daylight coming in through the tall windows, rather than by the subdued glow of candles set at regular intervals, but it was clear that David Archer's people had occupied this estate for many generations, and done well enough to hire artists to leave a lasting record of their lives.

Including those of the current generation. His eye was caught by a group portrait, three men and a boy standing beside a horse. The older gentleman—surely that would be the current Earl? And the two young, dark-haired men, one in the smart uniform of a cavalry regiment, were the elder brothers. That would mean that the fair-haired lad, perhaps ten years old, must be—

"Ah, you found it." Davy walked up beside him and rested a hand on his shoulder. "Evil little beast, wasn't I?"

"You look..." He considered the expression on the youngster in the painting, Davy's square jaw softer in childhood, his frame still small and narrow-shouldered. But the artist had caught that look Will had seen so often on his lover's face, the hint of impatience that said only self-control, or perhaps fear of official retribution, was holding in a sarcastic comment. "You look bored out of your wits."

"You must know him well, Captain." Lady Amelia came up on Will's other side. "He did not want to be in the picture at all. None of them did, I think. Our father had intended the painting to feature himself and Queen's Knight. The horse," she added, at Will's obvious perplexity. "But Mother asked him to include the boys, and by the time the painting was completed, he had decided it was a capital notion. Fortunately, the artist was able to complete much of the painting with only Father and the horse."

"Oh, Ronald thought it a fine idea," Davy said. "You'd have thought his being sent down for misbehavior was the occasion for the sitting—just look at that expression."

"On the right?"

"Yes. My father on the left, of course, at Knight's head, and me between him and Mark, where either of them could clout me if I moved."

"Mark had just joined the Army then," Amelia added.

The Earl's eldest son had been a younger copy of his father, with a roughly oblong face, heavy jaw, and ruddy complexion. The only sign of their mother's influence was a pair of keen blue eyes, and a nose that was perhaps a little less formidable than his sire's. His expression held considerable humor, and Will regretted that he had not been able to meet the man.

Ronald was another matter, and in his stance and arrogant stare Will recognized the self-importance that Davy had described so many years ago. He was probably the better-looking of the older brothers, but it was a cold, sterile regularity of feature that held none of Mark's warmth or Davy's charm. "He does seem rather pleased with himself," Will said, trying to keep his utterance free of negative opinion. "Your eldest sister has the same coloring as your brothers, does she not?"

"Yes," Davy said. "All the girls but Mary have Mother's hair. We're all blue-eyed, more or less, but only Mark and Ronald got Father's height. It's interesting how the traits fell out."

"I know nothing of art, but it seems to me an excellent painting. The artist certainly caught your personality."

"It's very accurate," Davy said. "And I am glad we have it. Not so much for my own youthful splendor, but I believe it's the best picture of Mark that we have."

Amelia nodded, and took his arm. "I know you are just as pleased to have left that age behind, but you always were my favorite playmate. And you were always a gentleman and took the blame if we got into trouble."

"But we so seldom did," he retorted. "Who'd have thought such adorable children would have such speed and cunning?"

She laughed. Will let them move ahead, reminiscing, and allowed himself to be distracted by various paintings. If Davy learned anything from Amelia that Will ought to know, of course he would share the information. Will tried not to let himself feel like an unwanted intruder. This was Davy's family, Amelia his oldest real friend as well as his sister. It was certainly not her fault that Will was not a part of this household. On the contrary, she was doing everything possible to make him feel welcome.

What concerned him more than the pictures on the wall was the picture he began to perceive of what the family was now facing. Davy had always spoken of his mother and sisters with affection, even though he was only close to Amelia in age or disposition. He'd seldom mentioned his father, except to say that he had joined the Navy because his father had determined set him on a course he dreaded, after Davy unwisely fell in love with an actress and proposed marriage to her—which proposal the young woman, with good sense far outweighing her station in life, gently declined. His brother Mark had received nothing but praise from his youngest brother. But Ronald...

Will had thought Davy was exaggerating when he'd compared his elder brother to the murderous pirate who had kidnapped them a few years earlier. Even the warning when they'd arrived seemed harsh. But having seen Amelia's obvious distress at the prospect of Ronald inheriting control of the family, Will was less inclined to wonder whether his lover had allowed his own dislike to color his opinion. The look on the man in that portrait was that of someone who felt entitled to have his own way, no matter what. That would not be a pleasant sort of attitude to see across the table, day in and day out. It seemed unlikely that Davy would choose to remain here at the estate when war resumed.

Still...looking at the two blond heads so close together, Davy leaning toward his sister with a look of deep concern on his face, Will was equally sure that Davy would not be able to simply walk away from his family in this time of crisis, even though there seemed to be very little he could do to help. As for Will himself, he felt entirely useless.

⚓ ⚓ ⚓

Dinner was interminable. David Archer had hoped to see his mother at the table, if for no other reason than the moderating influence she always had on her husband. The Earl seemed to view his offspring as unruly beasts in constant need of a set-down, but as he was the soul of courtly courtesy to his wife, her presence would have gone a long way toward relieving the leaden atmosphere. Unfortunately, she had not found the strength to dress and join the family, so Lady Anne was acting as hostess.

And Amelia was right. The Honorable Lord Arthur Wilton Archer, Earl of Grenbrook, Viscount Archer, a man well endowed with worldly means and secure in the affection of his devoted wife, a man whom his son had never seen as anything less than formidable...had indeed altered. David's father was no longer the man that he remembered. He was still tall, and broad in proportion; his iron-grey hair had lightened a shade closer to silver—but what startled David was the vacancy in his father's lined and weary face. It was like watching a painting of a fire, instead of the fire itself. The familiar image was there, without warmth or movement. Even his frown seemed more habitual than an expression of real feeling.

"So you've come home at last, have you?" was the Earl's paternal growl as they gathered before dinner.

David inclined his head. "As you see, Father. But you may rest assured I'll not be here for long. Like the Army, we are waiting to be called back to duty when needed. May I present my friend, Commander William Marshall..." He observed the proper form, Will expressed the appropriate pleasure in the meeting and was accorded a shake of the hand.

With a little of his usual energy, the Earl said, "Pleased to meet you, sir. Though I must say you'd have done better to finish the job! This country cannot get back to normal until that damned Corsican has been put in his place."

"I agree, my lord," Will said. "And there is not a man in the Navy who would argue with that proposition. It's quite clear that Bonaparte only signed the treaty to give himself time to regroup—a capital mistake, and one that will cost us dearly."

"Indeed," the Earl said, with a rare nod of approval.

That hurdle cleared, David allowed himself to breathe again as they proceeded in to the table and took their seats, an uneven arrangement as the ladies outnumbered the gentlemen. Under the circumstances, everyone except for Will being family, it hardly mattered. Will, poor fellow, had Eugenie at his right hand, but that difficulty was balanced by Amelia at his left. David found himself next to his cousin Jane, with an empty place between himself and Anne.

They might as well have each been dining alone, for all the conversation that took place. Every time someone spoke—Amelia addressing some harmless pleasantry to Will, David attempting to converse with Jane—the Earl glowered at the one who had broken the silence that he maintained from start to finish. It was not inappropriate for a family in mourning to be somewhat subdued, David thought, but this was positively moribund. Surely some consideration should have been due a guest.

Not that he could blame the Earl for his low spirits. From what Amelia had said, Ronald had been making a career of disaster—or, more accurately, doing his best to make a disaster of his military career. There had been two near-scandals that she had not wished to trust to the mail, one of them some dispute over a matter in which Ronald had challenged, shot, and wounded a man whose grievance was never explained but probably had some connection to gambling.

The other issue was far more serious, and as yet unexplained. Ronald's wife had died abroad, but the family had not been informed of that fact until months after the event, and as far as Amelia knew, no one even knew what had caused her death. David suspected the prospect of handing the family's future over to Ronald under these circumstances must be almost as appalling to his father as it was to David himself.

Whatever the cause, gloom reigned at the table. Anne eventually seemed to resign herself to the situation and rose; the ladies adjourned with her to the drawing room.

A footman brought the port around. The Earl pondered his glass for a few moments. "God save the King," he said finally. "That's what you say in the Navy, isn't it?"

"Yes, sir," Will answered.

"Well, God save him, then. God save us all." He took a drink, stared down into his glass, then said, "You must excuse me," and simply walked out.

David watched him go in disbelief. He had not expected any particular courtesy for himself, but such a snub to a guest was beyond his experience.

"Now what?" Will asked. "Shall we join your sisters?"

"Yes, of course, though it's my guess this merry gathering has set the tone for the evening." He sipped at his port, unable to find any solace in the drink. "This is not like my father at all. He has always been so strong. Amelia was right, Will. This has altered him, and not for the better…"

"I was very young when my mother died," Will said, "along with the baby she'd just borne, but I remember something my father said then. He told me that losing a child was the worst blow that could befall a man."

"My mother said something very similar this afternoon. Mark should have buried her, she said, not the other way around."

Will pushed his glass away, barely touched. "It almost makes me glad I shall never have children."

Rather than point out that it was never wise to challenge Fate, David changed the subject. "Come, we may as well join the ladies in the drawing room. Anne is very fond of whist and Amelia despises it, so perhaps we can brighten both their lives by allowing Anne to prove her skill against us. I'll even take Genie as partner, as a kindness to you. She enjoys the status of sitting down to cards with the adults, but she plays the worst game of whist I have ever seen."

"Worse than your own?" Will shook his head. "Is that possible?"

"For that remark, I leave you to find out for yourself, the hard way." David finished his drink. "But you have been warned, Captain Marshall. When she is fluttering her lashes in your direction and forgetting the cards in her hand, you'll have only your wit to blame."

He led Will off to the drawing room, but the only ladies remaining there were Amelia and Jane. David gave his sister an inquiring look.

"Anne begs your pardon," she said. "She has been suffering from a miserable headache for some hours, and wished to retire early."

"And Genie?"

"Anne advised her in the strongest terms to do the same," Amelia said with a half-smile. "I think she meant it for the best."

Jane spoke up. "I think she did not believe you could

keep your sister's enthusiasm within the bounds of propriety."

"Now, that, I can believe," David said. "Anne takes propriety very seriously. And in this case, that may not be a bad thing. I admit I have found it difficult to grieve—I am still stunned, and some part of me cannot believe that Mark is really dead. But I would have expected Genie to be more affected."

"It is still new to you," Amelia said, "and you have only the report of the accident, whereas our experience was much more immediate. The first shock has passed for the rest of us now, and we are trying to adjust to the change in our lives. I assure you, poor Genie wept for days without ceasing. I do appreciate Anne's wish to help, but I wish she would be more understanding. Genie is such a lively girl—she finds this solemnity hard to bear. She adored Mark, but I think she seeks distraction to ease the pain of our loss."

Wishing he could seek such a distraction himself, David suggested, "Perhaps we might go for a walk tomorrow, if the weather is fair. Solemnly, if necessary, but I think it would do us all good to get out of the house."

"Or a ride," his sister said. "The ground is too damp for a stroll, but if we drove we might show Captain Marshall some of the local sights."

"At this time of year? Not much to—" David broke off, hearing a carriage rattle by the window facing the drive. He almost asked who it might be, but a look at Amelia's face showed the same apprehension he felt. "Ladies, we have had a long journey, and started quite early this morning. Would you be offended if we all make an early night of it, and start fresh tomorrow?"

"Not at all," she said, rising swiftly. "Jane, shall we go?"

They made a strategic retreat of it rather than a rout, the ladies hurrying down the hall to the left while the men went right. As he followed Will through the door to their rooms, David heard the sound of boots in the hall below, and a clatter as if a walking stick had been thrown angrily to the floor.

"Your brother?" Will asked.

"Yes," David said, turning the key to his room with no concern at all for the possible discourtesy of such an action. "And you may call me a coward if you like, but I would prefer to let that reunion wait until tomorrow."

⚓ ⚓ ⚓

Damn their insolence! Granted, the fatted calf might have been a bit much to expect under the circumstances, but a certain amount of common courtesy was not too much to expect here in the home that would one day be his own. It was probably her fault, Daddy's little petted darling, too sure of herself by half. Well, that was going to change, and soon, and she had better learn which way the wind was blowing. A woman's duty was obedience, and if she would not conform herself to that ideal, she could be disposed of. That was easy, disposing of women. And strangely enjoyable.

Chapter 5

W ill Marshall woke to utter darkness, in a bed that was far too large and was not swinging with a ship's movement. There was no Davy beside him, either, which he would normally expect when sleeping ashore. He lay quiet for a moment as memory supplied the reason for these deficiencies, then sat up and reached out to where he believed the bed-curtains to be. The room was dark as well, but a little moonlight seeped in through the drapes at the window, and his eyes were used to making do with starlight. It felt late— somewhere in the middle watch, with hours left till dawn. What had wakened him?

A sound came again, a faint hint of movement from the direction of Davy's room. Uneasy at his lover's peculiar mood, he had not closed the dressing-room door, though it seemed absurd to behave as though they were in enemy territory.

He got out of bed, pulling on the dressing-gown that had been left on a nearby chair, and gratefully donning slippers that some unseen servant had provided while the family was at dinner. With as little noise as possible, Will slipped through the small room and hesitated. In all likelihood, Davy had only turned over in his sleep. He could simply look in, and be sure all was well.

But Davy was not sleeping. He stood at the window, bathed in silver light, gazing out into the pre-dawn darkness. "Hello, Will," he said, very quietly. "Sorry I woke you—I was trying to find my watch, to see what time it was. It's nearly six bells."

That was three in the morning, landlubber's time. Will had become accustomed to ordinary timekeeping in his months ashore, but he had quickly reverted to sleeping in four-hour watches aboard the *Mermaid*. At this moment, especially in the night chill, he did not feel inclined to go back to bed. He joined Davy at the window, standing close but restraining the impulse to put an arm around him. "When will we be awakened in the morning?" he asked. "That is, I assume someone will do so?"

"Yes, one of the maids will bring chocolate at eight," Davy said. "I remember you enjoyed that in Kingston, and asked them to bring chocolate instead of coffee."

"Thank you." They had gone immediately to bed after Ronald's arrival to discourage any late-night visitation, and Will had been left with several unanswered questions. But Davy seemed to be in a sober mood, and Will did not want to burden him with chatter.

After a moment, Davy let the curtain fall back. "I wish we had stayed away," he said, then shook his head. "No, that's not true. I must be here. But from what Amelia has told me..." He glanced at the door. "Will, I shall have to ask you to trust me."

Why did he have to ask? "I do, Davy. You know that!"

His lover's face was shadowed. "To trust me, no matter what the future brings. I fear that within a few days' time you may think I'm going mad. I wonder myself, for I have suspicions but no proof. Come with me."

Moving noiselessly, he led Will back to the small chamber between their apartments, a space that might be occupied by a lady's maid or a nurse to an invalid. It was close and dark, and Will was mightily tempted. "Davy..."

"There's no chance anyone might overhear us now," Davy said, and pulled Will down into a kiss, sweet but brief. Only a single kiss, and a lingering embrace that held more tension than passion.

"What is troubling you?" Will asked. "Is there anything I might do to help?"

Davy's breath was warm against his neck. "No, not yet. This is something so serious I dare not suggest it, even to you, until I have some basis for my suspicions. But Will, I thank God you're here with me, because there is no one else I could trust to guard my back."

They stood there for awhile, enjoying the closeness even though they dared attempt no more. Finally Davy drew back with a strained laugh. "I daresay I'll tell you to forget this in the morning," he said. "My mother would say I need a good night's sleep, and no doubt she'd be correct. Pleasant dreams, Will."

After one more chaste kiss, they returned to their separate beds.

⚓ ⚓ ⚓

The actual meeting with Ronald, the following morning, was put off once again. Davy came into Will's chamber with his own cup of chocolate, and they dawdled through their morning toilette, glad of the hot water but dismissing the offer of a shave from the late Viscount's valet, James. Davy made no mention of his worries of the night before, instead chatting lightly of what they might do during the day, which had dawned chilly but fair. Will expressed a strong preference for a walk rather than a ride, but they agreed that the ladies would have the last word on that matter.

At last, wearing their everyday uniforms, they made their way down to the dining room, where Lady Amelia and Miss Winston were enjoying a cup of tea following their meal. The footman minding the buffet invited Lieutenant Archer and his guest to sample baked eggs with a new cheese sauce Cook had concocted.

"Have you tried it yourself, Gavin?" Davy demanded of the footman.

"Oh, certainly, sir. You know she would never feed anything to the Family until she'd got it just so."

"Of course," he said with a smile. "I'd forgotten. I see you survived in fine fettle, too. Game, Will?"

"Certainly, thank you." Will was fond of eggs in almost any form, and perfectly willing to eat whatever was set before him. He was pleased to see that the dish was accompanied not only by cheese sauce, but ham, sausage, warm seedcake, and three kinds of jam.

They settled down beside the ladies, and Will applied himself to the eggs, which were surpassingly delicious, while Davy divided his attention between his relatives and his breakfast. "How are the parents?" he asked. "And where are our sisters?"

"Mother is still asleep, and Anne has not come down as yet. Poor Genie awoke with a sore throat, and Nurse decreed she must spend the day in bed. But Father was up early. He summoned Ronald to break his fast with him, and then took him out to see Thomas Legge."

"The estate manager," Davy explained to Will. "My father employs one, of course, though he generally keeps poor Legge on a short leash. In practice he's more an overseer than a manager—Father himself makes all but the most minor decisions."

"That had begun to change," Lady Amelia said. "Father gave over the Four-Acre field to Mark, to try some experimental planting."

Davy set down his fork. "He gave over control? You cannot mean that!"

Both ladies nodded. "It's true, Cousin," Jane said. "Hard as it was for him to stand back, he said that if Mark meant to be head of the family one day, he would have to make his own mistakes. And he was very proud to see the progress your brother made."

"You know his way," Lady Amelia added. "Never to say a kind word to our faces, but heap praise upon us when others are in earshot."

"Or not, as the case may be," Davy said dryly. "I suppose I should pity poor Ronald. He'll be happy to be called Viscount, but the only thing that interests him about the land is knowing what game it provides him for hunting."

"Truly, you should have a little sympathy," Jane said, assuming a look of piety. "Most men hereabouts prefer hunting to farming."

Davy shook his head in mock sorrow. "Alas, I cannot. Most men *prefer* play to work, but they also know which is a necessity and which a luxury." He polished off his toast and jam, and looked across to Will. "We spoke of an outing today. Would that suit you, O Honored Guest?"

"Whatever pleases the ladies," Will said diplomatically. "But I must warn you all, if we are on horseback and come to a hedge, you will have to wait for me to ride around it. I can hand, reef, and steer a ship, but I cannot steer a horse, much less stay aboard when it jumps, and I doubt I should fall gracefully."

"It's cruel of you to deprive of us of the chance for such a sight. Amelia?"

"Jane is too polite to say she would like to ride," Lady Amelia said with a sidelong look at her cousin, "but I can handle the gig, if you would ride with her."

For the first time since they'd arrived, Davy brightened. "I will, with pleasure," he said. "How is Dancer? He must be nearly nine now, but—" He caught a look that passed between the ladies, and his face fell. "What happened?"

"He is alive, and well," Lady Amelia said, "And he is at Bentley Hall."

"Why?"

She sighed and signaled to Gavin, still on duty at the sideboard in case one of them should require another morsel. After asking him to have a fresh pot of coffee brought for the gentlemen, and waiting until he'd gone, she said, "Ronald, of course. He was home on leave, and visiting at the Hall, and there was a card game. He was losing heavily, and he...bet the horse he'd ridden over on."

"My horse," Davy said shortly. "Not father's, but mine, the only animal here that was my own." He glanced at Will. "It seems petty, I suppose, but Dancer was born here; he was a birthday gift from my parents. I trained him myself, and I had my father's word that he would not be sold without my permission."

She nodded. "Yes, and of course Ernest Bentley realized what Ronald had done when he went out to the stable the next morning and recognized Dancer. He immediately rode over to return him. Ronald was out once more, so Mr. Bentley spoke to Father..." She smiled at Will. "I am sorry to draw you into this."

"I can see that it's none of your doing," he said. "Rest assured I shall forget everything you've said the moment we leave this room."

With a grateful nod, she turned back to Davy. "Father was furious, of course. At first he said that Ronald must pay Mr. Bentley full value for Dancer. But I could see that if he were forced to do that..."

Davy's face was white with anger. "He'd take my horse out again—which he had no business doing at all, in the first place—and there'd be an accident of some sort, and he'd be 'forced' to put him down."

"Yes, exactly. But you were at sea—in fact, this took place when you were convalescing in Jamaica. We had no idea when you might be able to return—"

"Or *if* I would ever return," Davy said cynically. "Convenient for him, if I had not. But he might at least have waited until my body had cooled!"

"We'd no idea *when* you would return," his sister said in a tone that brooked no argument, "to claim the poor creature. So I spoke to Father and Mr. Bentley, and they agreed on the details. He has the use of Dancer as a riding hack, and if you find yourself home on half-pay for a considerable length of time, Father will pay Squire Bentley the original sum, plus board, and Ronald will find his allowance rather scant at the quarter-day."

"Thank you, my dear," Davy said. "You have the wisdom of Solomon—Bentley's got a decent seat. I shall have to visit and give him my thanks. Not just yet, though. I think Dancer is safer at the Hall, for the present."

"I think so, too," Amelia said. "And I have been longing for a chance to spend some time out of doors, so if you gentlemen will excuse us, we will be back shortly. Shall we meet by the front door in half an hour?"

The gentlemen rose until the ladies had left the room, and Will turned to his lover with a look of disbelief.

"Yes, that's my beloved older brother," Davy said. "If you had any doubt of my objectivity regarding his character—"

Will said, with chagrin, "I had hoped you might've exaggerated a little."

"If only that were true. His behavior has become so infamous that I suspect Father would disinherit him—except, of course, he cannot now that he's the legal heir. And if he could, that would mean he'd be stuck with me, so even if the law of the land allowed it, his own judgment would leave things as they are."

"You slight yourself," Will said.

"No, Will. I do think I'm a better man than my father believes me to be—but up to the job of tending this place, with all these lives to care for? In all honesty, I believe that task is beyond my ability. But unless Mark has left a son, Ronald is the heir. If the baby is a girl, Ronald becomes Viscount Archer, by custom—though there's some consolation in knowing that is only a courtesy rank so long as my father lives. It galls me that you—or anyone—might one day be obliged to address him as 'my lord.'"

"Respect to the rank, not the man," Will said. "Just as a seaman with twenty years' experience salutes even the most dim-witted eight-year-old middie."

"He's a major as well, and never allows anyone to forget it. I tell you, Will, I pray that Virginia is carrying a strong, healthy son. Or better still, twin boys, hard-headed and belligerent."

Will laughed as Gavin returned with the coffee, and for courtesy's sake drank a cup he did not especially want, though its excellence made it a pleasure rather than a chore.

That finished, Davy sent word to the stable to saddle two horses and bring around the gig, then led the way back to their room to exchange their shoes for more durable footwear. In Davy's case, an old pair of riding boots had been brought out of storage and polished for his use. He had a complete riding kit as well, with snug buckskin breeches that clung lovingly and made Will's fingers itch to touch him.

"It's as well I lost a stone," Davy said with a critical frown in the looking-glass. "I was a bit younger when these were fitted!" He caught Will watching him and said, "Now, Captain—"

"I find myself wishing we could take a journey," Will said, keeping his voice low. "A long journey together, just the two of us."

A smile tugged at the corner of Davy's mouth. "In a closed coach, I suppose?"

"How did you know?"

"I've been wishing the same thing almost since we arrived. But duty calls, sir! Shall we go and see whether the ladies are ready?"

⚓ ⚓ ⚓

David took a slight detour to his mother's suite on the way downstairs, where Kirby informed him that her ladyship was still asleep. "And it's knowing you're here, sir, that lets her rest so sound," the maid assured him. "I'll tell her you stopped when she wakes."

"I doubt my presence serves as a sleeping potion," he remarked to Will as they descended the stair, "but it's kind of her to think so. I wish there were something more I might do."

"I think she was absolutely correct," Will said. "Your mother just lost a son. Having you here, whole and sound, may mean more to her than you realize."

"It's certainly pushed our other dilemma to one side, at least for now. I may have to consider finding lodgings in Plymouth, rather than Portsmouth, if she continues to do so poorly. If I can help her by my presence—"

"You would not stay here?"

"With Ronald at home? Not if I have any alternative." He preferred to avoid considering his own future, let alone that of the family. He had a modest competence, and for one who owned a home and had little interest in games of chance, it would be more than sufficient. But after a life at sea, he could not produce much enthusiasm for finding some snug berth ashore from which he might watch Will be rowed out to a ship that would set sail and carry him off. Sit there like a maiden aunt, with nothing to do but watch the *Naval Gazette* for the casualty reports? That was no kind of life for a man.

Amelia and Jane were waiting and ready at the door. "Our transportation is waiting, gentlemen," Amelia announced. "And as you see, we have confounded the rumor that ladies cannot dress quickly."

"So you have," David said. His sister and cousin were wearing neat, dark riding habits, their alacrity speaking volumes about how eager they were to get out of the house, even for so short an excursion. He held the door for them and gave Jane a boost up into her saddle while the groom held her horse; Will handed Amelia up into the gig. They started off without complication, but had barely gone halfway up the drive to the road when a pair of horsemen came trotting down it toward them.

David would have recognized them immediately, even if the scarlet uniform had not proclaimed his brother's rank. But the years had not been kind to Ronald. No longer the slender youth of the portrait, he had not only put on two or three stone but had also acquired the sort of coarse, reddened complexion that suggested too many late nights and too much drink. He was not quite thirty, but he looked years older.

Amelia brought the gig to a halt as the Archer men approached. "Out for some air?" their father inquired.

She nodded. "Yes, Papa. I proposed we show Captain Marshall our Devon countryside, but I was too lazy to walk in the mud."

He gave a curt nod. "Sensible girl. With your mother and sister both under the weather, you see to it that you stay in good health!"

Ronald had sidled his mount closer to the gig, to give Will an insolent looking-over. *"Captain?"* Ronald asked, with his usual down-the-nose stare. "I was given to understand your rank was *Commander.*"

"A courtesy title," David said before Will could speak—there was scarcely any polite answer to that sort of comment. "Similar to the 'Viscount' you stand to attain, except that in the Navy, a Commander must actually do a Captain's work aboard his own vessel. Hence the address."

"Oh, dear," Ronald said mockingly. "My apologies, *Captain.*"

"Do give me a chance to introduce our guest before you begin slighting him," Amelia chided. "Captain Marshall, this is my brother, Major Ronald Archer of the—"

Ronald interrupted her. "Not for much longer, dear sister. I am in uniform only until I can spare the time to return to my regiment and sell out." He reached down to shake Will's hand for the briefest possible moment. "I've heard that our lads in blue can form very tight bonds in all those months at sea," he said with a smirk at David. "I've no doubt you two are closer than brothers."

"Closer than some brothers, I suppose," Will responded. "At sea we've no time to indulge in childish jealousies."

"Oh, I'm sure you are always hard at work," Ronald said, with a lift of an eyebrow that said just the opposite.

The Earl cleared his throat. Oblivious to this family signal to change the subject, Will went on, "You know, Major, I find that every branch of His Majesty's service has foolish stories they tell about the others. Just last week I overheard one of my men relating a droll tale about Army officers' affection for their horses."

Amelia gave a strangled cough and put her hand to her lips; an unhealthy flush spread up Ronald's tanned face.

"Absurd, of course!" Will continued, as though the obscene implication was too coarse to have ever crossed the mind of an officer and gentleman. "And so utterly wanting in good sense. One would think that having a common enemy in France would encourage mutual respect among His Majesty's officers, no matter their uniform."

"Well said, sir," the Earl said, in a tone that closed the subject. "I'm pleased to see that *one* of my sons is now choosing his friends wisely. Come, Ronald. I want you to review the records of the work your brother began on the Four-acre field. I mean to see his plans continue without interruption. Ladies." He touched heels to his horse and was off, with Ronald throwing a venomous glare over his shoulder as he followed his father.

Always the left-handed compliment, David thought bitterly. *Now* choosing my friends wisely. Ah, well, it was a point in Will's favor and, if his father's sharp look at Ronald had been any indication, that line of discussion was well and truly closed while the old man was in earshot. Had his brother any real clue regarding his relationship with Will? Probably not; as Will surmised, it was the old rivalry between the services, as well as the old scorn for the weakling younger brother.

"Are they gone?" Amelia asked in a strained voice.

"Out of earshot, yes," Jane said.

"Thank heaven!" She let out a peal of laughter, and turned to Will. "Captain Marshall—oh, pardon me, *Commander!* – I had no notion you had such a deadly wit! My brother always writes of how serious you are!"

"But I am serious!" he protested. "That is, I was. In all the years I have been at sea, I have never heard an Army jibe that had any vestige of originality to it. I had expected something more creative from Mr. Archer's brother."

"Ah, but David is the bookish son," she said. "He inherited my mother's love for words, the other boys my father's love for chasing small animals on horseback."

David winced at her grammar. "You must admit, getting small animals to ride horseback is something of an accomplishment," he put in, and received a mock-grimace for his pains. "Well played, Will—but don't expect that to be the end of it!"

⚓ ⚓ ⚓

Will was relieved to be outdoors instead of cooped up in the elegant but oppressive manor house. The day was damp and grey and a sharp wind blew in from across the moor, but some sensible groom had put a couple of carriage robes in the gig, and his companions' conversation kept him from paying too much attention to his cold feet. Odd, how one noticed such things sitting in a carriage. It had been far colder aboard the *Mermaid*, but since he was constantly walking about the deck, he had seldom noticed the chill.

They followed the road in the opposite direction from the way the coach had brought them in. Grenbrook land, as far as they could see—the home farm that raised necessities for the manor house. Will had thought his lover was joking when Davy had given him a scarf one Christmas and said it was knitted from the wool of his family's own sheep, but here were those very sheep, nibbling away at the tough winter grass in a pasture that sloped gently up toward a wood, tall old bare trees with a few evergreens dark among the cold grey branches. It looked like a painting. It probably *was* a painting, come to think of it. He'd seen a few of this kind of scene back in the gallery.

"It's a pity we didn't come here in the spring," Davy said, riding beside him. "The orchard is lovely. Better in summer, of course, when the fruit starts to come ripe."

"If you should ever happen to visit when the peaches are ripe, Captain," Lady Amelia said, "be sure you do *not* let him persuade you to climb up after them. I nearly broke my neck that way, once—and tore my dress!"

"Why did you do it?"

"I knew that if I did not, he would climb up there himself—and he was only four. His legs were too short."

"You see, Will—I told you my sister was a heartless

wretch. To throw such a thing up at a man, after twenty years!"

Lady Amelia laughed. "Well, they *were* short, but you did finally grow, and very well, too."

"It was the nourishment in those peaches," Davy said. "And you know you'd have gone up that tree whether I was there or not. She was always a tomboy," he added to Will, "and if memory serves me, so was this lady. Cousin Jane, would you care for a race to the bridge?"

Miss Winston, who had said little thus far, brightened, gathered up her reins, and said, "Certainly!" She was off in an instant. Davy laughed and sent his own mount galloping after her down a long open stretch of road.

Will was enchanted by the sight of Davy on horseback, balanced in the saddle as though he'd been born to it. "I knew he rode," he said. "He's tried to teach me once or twice. I had no idea he rode so well."

"My brother never boasts," Lady Amelia said, "but he is every bit as good a rider as my father. How is it that you do not? Do you dislike horses?"

"The skill never seemed important," Will confessed. "My father was a parson and we had a horse and a gig much like this one, but my interest was all directed toward the water. I suppose I would have found time to learn to ride if I had stayed ashore, but I was off to sea by the time I was twelve."

"So young!" she said. "I think of my brother at that age, and he was ...well, I'm sure he thought himself quite grown-up, but I thought of him as a little boy still. Was that not a lonely life for a child, and frightening?"

"Oh, no," he said absently, still watching the riders, now a mile or more away. "It was a marvelous adventure. I had a very dutiful captain who saw to it that his 'young gentle-men'—what we call midshipmen—were properly looked after and educated. I was older when the war began with France, and even then I was too young and stupid to be frightened."

"But the battles—the cannon? It must be deafening to

have them firing off so close!"

He grinned. "Oh, it is, but to a boy, the louder the roar, the better. That may be different for girls, or perhaps it's only youth. I think understanding of the danger only comes with experience—it becomes real when one sees shipmates killed or wounded." He wondered if he had ever really known fear until he saw Davy shot. Yes, of course he had—but nothing that struck so hard or pierced so deep. "But the business of the Navy is war, after all. In a few years one becomes accustomed to facing danger, and the fear of being thought afraid is stronger even than the fear of death."

She gave him a curious look, but only said, "I have never been on a real ship, even on the Channel, and I would so love to have the chance. We Archer daughters are not allowed adventure; my father does not hold with women traveling except when absolutely necessary. That suits Mama. She is content to go to London and Bath and sometimes the seaside—but if Davy has inherited our mother's love of reading, I think I have a little of my father's thirst for activity. I do wish to sail, one day, for at least a short journey. For something so large to move so swiftly must be thrilling."

"It is," he said. "To run before the wind, with nothing but the sound of the sea rushing by..." He broke off as Davy came thundering back, his cousin close behind, both flushed and laughing with the sheer excitement of being alive. "It feels the way they look. To have such power at your command, not just for the function of movement, but the joy of it."

"My brother said you loved the sea. He never said you waxed poetic."

Will felt himself blush. "I do not, as a rule. Unless a man is inclined to write poetry—and I am *not*—we may feel such things, but we hardly speak of them. Perhaps it's your brother's influence. He introduced me to Shakespeare, and I think such exposure must improve a man's vocabulary."

"Captain, the best vocabulary in the world cannot express what is not felt."

He had no reply to that, but didn't need one. Davy slowed his horse as he drew closer. "That was more like it! Will, you must ride at least a little while we are here. I know you would enjoy it once you've had a bit of practice."

"Yes, do," Lady Amelia said. "The most beautiful places on the estate can only be reached on foot or horseback, and with my brother as chaperone Jane and I would not need a groom as escort."

The riders fell into step on either side of the gig, and Davy smiled sympathetically at his sister. "Old Mother Hubbard?"

"Of course. A little older and browner, but every bit as excessively solicitous as ever!"

"Mother?" Will asked.

"Our head groom," Lady Amelia explained. "He is married to our housekeeper. Hubbard taught us all to ride—and taught my brother how to train his horse, Dancer. We call him 'mother' because he is like a broody hen when I or my sisters go out riding. He keeps us much safer than we need to be."

"What has become of Mrs. Hubbard?" Davy asked. "I'd expected to see her by now."

"Gone to Tavistock," Jane said. "The Countess gave her leave to go home at Christmas, and she found her mother dreadfully ill, not expected to live. Your mother told her to stay as long as she was needed. But it seems her presence has cheered the old lady up, and she is beginning to recover."

"That was before the accident," Lady Amelia added. "And after the bustle of Christmas, so we found she could be spared for awhile."

Davy frowned. "And now Mother's on the sick list and I can guess who's shouldered the burden. It's no wonder you wanted to get out of the house!"

She shook her head. "It has not been the chore you may think—I've found it easier to have something to occupy my mind. But speaking of burdens reminds me that there is something I meant to ask you yesterday evening. This may not be the best time—and no, Captain Marshall," she said, her gloved hand moving quickly to his wrist, "please do not feel you need to absent yourself. I do not mind your hearing this."

"What is it, then?" Davy asked. "By heaven I charge thee, speak!"

"Hamlet," she said. "And far too close to the mark, don't you think? Ronald is behaving exactly as I'd thought he would, and I am fearfully reminded that, God forbid, should anything happen to Father, he would be my legal guardian...and Genie's, as well as Jane's."

Davy winced. "Heaven protect Father! What would you have me do?"

"I know that you will most likely go back to sea, and soon," she said. "But—would you permit me to ask Father to make you our guardian, instead of Ronald? I hope that Genie will have married before you would ever need worry about her—"

"And so will you both, I imagine," Davy said.

"Oh, no," she said lightly. "We shall be the maiden aunts, and dote on our nieces and nephews—or cousins, in Jane's case. I thought that perhaps I might keep house for you, at least until you marry."

"There's no likelihood of that in the near future." Davy laughed. "Or the distant future, either, so far as I can see." He gazed thoughtfully across the fields, toward a far-off wood. "Yes, ask him, if you like, though I despair of keeping you firebrands in order if it were to come to that. But I would not hold out much hope of Father's consent."

"A year or two ago, you would have been correct. After Ronald's recent misadventures—and that troubling silence about Lenore—I think Father will be less trusting of his judgment. And the burden would not be yours alone; I mean to ask that you and Mama be joint guardians. In that way, we would have a responsible gentleman making decisions, but she would have the authority to act if you happened to be at sea."

"So you girls and Mama might remove to the Dower House if Ronald became unreasonable, or if he were to find an uncongenial bride."

"The Dower House at the very least," she said. "Or perhaps the town house. I should prefer as much distance as possible, since I do not trust our brother any more than you do."

Davy gave Will a wry grin. "Did I ever explain that the Archer men tend to action, and the ladies to strategy?"

"You did not," Will said, "but I begin to think it a pity that the Admiralty has no positions open for members of the gentle sex."

"When gentlemen have all the power, Cousin," Jane said, "ladies have no recourse but strategy." Although her tone was light Will did not think she was joking. There was an edge to her, somehow, that the Archer ladies did not have, and he wondered what lay behind her quiet countenance.

"I think our mother has more power than meets the eye," Davy said. "I cannot recall ever seeing her quarrel with our father, or him lay down the law to her the way he always has to us. Of course there are areas outside her interest—she knows nothing of financial matters, and little about farming—but in nearly everything to do with the house, her will prevails."

"Of course it does—so long as the house is comfortable and we dine on schedule, he is content!" Amelia cocked an eyebrow at her brother. "Can you imagine Father having the slightest interest in new draperies, or selecting the menu for a dinner party? He would dine on chops every night and think nothing of it, if it were left to him. I think our parents do so well together because they have their own spheres of influence, and have little interest in meddling outside them. And, of course, they adore one another."

"They are the best-suited couple I have ever met," Davy agreed. "I hope Mother is feeling better today. Enough, at least, to come down and dine with the family. Have things been as somber lately as they were last night?"

"Not often," she said. "With no other gentlemen at the table, Papa has been eating very little, then going off to his study, or to sit with Mama in her room. I expect dinner will be interesting this evening."

"Yes, so do I," he agreed. "And I think it might be a little less *interesting* and a bit more comfortable if our mother is present."

They followed the road a little while longer, past a few cottages where Will volunteered to hold the reins while the Archers stopped to look in on their tenants.

"Oh, no," Davy said. "You'll not get out of meeting people that easily! We shan't stay long. It's too cold to leave the horses standing for more than a few minutes."

Will gave in with as much grace as he could, and the visit was brief enough; most of the men were out working, and the cottagers' wives were busy with their own chores. But the look of awe on one little boy's face convinced Will that allowing himself to be exhibited as a Famous Naval Commander was perhaps not such a bad thing, after all. If the youngster had had his way, they might have stayed at that cottage the rest of the afternoon and beguiled the time with sea stories, but his mother sent him off to fetch his father and brothers when the sky began to darken.

Amelia decided that the strengthening wind and heavier clouds were reason enough for them to head homeward as well, and Will found himself with food for thought as they turned the horses around and retraced their path.

The long list of servants and tenants he'd met thus far was more than Will could keep in his memory. Even bearing in mind that as the younger son Davy had no claim here, Will was nonetheless daunted at the difference between their positions, the lands and people that were a natural part of Davy's life. Had it not been for the Navy's system, which gave as much credit to ability as to birth, he would never have met David Archer under any circumstances that would have allowed them to speak as friends or equals. He'd never have earned a rank superior to Davy's—in fact, he'd have had no chance at all to become an officer. And it was probably best to keep that in mind while he was here.

He put those thoughts aside when they reached the house. After they had helped the ladies down, Davy invited him to visit the stables. "We shall have to change for tea, of course," he said, "but I thought you might like to see if any of the horses strike you as agreeable."

"If you like," Will said. "Not that I would know one from another, but since you've offered me the chance to learn, I shall be happy to take you up on the offer."

Davy handed his hack off to a waiting groom, who also took the reins of Jane's horse, and climbed into the gig with Will. As soon as the groom was out of earshot, he said, "Oh, Will, you're going all stiff and mannerly on me. I know you too well to believe that! But while you needn't be *happy*, I do think the practice will be of some use to you."

Will sighed. "I hadn't meant to be distant, Davy. I just thought it best to maintain...a sort of quarterdeck formality. Particularly after that remark about 'closer than brothers.'"

"I expect you're right." Davy let his hand slip over to Will's thigh, and gave it a quick squeeze. "But only as a precaution; Ronald's been making that sort of remark about me ever since he realized I would rather sit indoors and read than chase some benighted fox to its death—I generally felt more kinship with the quarry than with my dear brother." He smiled wistfully. "I wish, now, that we had traveled by postchaise from Portsmouth, and been able to spend a few more evenings in quiet inns along the way."

"As do I. But you're needed here, I can see that—at least by your mother and your sister. Lady Amelia, I mean; your other sisters—"

"Anne is closest in age to Ronald," Davy said. "I think she feels some sympathy for him. Though I do not believe she knows him well; she married while he was off at school. She barely knows me at all. When Anne was presented in Society, I was crawling around the nursery. And when I went off to sea, Genie was a sweet child whose life had very little to do with mine. I suppose it is often so in large families when the children are born so far apart."

"I feel like a visitor in a different country," Will said. "Before I met you, I was so often alone that I used to wish I had had brothers and sisters."

"I could say the experience is overrated," Davy said, "but it most likely depends on the brother or sister. I love Amelia dearly, and I do wish you had been able to meet Mark. We were so far apart in age and interests that we were never very close, but he was kind enough, and he never tormented me the way Ronald did. Both of them were mad for any form of sport, though, and to me anything but riding always seemed a waste of time. I wish now that I had spent more time with Mark, even though I suspect he found me rather dull."

"I cannot see why he would," Will said. "And to my untutored eye, you ride very well."

"Oh, that's nothing. All Archers ride, by my father's decree—except for my mother, who gave it up after Anne was born. For me, it was mainly a means of taking myself out of harm's way—to be elsewhere when Ronald was spoiling for a fight."

Will felt he needed to ask the uncomfortable question. "What ails him, Davy? Is there a reason for his animosity, or has he always been so distempered?"

Davy shrugged. "Partly disposition, I think, and partly spoiling. My maternal grandmother lived with us for some years. She made a pet of Ronald, taking his part and making excuses for him, giving him money from her own allowance so he never had to learn to make do with what Father provided. She always supported him in the quarrels he picked with us, even lied for him, and in turn he spied for her."

"I'm sorry," Will said, sorry indeed that he had asked.

"It's a complicated story, Will, and I doubt I know all of it. She was a discontented old woman, and I think she had reason to be; her marriage had not been a pleasant one. But I never did understand why she seemed determined to make everyone else as unhappy as she was. She disliked my father, too, though I never understood that, either—perhaps it was only that he treated my mother so well and proved Grandmother wrong. I suppose he tolerated her for my mother's sake."

"What are you going to do now? This must affect all our plans—" He caught himself. Back on the Mermaid, at Christmastime, he and Davy had exchanged promises that to Will could have served as marriage vows, but it was his own fault, and his alone, that Davy could not go back to sea with him. "Your plans, I should say. I don't mean to intrude."

"This changes everything," Davy said somberly. "Mark was a good man, steady and responsible. With him at the head of the family, I would have been able to range as I liked, knowing that everyone was safe in his care. Now…"

"Now you have responsibilities. It would be wrong for me to try to interfere."

Davy turned on him suddenly, the hurt plain on his face. "No! How can you call what we have between us 'interference'? Will, I mean to keep *our* plans, even if we must adjust them to some degree. I cannot bear to think that you'll vanish from my life. I may someday wind up as my sisters' guardian, but you heard Amelia—the girls would be in Mother's care, not mine. There must still be a way for us to salvage something." He kicked at the edge of the gig, dislodging a bit of mud from his boot. "Or perhaps there is no way, and I'm a fool to think there might be. You'll be off to sea before long, and I had better get used to the idea."

He looked so sad that Will made a clumsy attempt at levity. "Well, Lady Amelia seems to have set her own course. We can but hope that your mother makes a quick and lasting match for your sister Eugenie."

"Oh, I do," Davy said. "Fervently. I hope she falls in love with the perfect man at her very first ball."

"And vice-versa, of course."

"Lord, yes." He smiled. "But knowing Genie, I pity the gentleman who tries to ignore her!"

⚓ ⚓ ⚓

As David might have expected, Will made polite noises when shown the various horses in the stable but showed no sign that he saw any difference, other than size, between the Earl's prize hunter and the dappled pony that would soon be bearing Anne's little girls around in careful circles.

David enjoyed the warmth and scent of the stables, one of the places he'd always felt comfortable as a child. He hoped he'd be able to find Will a mount that would let him learn how to enjoy riding. Odd, he thought, that a man who could walk on a yardarm a hundred feet above a hard and unforgiving deck would be nervous sitting atop a horse, a mere five feet off the ground, but Will was so confident at sea that the small weakness was all the more endearing. And it could be cured, David was sure of that.

They were halfway down the line of stalls when a spare, grey-thatched man called down from the hayloft. "Master David! Good to see you, sir!"

"Afternoon, Hubbard! That's Hubbard," David said, unnecessarily. "We'll need to find a good teacher for Captain Marshall," he said after introducing Will. "He's death to the French on a quarterdeck, but went to sea too young to learn horsemanship."

"Fair enough," Hubbard said. "I've no sea-horses just at the moment, but I think Pennant will do. My lady Anne found him a very biddable mount."

"If he's patient enough for my sister, he'll do for you," David assured Will. "She fidgets, and you don't. I think we shall go out tomorrow, Hubbard, in the late morning or early afternoon, if the weather's fair. Just for a short while."

"Aye, sir. I'll be sure to let out the stirrups for him." He seemed about to fidget himself, then blurted, "Master David, about Dancer…"

David brushed it away. "No need to apologize. My sister told me what happened. There was nothing you could have done, and it's all worked out for the best. Perhaps I'll ride over to Bentley Hall tomorrow and sort things out."

Hubbard nodded his thanks, and returned to his work. David watched him go. "It's going to be hard on our people when Ronald takes over," he said. "My father is a stern taskmaster, but he's always looked after them—made sure the cottages are kept in repair, brought in the doctor if they fall ill... Ronald seldom thinks of anyone but himself. I wish there were something I could do, but anything I might attempt would only make things worse."

Will said nothing, only put a hand on David's shoulder as they turned to leave the stable. He let it drop as a shadow moved across the doorway.

Chapter 6

Ronald was standing outside. Had he been waiting for them? Or only trying to eavesdrop? He fell into step with them as they headed back toward the house, the wind blowing cold in their faces. "Did you enjoy your ride, 'Captain?'" he asked blandly.

"Indeed," Will said neutrally.

"I was sure you would. My sister is a very pleasant young lady, is she not?"

"Indeed she is."

"Yes, indeed," Ronald mimicked. "I hope you are not getting ideas above your station," he said, after Will made no further comment. "I have plans for my sister's future, and they do not include her being leg-shackled to a common sailor."

Will gave the insult the response it deserved—an indifferent silence.

"Have you consulted our sister about your plans?" David put in. "I recommend you do so before posting any banns. Of all the people she might consult on the matter of choosing a bridegroom, I doubt your name would be first on the list. In fact, I doubt it would appear at all."

"I don't recall asking your opinion," Ronald said without looking at him.

"When did you ever seek an opinion that was not an echo of your own?" He expected no answer, and got none. "Nonetheless, you might bear in mind that though you are heir to Grenbrook, our father is still alive and in full possession of his faculties." Some evil impulse prompted him to add, "Or do you have some reason to think that might cease to be the case?"

His brother whirled, his face ugly. *"What did you say?"*

"I think you heard me," David said levelly. "It appears to me that you've had a very profitable year, Ronald. First Lenore—so soon after she inherited her grandfather's wealth, and before she could bear a child who might take some of it away from you. Did you ever tell anyone precisely what became of her?"

"That's none of your concern!"

"And now Mark is gone, and you stand poised to take his place. I know that Society sees you as one who is deserving of sympathy, but you hardly strike me as a man bereaved. On the contrary—"

He blocked the blow his brother aimed at him, and took a step to one side, out of arm's reach. "I shouldn't try that sort of thing anymore. You don't have me outnumbered the way you did at school, and I've killed better men than you in battle."

Ronald started to speak, then glanced at Will and visibly restrained himself. "So have I, little brother."

Will spoke suddenly. "And out of battle?"

"I was in London! And what business is it of yours?"

"I do not understand what you mean by that, Major," Will said punctiliously. "I was referring to matters of honor; I have called a man out and killed him for sufficient provocation, and I thought you might have, also."

"That, too, seems to me to be none of your affair."

"I fear that it is." Officer and gentleman, Commander Marshall could speak from his own authority when the occasion warranted. "I am aware of the courtesy due one's host, and would have thought it infamous to transgress upon your father's hospitality. But if you and I should meet when I am not a guest in your father's house, I suggest you refrain from crude jokes that impugn your brother's honor and my own. I have received such insults before, and I have dealt with them."

David felt a thrill of pride at Will's firm, level tone, and found it hard to maintain an impassive expression in the face of his brother's frustrated ire.

"What are you doing here, anyway?" Ronald flung at him. "And why have you brought him?"

"I don't believe I need explain myself to you," David said without raising his voice.

"You will, brat. Remember, you are dealing with the future Earl of Grenbrook."

"And the present horse's arse." He was angry with himself for allowing this quarrel to escalate, but on the other hand, he was relieved—and not only because Will was here beside him. Until now, he had been burdened with a dread of his brother, leftover memories of childhood pain, but life in the Navy really had made a man of him. After sailing into the face of cannon fire, he had no fear left for this fuming bully. "The future is a long way off, Ronald."

"Not so far as you think." His brother turned on his heel and strode back to the stable, with a touch of tantrum in his furious steps.

"Well, I had been willing to like him, for your sake," Will said, "but somehow it seems that is not to be. Whatever possessed you to accuse him of murder?"

"I didn't, Will," David said. He waited a moment to be sure Ronald did not follow them, after all, then headed for the house. "I asked him what his plans were, not what he had done. I wanted to see what his reaction might be. It was you who elicited an alibi, and you were not accusing him of murder, either—I took for granted that you were referring to his duel. Isn't that interesting?"

"What duel?"

"That's right, I never mentioned that to you, did I? And I'm sure Amelia did not."

"No. Neither of you have said anything to me about such a thing."

David glanced around, but there was no one within sight or earshot on the long path back to the house. "I hate to draw you into the family muddle, but after I think it best that you be aware of the situation. Yesterday, my sister told me that Ronald's wife Lenore died some time this past year when she was abroad, near where his regiment was stationed. There's been no explanation of what happened, whether she died of illness or accident...and shortly after that, Ronald was apparently involved in an affair of honor and wounded someone."

"Do you think the two events were connected?"

"Good Lord! That had not even occurred to me. I don't know, Will, and unless we were able to find someone who was on hand at the time, I see no way of finding out. The impression Amelia had was that the quarrel was over some debt or other, and getting Ronald out of that fix was expensive. She doesn't know the particulars, but she overheard Father laying down the law when Ronald was home last year. Even though that visit occurred shortly after his wife had died, he never saw fit to mention it when he was home."

"What? Not a word to the family?"

"Not one. Apparently he acted as though she was still alive but unable to travel—Amelia says he gave the impression that she was expecting a child."

"That seems ..." Will shook his head. "That is a very peculiar omission."

"Is it not? I wondered how he was planning to explain himself when the truth finally came out, but apparently he has managed to avoid a reckoning. If my father was able to pry anything out of him, I've heard nothing of it. Mark's death seems to have pushed all the old questions aside."

"When did you learn of his wife's death, then? And how?"

"Mark found out, according to my sister. He received condolences from a friend whose brother was in Ronald's regiment, but he could hardly inquire further without revealing that he'd known nothing about it. Ronald has also been bringing home gambling debts for my father to pay, which is why Amelia thought that might have had something to do with the duel."

"Should you be telling me all this?" Will interrupted.

"Who better? I need to talk to someone I can trust, and after all the hints my sister was dropping, it's only fair to be sure you understand the situation. I've been asking myself just how desperate Ronald might have become, and to what extent he would go to secure his own future."

"You know you can tell me anything in confidence." Will said. He walked on for several paces, studying his own boots. Then he said, as though making it clear to himself, "Do you mean to suggest that your brother Ronald might have had something to do with your brother Mark's death? Davy, do you truly think that a serious possibility?"

"Put so bluntly...Yes. I hate to think it, Will. I know I sound like a complete scrub for making the suggestion, or even thinking it, and if he really was in London at the time, then of course it's impossible. I know my dear brother well enough to be certain he would never hire an assassin and leave himself open to blackmail. He would do it himself."

"You are serious, then."

David sighed. He didn't like the tone of Will's voice. "Perhaps I should have kept silent. But Cain and Abel is the oldest story in the book, Will. Apart from the talking snake and the apple, of course, and I've always had my doubts about that one."

"If it were true..." Will stopped and turned. "If it *is* true, then your duty is clear. But, Davy, just because he goes out of his way to be rude and offensive, even if he had wished his brother dead...or was vile enough to rejoice in it...that still does not make him a murderer."

"I know." David kicked an innocent stone that lay on the path, and sent it hurtling into the grass. "I know that, Will. But it's not just Ronald's character, or lack of it, or the fact that I know him to be capable of considerable cruelty—that's not what has nagged at me from the start."

"What, then?"

"My brother Mark taught me to shoot. And you would be hard put to find a man who had more caution and respect for the destructive power of a gun. He would not let me even *touch* one until I could recite his rules for safety—never point it at anything I did not meant to kill, never kill any creature without a reason, never assume a weapon is un-loaded...even such things as being sure to put the gun through a fence before climbing the fence, and place it far enough away that there was no chance of stepping or falling on it, and—dear God, I had forgotten this—he taught me that if I should slip and fall, I must make certain to thrust the bar-rel away from me, to avoid just such an accident as they claim took his life. Mark was as careful and painstaking as the captain of a powder-room. Of all the people in the world who might die accidentally of a gunshot wound—of an in-jury from the careless handling of his own gun—his *own gun,* Will!—Mark is the very last person. I cannot believe his death was an accident."

Will nodded. "I must accept your knowledge of his char-acter," he said.

David's heart sank at his tone, and at what was left un-said. Will Marshall was a fair-minded man, a decent man. Faced with something this genuinely evil, his mind refused to accept it. David envied Will that innocence, but felt de-serted in the face of enemy fire. "You don't believe me." It wasn't even a question.

Will stopped, turned to him. "Davy, I trust you. I love you, sir. I know you to be a fair and honest man, and I be-lieve you are telling me the truth about your brother Mark. But accidents do happen, even to the most careful of men. And...yes, I do think you may be less than perfectly objec-tive in this situation. Ronald is arrogant, condescending, he seems to have no respect or regard for you—it would be amazing if you did not think the worst of him."

"With reason," David said, pushing away the memories of what Ronald and his friends had done so many years ago. "I haven't told you half the things he's capable of."

"If you did, I am sure I would believe them. I do not like him in any way, and he looks as though he's gone badly to seed since that portrait was painted, so no report of debauchery would surprise me. But *murder?* Of his own brother, Davy? That is so very...To say it's far worse is the most pitiful understatement. It is unthinkable!"

"Do you think I do not know that? And what of his wife, Will? What happened to Lenore, and why has he never even mentioned her?"

Will threw up his hands. "I don't know! Perhaps it was nothing more than guilt at having failed to protect her. He might have felt ashamed."

David laughed harshly. "Oh, Will...No. Not possible. He is not like you, he never feels shame, he only regrets being caught. I know for *certain* that he would torture his own brother."

"What?"

"From personal experience," he said shortly, "and that's all I mean to say about it. Perhaps you see that as less serious than murder—I did not, and do not. But even setting that aside, please consider what it means if my unfilial suspicion is correct. I fear for everyone over whom he will have power—especially for my father, who is now the only one standing between him and the title. It isn't just that I do not know what evil Ronald may have done. I do not know what more he might do."

"But we are not certain that he has done *anything.*"

If I cannot even depend on you ... "Will, I warned you of this last night, and asked you to trust me. You said that you would. If you find you cannot...then at least tell me so, and tell me now. I must find out what happened to Mark, with your help or without it. I *will* find out. If you are unable to help, at least don't hinder me."

Will studied him for a moment, then sighed. "You know I could never do that. But this enmity between you is so strong—and well-deserved, I certainly take your word for that—"

He stopped suddenly and turned away, and David could almost hear what he did not say. *You cannot be objective.*

Well, that was true. He was not objective. He was too familiar with Ronald's character to be so naïve. But there was no
point in trying to make Will see that, and no point in feeling
hurt and angry that Will seemed to be taking Ronald's part
against him. Will was trying to be fair. He could only wait
and try not to hope for more than Will could give.

Finally Will turned back to him. "Davy, I trust *you,* but I
cannot adopt your conviction as my own. I need proof to
convince me that such a loathsome charge is true. If you can
accept that, I will do what I can to help you find that proof. If
he did murder your brother simply to gain the title, of course
you must find a way to prove it and bring the murderer to
justice, and I must help you. Even if you were not dearer to
me than my own life, I should be obliged to do that."

The words were all David could hope for, but the re-
straint in Will's manner felt like a wall rising between them.
But Will was doing his best, and could not know how much
hurt accompanied this loss of intimacy. Will was being himself, and entirely honest. There was nothing to do but try to
meet him halfway. "Thank you. Will you come with me tomorrow, then? I want to see where this so-called 'accident'
took place, and if there is any proof that it truly was an accident, you will hear no more about it from me."

"Gladly," Will said.

⚓ ⚓ ⚓

Dinner that evening was as cheerless as that of the night
before, with the added discomfort of Ronald's presence. The
Countess did not feel well enough to join them, and the ladies Virginia and Eugenia also remained in their rooms.
David concentrated on his dinner and exchanged a few quiet
words with his cousin Jane. Amelia relayed the greetings and
condolences of their tenants, and received a nod from her
father in return. Ronald made a few abortive attempts to
quarrel, but Will presented a face of such bland courtesy that
none of his darts appeared to stick, and the Earl at last
snapped, "Mind your manners or go to your room!"

"Thank you!" Ronald answered icily. "I shall see if I cannot find more congenial company elsewhere." The Earl's son and heir rose, made a mocking bow to the ladies, and departed.

Becoming heir apparent, David reflected, had only worsened his brother's behavior. In the past, Ronald would have left after dinner to go inflict himself on his friends, or wherever it was he got to—but he would have waited until the ladies had left and would never have been so disrespectful to their father, who was looking decidedly dyspeptic.

To his surprise, though, his father did not make an early exit from their company. He stayed behind until the ladies departed, the port had been passed, and they were on their way to rejoin their womenfolk. As Will passed through the dining room doors ahead of them, the Earl stopped his youngest son with a glance. "A word with you."

David nodded to his friend to go on, and turned. "Sir?"

"Your sister spoke to me today. I imagine you know what she had to say?"

"Yes, sir, I do. But I would like you to know that this was not my doing—"

His words were cut short. "Nothing to do with you," his father said, staring at him with a measuring eye. "All her own idea, I know that. That one's got spirit enough, she should have been another son. Seems to think you'd do a better job of looking after her than your brother would, if I should stick my spoon in the wall. I told her I didn't see how. She said you couldn't do worse."

"I thank you both," David said gravely.

"Hold your tongue!"

David bit back a retort. There was nothing to be gained by starting a quarrel with the old man, not with the girls' future at stake.

"The pity of it is," his father continued, "she's right. He's no fit guardian for my daughters, and you're finally showing some sign of becoming a man. I've sent for Beauchamp to come by tomorrow. I shall be altering my will to remove

Ronald as the girls' guardian and transfer that responsibility to you. If you're not willing to take the job, you'd better say so now."

It was hardly the sort of conversation he'd ever expected to have with his father, but it was the first time he could recall ever having been addressed as a competent adult. "I am willing," he said, "if by 'the job' you mean what my sister proposed to me—that my mother and I be made joint guardians of Amelia and Eugenie, in the event of your death. My expectation, of course, is that Mother would exercise actual control over their activities, and I would merely act as needed in those areas outside a woman's domain."

"Yes. And Jane as well. She's doomed to be an old maid, but I'm damned if I'll send her back to that drunken lecher of a father—I told Eustace I'd take a horsewhip to him if he came near that girl ever again, and he knows I meant it. He signed her guardianship over to your mother and me, with an irrevocable trust for her marriage portion."

"So Jane is now a permanent member of our household?"

"Yes, until she marries or your uncle dies. Not that anything will change then—her brother's just as big an oaf as his father and grandfather before him, but the legal matters are sealed up too tight for him to get his paws on her money. How that clot of barbarians ever managed to produce an angel like your mother—but never mind that, it's three of them to look after. Do you think you're up to the job?"

"I believe so. But I hope and pray that the girls will have presented you and Mother with grandchildren before it ever comes to that."

The bristly eyebrows drew together over a suspicious stare. "Think you're smart, do you?"

That was simply too much. "Father, I have no idea whether I'm smart or not," he said, exasperation getting the better of his self-control. "But I don't believe I'm stupid, and I do love Mother and my sisters and will do my best to protect them if necessary. And—" He stamped hard on his anger and tried to find something conciliatory. "I am sorrier than I can say that we've lost Mark. I don't believe I ever realized how much we all depended on him."

For a split second, his father's face crumpled in pain, then returned to the lines of scorn and anger David knew too well. "Of course you didn't. You were oblivious. I doubt you ever gave a thought to this land, or anyone on it."

"And why would I have had reason to?" David asked, still trying to keep this discussion on even ground. "The land is yours, sir, and I knew it would be Mark's one day. If you know nothing else about me, you know full well I never envied him the title, or the estate, or the burden of responsibility." *Which is more than you can say for Ronald!* He thought that last, but hardly needed to say it aloud; he could read the old man's face well enough.

"Well, you'll have your share of the burden," the Earl growled. "And you needn't worry about supporting them on your Navy pay, I'll see they're all provided for."

"Thank you, sir." He waited, knowing that he would not get a word of thanks in return, but willing to be proven wrong. He almost said, "Will that be all?" but knew his father would twist that into sounding like he was seeking something for himself.. Which he was not. He knew better. If he said nothing, he would regret nothing.

After a long moment, the Earl said, "That's all. Go tell your sister she'll get her way. I need to go to my study and draft the changes."

"Yes, sir." As always, his reply was made in the privacy of his own mind. *I am doing you a service and am expected to thank you for it, and know that you respect me no more for this than you would if I had refused. Thank you, Father! It's nice to know that something in this house has remained constant.* As he hastened to the drawing room, David Archer reflected that at least his upbringing had made life in the Navy a little easier. One who expected nothing from Authority was seldom disappointed.

And now, at least, he'd be able to keep the girls safe.

Chapter 7

"It happened there." Davy paused at the top of the slope that led down to the stream, and the pool that formed where the swift-flowing water had scoured out the hollow between half a dozen boulders. "Not really a difficult climb, is it?"

"But there are rocks," Will pointed out. "Easy enough to trip and fall. Oh, get back, will you?" He gave a gentle shove to the liver-and-white spaniel that had accompanied them— Spark, the dog that had been with Davy's brother on his last ill-fated hunting trip. Davy had suggested they take a walk after breakfast and bring the beast along. He had stuck close to them, whining now as they descended to the area where the grass had been trampled into a churned-up mass of refrozen mud.

"They've made a mess of it," Davy said. As if agreeing with him, the dog went straight to the middle of the disturbed area, sniffed around at a darkened patch of ground, then sat down and howled. "Hush, old boy. That won't bring him back."

The animal shook itself and ambled over to Will, leaning heavily against him, panting. "Too bad he can't speak," Will said.

"Isn't it, though? All we need is one witness." Davy climbed back up to the highest point and looked around him, down the other side of the hill to a small patch of woods. "Out of sight of the house and the Dower House, the barns are behind that spinney..." His eye seemed to stop at a point in the woods. "Oh, not that."

"What is it?"

"The way the land slopes, there's no place in cover that would give a clear shot at a man standing here," Davy replied, "except one. D'you see that tree—the tallest one? It would be a clear shot, straight across, from up in the branches. A long way, even with a rifle, but not impossible."

Will walked up the grassy incline with the dog gamboling around him. "What do you mean?"

"There's a perfect sniper's post in that tree. I never thought of it that way as a child, but it would be ideal. If it's still there, of course. It might not be. And we must find out if it is. Come along."

Puzzled, Will followed, expecting it would all make sense at some point. "And how shall we do that?"

"Didn't you ever climb trees when you were a boy, Will?"

"Of course."

"So did I. In fact, I persuaded one of the stableboys to help me build a treehouse, in that very oak." He pointed to a venerable giant that grew amid a stand of smaller trees, its trunk so wide he and Davy would not be able to span with their arms it even if they reached around from opposite sides. "I used to sit up there when guests were expected—you can see all the way to the main road—then climb down with just enough time to run back and change into proper clothes before they reached the house. I could see for miles around, including the pool. I never thought that Ronald would discover my sanctuary."

"Unless he's much more agile than he looks, I would not think it now. Shall we go up and find out?"

"Yes." Davy grinned at the worn shooting jacket Will had borrowed, and his own old clothing. "Just as well we wore these, is it not? The trick is that you must begin on the smaller tree beside it, and climb across." He suited the action to the word, seizing a branch just over his head and swinging up to it. "Come, Will!"

Ascending the oak presented no difficulties to two young men who had spent their years as midshipmen skylarking among the shrouds of a frigate. The day was mild and sunny, with very little breeze, and the rough bark provided plenty of handgrips. Will felt entirely alive for the first time since they'd arrived, finally able to challenge his body in an activity he enjoyed.

He let his lover lead the way, admiring the view from below. From the speed and ease with which he moved, Davy had clearly recovered from his old injury. On the ground below, the abandoned spaniel barked a couple of times, then forgot all about them when a squirrel ran across his path. The squirrel sped toward another tree with the dog on its tail. Will laughed under his breath, and kept climbing.

Davy stopped suddenly, some thirty feet in the air. "It's still here!" he said. Peering past him, Will could see a loose heap of dead leaves. As Davy brushed them away, he could make out the corner of a wooden structure that was clearly not a part of the tree's natural form. "Still here, and in better trim than I expected." He cleared away the rest of the debris and waved an arm. "Welcome to my fighting top, Captain!"

Two branches of the tree grew within a few feet of each other, and several boards had been laid across them and nailed down, forming a platform five or six feet long and three or four wide. A snug little hideaway any boy would be proud of, it was nearly undetectable from below even in winter, thanks to the heavy branches that grew out on either side to serve as rails. When the tree was in leaf, this nest would be completely invisible.

"All sound," Davy said, walking about and testing the boards. No fool, he was keeping a prudent hand on a smaller branch, thicker than his arm, which stretched across the top of the platform at shoulder level. "I shouldn't wonder if young Jesse's father added more nails than we ever did. I thought this would be long gone by now."

"Who is Jesse?"

"One of Hubbard's boys. He's at the home farm now, I

believe, looking after the draft horses, but this would be a grand place to get away on a Sunday afternoon." Davy sat down upon the boards, leaning against a sturdy limb. "Have a seat, Will. It's not so impressive as my father's house, but I confess I'm more comfortable here than indoors."

Will joined him, finding himself at ease for the first time in days. "A very fine retreat indeed, Mr. Archer. Did you ever bring your sister up here?"

Smiling, Davy shook his head. "Lord, no. At this height, in her skirts? Far too dangerous. You would not credit how careful I was, Will. We had a rope that we slung down to the lowest branches, just in case we should lose our grip on the tree itself. Jesse would have been held accountable if I'd broken my neck, you see, and of course I was responsible for his safety. And really, it is a long way up."

"This is good work for a couple of youngsters."

"Better work than we did, I'm sure—that's why I think his father may have come up and made sure we wouldn't kill ourselves in the pursuit of adventure."

That answered a question Will had not wanted to ask; he knew it was ridiculous to be jealous of Davy's childhood playmates. "How old were you?"

"Oh, ten or eleven. Just old enough to handle the lumber and tools. I never told anyone we meant to put the thing so far up in the tree, of course, but the branches made a natural frame for it. And no one ever found me up here."

He looked very pleased with himself, and far more re-laxed than at any time since they'd come to Grenbrook. Will looked around, saw nothing but branches and sky. He leaned over to look down the way they'd come, and saw only Spark, making himself comfortable among the gnarled roots below. "I suppose the dog would bark if anyone were to approach," he said.

"He would if it were Ronald. Why do you ask?"

Trying not to raise his own expectations, Will leaned over and captured Davy's lips. After a moment's hesitation, they opened beneath his. He took his time with the kiss, hungry after all the time they'd been together when he dared not even think of touching him. "I know we agreed not to do anything improper in your father's house," Will murmured, "but since you say this is *your* sanctuary…"

"You're mad," Davy said, throwing an arm around his neck. "Come here."

Will had not realized how much he'd missed his lover's touch. As their lips met again, his whole body felt aflame. He slid a hand down to Davy's rear, pulling their bodies together, and felt Davy's fingers tighten on his thigh. "What would you like?"

"Nothing too complicated, it's cold and I've no grease. Doesn't matter." His hand traveled over to Will's fly and began fumbling with the buttons. "Just want to touch you. Never thought we'd have a chance here—"

"It's been too long." Will didn't bother with buttons; he slid his own hand down the front of Davy's trousers and felt the warm shape of his cock standing at attention through the heavy fabric. Davy sighed and arched upward. Will reached a little farther, and cupped Davy's balls while pushing him flat to administer a deep, thorough kiss. The moist heat of his mouth was a sharp contrast to the winter breeze on their faces. "God, I've missed this."

"Watch out," Davy warned. "My hand's cold." And it was, but after a startled gasp Will simply relaxed into the sensation of his lover's hand around him. Cold or warm, he was not going to complain.

He managed to get Davy's fly open to return the favor, but gave up his original plan when Davy pulled him down atop him. "Cold, are you?"

"Not in the least." Warm breath sent a tingle through him as Davy nuzzled his ear. "Warmer all the time." He thrust up, and Will found himself drowning in the delicious urgency. So good…and it would be over so quickly…

He caught himself, and gazed down at the dreamy face beneath his own, Davy's lips parted a little, his face flushed. "Must we hurry?"

Davy squeezed his arse with both hands. "Yes!"

"No." He softened the word with another kiss, pressing down to force their cocks tighter together. "Who knows when we'll get back here? Let me—" He ran out of words; he was never good with words. Instead, he moved back a bit and opened Davy's coat, unbuttoning the waistcoat beneath and pushing his shirt up far enough to slide his hand up under the shirt. As he'd expected, the nipple he found was hard and sensitive, and he muffled Davy's cry of pleasure with his mouth. All these were things Davy had taught him, in the slivers of time they had together; it really was better to give than to receive. Cradling Davy's head on one arm, he let the other hand travel over chest, belly, and lower, letting his fingers touch and tease, moving from one place to another until Davy was writhing in sweet frustration.

Davy got hold of him again, and that was sweeter still, but he resolutely pushed the hand away and shifted so he could kiss where his hand had been. When his mouth reached its target, Davy rebelled, rolling to one side so he could reply in kind.

And he returned the attention with interest. Will lost himself in the overload of sensation, each move of Davy's quivering body setting off a spasm in his own. It seemed to go on forever, but ended much too soon.

When the world began to spin back into place, he sighted along the length of his body and saw Davy's wicked grin. The first words out of his lover's mouth were, "Good thing the boards held, wouldn't you say?"

Will groaned. "A fine tangle we'd have made below."

"Yes, and proved all my brother's worst suspicions. But I did check her for soundness, Captain, and she proved steady after all."

"Mm." Will fished out his handkerchief and tidied up as best he could, then stole a few kisses that were surrendered without protest. When he got his breath back, he recalled the original purpose of their visit and raised his head above the railing as a sniper might. "Davy."

He was doing up his buttons. "Hm?"

"Do I understand that you have not been up here for some years?"

"Yes. Seven or so, at a guess. Why?" He gathered himself together and sat up, brushing dust from his jacket.

"It seems the tree went on growing after you left. Look here." It might have been possible to fire through the tangle of young branches that stretched between the aerie and the fishing pool, but only a madman would have expected to hit his target with a single shot. "No one could shoot toward the pool from this angle. If anyone tried, there's no telling where the ball might go. If he had several shots to find his range, it might be done, but even then, firing downward, through obstruction...It's too much risk with too little chance of success."

"What?" Davy scrambled to his knees and followed the line of Will's finger. "I see. Well, we must look around below, then." He shook his head in mock regret. "I suppose coming up here was a foolish thing to do."

"Not at all," Will said, still happily mellow with the afterglow. "I think this is the finest place on the entire estate."

"It's always been a favorite of mine," Davy agreed. "Though I admit, never for the same reason. But..."

"What of that building? A gazebo, perhaps?"

"What gazebo? There's nothing built out here."

"There, beyond the shrubbery." A dense hedge of tall evergreens—holly, Will thought—had screened it from view as they'd approach the oak, but from above he could see a roof of some kind, indistinct amid the lower branches of smaller trees. "If you were thinking of a shot from cover, what could better serve the purpose?"

"That's new to me. Let's go down and have a look."

Once on the ground, Will had to deal with the enthusiastic welcome of the spaniel, who acted as though he'd been abandoned for weeks. When the dog finally settled down, Davy led the way around the holly bushes and trotted up to the top of the stairs. The structure was set high, no doubt with the same purpose as the crow's nest up in the tree, and the cast iron framework blended with the grey-brown trunks and branches around it. "This would be a good place for a picnic in summer. Shady and cool, with a view of the water. I wonder if it was Mark's idea."

Will ascended to the platform with the dog still tagging at his heels. His assessment was military, not pastoral—if one wanted to set a sniper in ambush, the placement could hardly be better, save for the distance. It was high enough, just barely. "It's a clear shot, but not an easy one. How good a marksman is your brother?"

Davy moved closer, sighting along the line of fire. "Good enough. Dangerously good. And he could wait comfortably, out of sight." He motioned toward low benches set along the railing on three sides. "Easy to brace the rifle and take aim— Will, look here!"

At his feet was a small dark patch, black against the floorboards. "I think this might be—" He touched it experimentally, and his finger came away with a smudge that he sniffed. "Gunpowder." Brushing his fingers together, he said, "Very fine-grained gunpowder."

Will frowned at it. "So it appears someone loaded a gun here. But your brother was shot—what, a month ago? Would it lie undisturbed that long?"

"Not so long as that, Will. Less than three weeks. And this site is sheltered by the roof as well as this bench, and this powder was ground into the floor. I'd say someone spilled a bit, then stepped in it when he rose." He tried to shoo Spark off the gazebo, but he and Will both had to leave it in order to get the animal to follow them.

Will began to have second thoughts about the assumption they were making. "This could mean someone lay in wait for your brother, but it's by no means certain. What if someone else—"

"Who? And whatever for? Will, there's nothing to hunt right now but rabbit and wood-pigeons. At this time of year there's not much in the garden for rabbits to destroy, though

I suppose some of the men might hunt for the pot. Even so, this is hardly the place anyone would ambush a rabbit."

"Could you discover for certain whether anyone did go out?"

"I can ask Amelia, and the gamekeeper ought to know, but only consider—Mark died in a hunting accident at the very end of the hunting season. I think it will be spring before anyone can pick up a gun without thinking of that. I know this powder is not proof of anything, but you must admit it's damned peculiar."

"It is that. But as you say, the only thing it proves is that someone had powder here. It wouldn't even necessarily mean there was a gun. Someone might have shaken a little loose powder out of his pocket when he sat down."

"Out here? In the dead of winter? Why?"

"Why not?" Will caught himself, trying not to show his impatience at the circular argument. "Davy, only think a moment. If it's been here since that day, why could it not have been your brother Mark, resting his feet? We know *he* was out here."

"We also know that Mark never stopped to rest when he was hunting. He was always active, always on the move." Davy's hand flashed in an impatient gesture. "I'm sorry, Will, of course you don't know that. But when he was out in the field, Mark's motto was 'If you need to sit down, you ought to go home.'"

"Oh, was it?" The last thing they needed was a quarrel with one another over something so insignificant. "I didn't mean—"

"No, no, my fault," Davy said quickly. "And of course anything is possible. Knowing Mark, it's unlikely, but I shan't argue the point. If you can't believe me, you can't; that's an end to it. We can only be sure that someone was here with gunpowder. If you insist, I shall even admit that there is no proof he had a weapon with him."

"No, that would be foolish. It is fair to assume the presence of a gun, but the identity of its owner is all conjecture."

"And no way to prove or disprove my suspicion, I know. No proof of anything." He seemed about to continue along that line, then said abruptly, "We had better get back to the house and change out of these damp clothes."

"I agree. We have learned all we can for the present. Am I fit for polite company?" Will asked, turning around so Davy could see if there were still leaves clinging to his back.

"No more than usual, though I detect a hint of satisfaction in your manner. Nothing that suggests improper activity, Will. And I?"

Will checked him over with loving care. Buttons done up properly, a few smudges on the back of the jacket...and a faint lessening of the tension that had been riding his shoulders since they'd arrived, though he was obviously disappointed that their expedition had not been more successful. "You'll do."

⚓ ⚓ ⚓

They managed to detach Spark when they were leaving their boots and heavy coats in the back entryway, near the kitchen. The dog's sudden attachment to Will proved a frail reed in comparison to the allure of a ham bone the cook had saved for him. "Fickle beast," David said.

"I take no offense. He's a friendly creature, but I've never hunted with a gun dog, so I can't give him any amusement. Is he allowed in the house? I've not seen any pets about."

"Oh, you'll see them, from time to time. Genie has a canary, and Mama has an old pug who spends most of its time sleeping by the fire. You walked right by him when we went to visit her—he's three-quarters deaf and almost never stirs. There were more animals about when I was younger; Mark would have a dog or two at his heels all day, indoors or out. I'm sure the poor animal is grieving now—you saw him down at the pool."

"So he's drowning his sorrows with a juicy bone instead of a pint of ale?"

David shrugged. "Why not? Come, let's go upstairs. We need to change into more presentable clothing." Will was a little way behind him as he started up the stairway, but he had only gone a few steps when he realized that there was an argument underway in what he thought of as the "gentleman's wing."

Amelia's voice was low but clear. "No, I will *not!* And if you think Father will allow you to simply walk in and begin rearranging our lives to suit your fancy, you had better think again!"

David stopped short, moving closer to the railing, and motioned to Will to get out of sight.

"You may as well accept this, Amelia." Ronald's voice. Of course, who else? "Once Father is gone—"

"Which, God willing, will not be for many years yet!"

"You will do as I bid you," he continued, ignoring her words. "Dixon would be a better husband than you deserve, and I would find the alliance very useful. It's not as though you've snared any prizes on your own—you may as well do your duty to the family."

She produced an unladylike snort. "Duty? What do you know of *duty,* Ronald? You never saw this family as anything but a purse to support your amusements!"

"It's a great deal more to me now, is it not? I'll be head of the family, and you and your dear Jane had better –"

"And you can leave Jane out of this, too. She didn't escape one monster just to tie herself to another—"

The sound of a slap and a cry from his sister broke David from his stillness. He gained the top of the stair in two leaps and erupted into the hall in time to see Amelia return the slap with considerable interest—that cry had been more of anger than pain.

He caught Ronald's arm and swung him around, dodging the blow his brother flung at him. "What do you think you're doing?" he demanded.

"Putting on airs," Amelia said breathlessly, her fists clenched. "He seems to think Father is already in his grave, and he's been promoted not only to Earl, but Archbishop of Canterbury!"

David moved between them. "You've spent too long in foreign parts," he said. "Perhaps you've forgotten that an Englishwoman's consent is required for a legal marriage."

"She'll do as she's told!"

"By you?" she flared. "I very much doubt it!"

"By God, you need a keeper, not a husband!"

David turned slightly, extending a hand toward each of them, and was pleased to see Ronald take a step back.

But that did not put an end to the argument. "I've Father's promise that I need not marry unless I choose to, and that if I do, I shall marry *whom* I choose," Amelia said, her voice low and razor-sharp. "And I can tell you, Ronald, I'd marry that butcher Bonaparte before I'd lower myself to any creature vile enough to win your approval."

"Perhaps you'd best talk to our father about that," Ronald said. "He was closeted with Beauchamp half the afternoon— no doubt he has your future assigned to my loving care."

"Really?" David caught his sister's eye; she gave him a grim smile and a slight shake of the head. He had done it, then. "How much would you care to risk on that, brother?"

Ronald's eyes narrowed. "The old man's nearly seventy. It's only a matter of time. I cannot be cut out of the succession."

"Grandfather was eighty-five when he died," Amelia reminded him. "And if he hadn't tried to take that last fence, he might be with us still."

David decided to send his brother off on a false trail. "I don't think Father has been pleased with your career, Ronald. My money's on Mr. Beauchamp as trustee. At any rate, why this sudden solicitude toward Amelia? She seems to have no fear of the spinster state. Do you crave more nieces and nephews?" He felt a movement behind him, and Ronald's scowl told him that Will was at his back.

"I know she's got no chance of finding a husband without help," Ronald said. "Dixon's a good man and he's willing to saddle himself—"

"He's a lecherous swine, and you know it," Amelia said,
and added to the others, "Ronald once brought him to visit at
the town house. Captain Dixon not only proved to be a dolt,
his manners were foul. He mistook Cousin Jane for a governess and tried to take liberties—particularly stupid with
Father in the next room, which meant that before Dixon
knew what struck him, he was standing out on the street,
where he waited for half an hour while his valet packed his
belongings."

David could easily imagine his father's comments, too.
"Not an auspicious introduction," he said.

"Precisely what he deserved. That creature is not welcome in this house."

Drawing himself up, Ronald declared, "Another thing
that is going to change when I'm master here."

"He does not sound like the sort of man I'd choose to call
brother," David said. "What is it, Ronald? Do you owe this
Dixon money and mean to pay him off with your sister's
dowry?"

Ronald's head snapped around. "*Damn* you!"

Got it in one, David congratulated himself. "Too near the
mark?"

Amelia laughed, not happily. "I had not thought of myself as a bargaining chip, Davy, but I think you hit the gold."

"Suit yourself, sister." Ronald snarled. "You should be
happy leading apes in Hell." He pushed past them and flung
off down the staircase. A moment later, they heard a door
slam.

"Off to the stables, to take out his ill-temper on his
horse." David realized his sister was shaking and put an arm
around her, but a glance at her face made him aware that she
was not frightened, but furious.

"It seems His Lordship Presumptive has all our lives
planned out for us." Amelia said. "So kind of him! I am to
marry his bosom-bow, and he himself means to marry Jane."

"Whatever for?" Will asked, clearly at sea. "She cannot
be in favor—"

"She most certainly is not. I suspect he's got his eye on

the money she would bring to the marriage. And no doubt he wishes to prove that he can do as he likes—but he cannot, not in this case. Jane despises him."

"Where are all the other ladies now?" David asked.

"Anne is with Mother, and I believe Jane is helping Genie with her piano practice. Why do you ask?"

"Only in the hope that none of them overheard all this." He moved farther into the east corridor, away from the wing that held their parent's chambers. "Are you certain Father has named me guardian for you girls?"

"Yes. He spoke to me just before Mr. Beauchamp arrived, and asked me once more if I was very sure I could rely on your judgment. I said just what I had before, and he replied that I had better be completely certain, because by the end of the day I would have my wish. And he said—Davy, he means to leave *all* unentailed property to the rest of us, divided, he said, according to need."

David blinked. "He told you that? All of us?"

"Yes. I asked if he meant me to keep that secret, and he said, 'I shall inform your mother when she is able to discuss the matter. I should prefer you not tell your sisters.'"

Astonished, David said nothing. Was that what the Earl had meant when he said that he would see to it that the girls were provided for? He was inclined to believe that their father had made the bequest to his daughters, equally, and Amelia had interpreted that more broadly, but what of it? It was her welfare, and Genie's, that really mattered.

Will didn't seem to notice his silence. "So, my lady, you do not believe he told your brother?"

"Not if he has made the changes as he promised—and I have never known Father to break his word. It seems to me that he is keeping his conversations with Ronald to the very minimum."

"I hope he does tell Ronald," David said. "And soon. That is the one thing I can imagine that might turn our brother sweet—and safeguard Father's life. He'll want to be sure the will is changed again, in his favor."

Will frowned, but Amelia nodded. "To hear him talk, one would think Father was already in his grave. Ronald was always selfish, but this surpasses all—to write his own father off so blithely!"

"'Only a matter of time,'" David said. "He is quite looking forward to our loss."

"Indeed!" She hesitated, then said, "Would it be harsh to say this makes me wonder about Mark's accident? It was the last thing in the world one would anticipate; he was always so careful with guns!"

"I've had the same thought," Davy said. "It seems Ronald was in London, though, and we've no way to prove otherwise, or even inquire."

"Of course you can inquire," Will said. "Why could you not? The Army must keep records of officers' leave, and where they may be reached when they're away."

"Father," Amelia said simply.

"But surely, in so serious a matter..." Will's protest dwindled away as both Archers shook their heads.

"We might hire a solicitor to make very discreet inquiries," David said. "Though it would have to be done without my father's approval. He may not be pleased to have Ronald in Mark's place, but he would never approve of an inquiry."

"Still..."

"No, Will. Mark's death was ruled *accidental*. No one needs an alibi for an accident. I can only imagine the uproar if we were to be found investigating Ronald's whereabouts at the time of Mark's death."

"I wish that we might do it, though," Amelia said. "And I wish that I could be shocked at the thought of it being necessary, but Ronald has changed for the worse since he joined the Army. I never thought he cared much for the rest of us, except Grandmama, but he was not so utterly hateful. It seems that none of us matter now, save to serve his purpose. But Davy, really—to kill his own brother!" She faltered, looking from David to Will as if hoping for a contradiction. "Even he would not do such a thing...would he?"

Was there any point in lying? David shrugged. "We both know that answer, Lia. Of course he would, if he thought he could do so without being caught. The question is not would he, but *did* he? And if so, how?"

"That's not the only question," Will said. "The critical one is—if he did, how can we prove it? It would take a local magistrate to hand the case over to the Assizes. Who is that, in this district?"

David sighed. "The Earl of Grenbrook, of course. My father."

⚓ ⚓ ⚓

A conspiracy, that's what it was. And Dearest Mama, of all people, to thank for it! Of course she had always coddled that superfluous whelp. The runt of the litter...if he had come home alone, dealing with him would've been a trifling matter, but he'd found himself a protector while he was away, and apparently found a backbone as well. It would be a challenge to hunt the pair of them...But no. Best to get over heavy ground as lightly as possible. The war would resume, they would depart, and the women could be brought to heel easily enough. Compromise the cousin, by force if necessary, and once her belly started to show she'd marry readily enough; her marriage portion would pay off all outstanding debts.

If one had any belief in a power higher than oneself, one would pray for war.

Chapter 8

R onald's absence at tea provided a much-needed break in the domestic drama. The Earl, Lady Anne reported, was having tea with his wife in her chambers, so the only gentlemen present were Davy and Will. Lady Eugenie seemed to be feeling more herself, and more determined than ever to practice her feminine wiles on a hapless naval officer. She fluttered, she gazed upon Will with wide admiring eyes, she spoke in reverent tones of the pride a woman must feel to know that the lord of her household was off fighting His Majesty's enemies...until Davy kindly turned to his baby sister and said, "You'd hate it, you know."

She faced him with all the injured dignity of naïveté. "How can you possibly say that?"

"Genie, you are not the sort of young lady who enjoys being left alone. Think of how long it's been since I was last here at home. I'll give you a five-pound note if you can even remember the date you last saw me."

The dignity vanished as she strove to summon a date from her memory, without success. "Well—but—but you are my *brother!*"

"I am well aware of that, and glad of it. The year, please?" He gave her plenty of time to respond, to no avail. "I know men who have not seen their ladies in two years' time—and I mean officers, not those poor foremast devils who only have their wives in to visit on board when the ship's in port. And even when his ship is in port, a captain is obliged to sleep aboard, as an example to his crew."

Her eyes widened. "You cannot mean that!"

"I can and I do, little sister. Exceptions are made if a captain is required to travel far from port, but that is the general rule...a captain is married to his ship. If you give your heart to a sailor, you will spend most of your life alone."

Did the tone of his voice have a tiny edge of pain to it? Will wasn't sure himself, and no one else seemed to notice as Davy continued, "A Navy wife can go from bride to widow without spending one week of the year under the same roof as her husband. That may be an honor, but I think it must be a lonely one. I cannot help but believe that when you give your affections to a gentleman, you will expect him to be on hand to appreciate you."

Jane Winston asked demurely, "So, Cousin, is it your opinion that sailors ought not to marry at all?"

"No, of course not," he said. "It would be disaster for the breed to die out. But I do believe that ladies should be aware of the disadvantages. We may have splendid uniforms in His Majesty's Navy," he brushed a nonexistent speck of lint from one shoulder, "but you must not be swept away by them."

"Perhaps Genie finds the notion of being her own mistress an attractive proposition," Lady Amelia said. "If one must have a husband, it might be convenient to have a spouse who spent all his time aboard his—" She glanced at Lady Anne and said, "Oh, I am sorry, dearest. Forgive my poor attempt at humor."

"You needn't apologize. I will concede your point," Lady Anne said. "Of course I would prefer to have my husband at home, but when I was increasing, and now, with the girls so young, there is much to be said for Gilliam being in the Service. My life is more serene than if he were present to take me out on the social rounds, and domesticity has made me so content that I must seem rather dull. I truly prefer a quiet life, spending the day with my sewing, or perhaps visiting with a friend or two."

Will caught the twinkle in her eye, and did not miss the

consternation on Lady Eugenie's pretty face. "That sounds much more pleasant than what befell Lady Pellew when Sir Edward made his famous rescue of the *Dutton*," he said. "Do you know the story?"

"I know he saved almost the whole ship's company," Lady Anne said. "Several hundred souls, was it not?"

"Over five hundred," Will said, "the youngest a baby who had been born during the voyage. The ship ran aground in a storm, and all her officers were able to do was get a hawser to shore. Merchantmen, of course," he added. "Not Navy. The ship was in confusion, and being knocked to pieces."

"I had heard nothing of Lady Pellew. What was her part in the rescue?"

"Prayer and patience." He saw that he had Lady Eugenie's rapt attention as well, and explained, "Sir Edward was taking her to dine with the vicar when their carriage was halted by the hubbub of people watching the wreck of the Dutton. He went off to see what the trouble was, and immediately took command of the situation—leaving her ladyship in the carriage whilst he swam out to the ship along the hawser and organized a rescue. His own ship—the *Indefatigable*, I believe—" He looked to Davy, who nodded, "was also attempting to assist the *Dutton*, and eventually they brought everyone safely to shore."

"But Lady Pellew," Eugenie said. "What became of her, that night?"

"We must assume she either continued on to dinner or went home to await news and notify a physician to stand by. Sir Edward injured his back on the way out to the ship, and spent a week in bed afterward."

"Ah, that foils my argument," Davy said. "He *did* spend an entire week at home. And I'm sure her ladyship was gratified when Sir Edward was made a baronet for his heroism."

"I think I should rather have my husband whole and sound," said Lady Anne. "I am proud enough of him without such extraordinary exploits. What a long night that must have been for Lady Pellew!"

"Sir Edward has always had a reputation as a fire-breather," Will said. "I believe her ladyship is well accustomed to sitting at the hearth, waiting for news of his latest exploit."

Lady Eugenie shook her curls. "How could anyone be accustomed to being left on the side of the road?"

"Well, I'm certain you would not appreciate it," Davy said. "Nor would you like to see your spouse lying prostrate, unable to squire you to a ball."

She bridled. "If he had come by his injury so honorably, I would sit beside him and tend his injuries! I am *not* a silly little girl, you know."

"Of course not," he agreed. "You are a silly young lady."

She turned to Will. "I am convinced, sir, that if you had sisters you would not tease them so!"

"No, never," he said quickly. She smiled, and he added, apologetically, "I should probably be much worse."

Lady Amelia took pity on him, and addressed her elder sister. "Anne, you said you had a letter from Gilliam this afternoon. Is there any chance he will be given leave to come home?"

The conversation wandered away into more general channels, and Will was able to stop feeling like an East Indiaman with a privateer bearing down with the weather-gauge. But the mention of letters reminded him that he had not yet written to let Sir Percy know that they had arrived safely, and he decided to put pen to paper as soon as he had a chance. There was still a world outside Grenbrook Manor, even if its crises were taking up all his attention.

⚓ ⚓ ⚓

The Heir Presumptive chose once again to deprive them of his presence at the dining table. If anyone noticed, they did not object. Afterward, the long-delayed game of whist was proposed and entered into, and David Archer had the immense satisfaction of seeing Will foiled at last, and by his own partner. Genie understood the game no better than David did himself, but he, at least, had experience enough to keep from disgracing himself. When they exchanged partners he persuaded Jane to take his place to give poor Will a respite, and joined his sister where she sat knitting some sort of fluffy thing for the imminent nephew or niece.

"Had all you can stand?" she asked slyly.

"It was never my favorite pastime," he said. "Poor Will!"

She chuckled, tsk'd as she dropped a stitch, and said, too quietly to be heard over at the card-table, "Father has made the changes. He has his draft copy, and the signed original went off with Mr. Beauchamp. I must say I am very much relieved."

"Do you know if he explained the changes to our beloved brother?"

"I believe he has. The subject arose when I told him that Ronald had proposed a match for me with his friend Dixon."

Her matter-of-fact tone surprised him. "How did you ever manage to bring *that* up without a tempest?"

"Why, gratitude, of course. I thanked him for taking such swift action to protect us from Ronald's ill-judgment—and of course he wanted to know what I meant by that."

He nearly whistled, but caught himself so as not to attract attention. "My God, Lia, you're a veritable Hercules."

"I had to let Father know of Ronald's intentions. How would it be if the odious Mr. Dixon were to show up at the door with his luggage and servants, and say that the heir of Grenbrook had invited him to come courting?"

"To a house in mourning? I can't believe anyone would be so graceless. That reminds me, thank you for putting Will at his ease. When he saw the black bunting, he was mortified at the thought of intruding."

"You needn't thank me, dear. I have been dying to meet him. As for Ronald's friend, well...I would not rely on his good manners."

"You've met him, not I. Poor girl! But that reminds me, where has Ronald hidden his batman—that slinking little weasel? I would expect to see him lurking behind th' arras, or listening at keyholes."

"Our brother arrived without servants this time. Isn't that curious? He told Leland that because he would be selling out soon, his man had been assigned to another officer, but Ronald is the last one I'd expect to see doing without a servant to look after his every need."

Unless he meant to do some surreptitious reconnaissance, David thought. Or any activity for which he was unwilling to chance a witness who could testify against him. "He's got poor James doing for him now, I believe."

"Yes, and James has already asked Father for a character. I don't suppose you know any gentlemen who would be in need of an excellent valet?"

He shook his head. "I can write to Kit, if you like. His wife's father has just decided to settle in England and marry again. He's a mere physician, though, and father-in-law to a baron, so I'm not certain if his blood's blue enough for James."

She smiled, but he could see her heart wasn't in it. "I hope James can bear with him until Mother's up and around—she hardly needs to have servants vanishing, on top of all the other troubles."

"I'll speak to him, if you think that would help. Would you like to go riding again tomorrow?"

"Oh, yes, if the weather permits. You had best warn Captain Marshall, though—I am sure Genie is well enough to go with us."

He glanced over to the card table, where Genie was blinking helplessly at the cards in her hand. "Never. My bold Captain needs to learn how to defend himself in situations where a sword or pistol is out of place."

"Your bold Captain." She glanced at Will, then back to David. "He's a quiet gentleman, but there's no back-down in him, is there?"

He raised an eyebrow. "I hope you're not getting ideas," he said, truthfully.

She opened her eyes wide, doing a fair imitation of Genie at her least subtle. "Would *I* do such a thing?"

Normally, David Archer could read his sister's meaning. This time he could not.

⚓ ⚓ ⚓

The next morning's weather did permit them to ride, but only for an hour or so; a line of turbulent clouds made its way across the landscape so speedily that their party barely had time to reach the safety of the stable before a cold, drenching rain began to soak the earth. Lady Anne was waiting for them at the door, and bustled her youngest sister, who had begun sneezing, off to change her clothing. The other ladies went along with them, and Will was happy enough to follow Davy back to their quarters.

"You're showing some improvement," Davy said encouragingly. "If you could only find the rhythm to post when he trots, you'd soon find the other gaits more comfortable."

"I'll never make much of a rider, I know that," Will responded. "But it was good to get out of the house and into the open air. I do believe my balance is improving—at least, the horse's movements are becoming less of a surprise. The boots help, I think."

"I hoped they might." In the course of keeping some promise to his sister, Davy had gone off to consult with Mark's valet the evening before, and had begged the use of a pair of his late brother's old riding boots—*not*, he had been careful to explain to Will, the top-boots that might make him look as though he was putting on airs.

Davy pulled a chair close to the fire and stuck out his own booted foot. "Here, give me a hand with these, would you? I know you'd rather not call for a valet. I'll help you with yours, too."

"Thank you!" Will dropped to one knee and smiled up at him wistfully as he drew the boot off. He ran an admiring hand down Davy's buckskin-clad thigh. "I'd be happy to help with any other articles you might wish to remove, sir, but..."

"Alas, just the boots," Davy said, returning the smile. "Where's a handy tree when you need one?"

"Out in the downpour," Will said, propping the second empty boot beside the first and restraining his impulse to offer more personal services. "My turn."

"As we came inside, I was thinking of what that squall would be like at sea," Davy said, trading places with him. "Hatches battened, the rain falling sideways, and next to no difference between being soaked on deck or dripping wet in the cabin."

Will glanced at the fire, appreciating the warmth and the clean, dry room. "If we were at sea, we'd be too busy or too weary to think of the damp, but I can't say I miss it. This is certainly more comfortable."

"Physically, yes." Davy picked up both pair of boots and took them over to leave outside the door for cleaning. He came back to the other chair and stretched his own feet out to the fire. "I think we may both wish we were back on the *Mermaid* by the time we're finished with supper. My sister-in-law Virginia is planning to join us."

That sounded as though it ought to be a good thing, but Davy's tone suggested anything but. "She is feeling better, then?"

"I couldn't say. Amelia says she is 'determined' to join us, and I hate to imagine what that may mean. It might simply be that she's grown bored, but I have to wonder..." Davy bit his lip. "Let me put it this way: all the charm she exerted to extract an offer from Mark vanished once the ring was on her finger. If he had not been the heir to Grenbrook, I doubt she would have made the effort, and she has always been certain, up to the moment each of her daughters was born, that she was carrying the next heir. Lia suggested I warn you that Virginia might well express some very strong opinions on the succession."

Will had no idea what that might mean. "And how should I respond?"

"As noncommittally as possible, I think. I don't like Virginia very much, Will, but I do pity her. The poor woman's lost the chance to achieve her life's ambition. She may still be the mother of a future Earl, but unless she has a son and he produces an heir of his own, her place here is not secure. And if the baby is a daughter, she's lost it all."

Will's knowledge of succession in noble houses had always been vague at best—it had, after all, never been something that was likely to affect him personally. "Your father would not turn her out, would he?"

"Of course not. But Ronald would find a way to make her so uncomfortable here that she would leave—which she would likely do in any case. They've always had a cordial hatred for one another." He laughed at Will's obvious dismay. "My poor Will, I apologize for bringing you into such a tangle. I grew up with all these conflicts and undercurrents, and never gave them much thought—no more than a fish would think about the rocks and rapids in a stream."

"It's natural enough, I suppose," Will said. "Much like being First Lieutenant on a man o' war and then being pushed back to Fourth when a few replacements with more seniority come aboard."

"Except it's not likely Virginia would be able to work her way back up now, and she'll never make Post Captain in this command."

Will was glad enough for the warning when they were gathering to go into the dining room, and before very long he found himself churlishly wishing that Lady Virginia had stayed sequestered in her suite. When he was introduced to the widow, she seemed barely aware of his presence, which he found perfectly acceptable. But the moment Ronald Archer walked into the room, her hostility was made quite palpable with an indrawn hiss. She drew Lady Anne aside, and a moment later Davy's sister quietly asked Will to sit beside Lady Virginia instead of Lady Amelia, adding in an undertone that it distressed the widow to sit beside the man who would one day take her husband's place as head of the family.

"Of course," Will responded immediately, wondering how the Honorable Ronald would react to giving up pride of place to a mere naval commander. But Lady Anne was speaking to him now; his brows drew together, but he nodded, obviously displeased but not willing to make a fuss about it.

If one took a step back and observed the lines of communication, this small change became a demonstration of social tactics. Lady Anne received the instruction, no doubt couched as a request; she passed it on immediately, then shared it with Lady Amelia, who spoke to her father, and the two ladies disseminated the information to the rest of the fleet. By the time the family proceeded in to dine, there was no sign that the order of their going was in any way out of the ordinary.

That façade of serenity began to crumble as soon as the first course was served and everyone began to make conversation with their companions. Lady Virginia did not bother to even touch her food. She fixed Will with an intense gaze and said, "You must help me."

"In what way, my lady?" he asked, wondering if she had dropped her napkin or some other small item.

"My son," she said, placing a hand just below the ribbon marking the high waistband of her gown. "David is a loyal brother, and you are his friend. I know that I can place my confidence in you." She had high cheekbones and rather deep-set blue eyes that made him think of pictures of some of the more fanatical martyrs. Will really did not wish to be the repository of her confidence.

"I...shall do everything possible, my lady," he said uneasily. He glanced across the table to Davy, who appeared to be considering what Eugenie was telling him. But Davy had his eye on Ronald—who was listening attentively to Virginia's rambling.

"That would be precisely nothing, Commander," Ronald drawled. "Virginia, you must be taking far too much cordial, or whatever you've been quacking yourself with. With all respect, madam, you have no son."

"Ronald—" his elder sister said warningly. He subsided, but the damage was done.

"What he says is quite true," Lady Virginia said, leaning toward Will as though it would keep her words from her brother-in-law. "I have no son as yet. But soon I shall, very soon, and we will need protection, for the same hand that struck my husband down will seek to destroy my child." She clutched Will's arm, darting a venomous glance across the table. "He sits there as though he deserves to take my husband's place, when the law must not permit it. He must fear my son, who will grow up and avenge his father against the mark of Cain!"

The Earl seemed to decide that things had gone beyond tolerable. "Virginia, that is quite enough. You must not allow your grief to lead you into foolish accusations." To Ronald, he said, "Such harsh language to a woman in your sister's condition is inexcusable. I demand you apologize."

If he intended to do so, Lady Virginia gave him no chance. "What does he care of my condition? He would like to see me lose my child!"

"Virginia, your husband—*my son*—suffered an unfortunate accident. It is tragedy enough for us all, but it was an accident, and no more. Ronald was in London at the time."

"So he says!" Lady Virginia put her cutlery down, bright spots of color appearing on her cheeks. "And do you believe him?"

"You are overwrought," the Earl said.

"And you are a fool!" she retorted. "Look at that creature. *Look* at him! Smug! He has what he has always wanted, the jealous beast!"

He did indeed have it, if what he wanted was to make Lady Virginia appear to be hysterical and discredit her accusations. And from the bland satisfaction on Ronald's face, he knew it, too.

"Come, sister." Amelia was suddenly beside the furious, bereaved woman. "Let us go back to your room, where you can finish your meal in peace and safety." Virginia was reluctant, but with Jane's help Amelia managed to persuade her to leave the table.

An uneasy silence fell after they left, finally broken by their hostess. "The accident was a great shock to her," Lady Anne said to Will. "I believe her reason is a little unsettled at the moment."

What could one say to that? Agree or disagree, it would sound insulting either way. "I have seen sudden grief lead men to rash behavior," he said carefully. "Such a terrible loss for her, at such a time…"

Lady Anne nodded approval of his tact, and let the subject lie. Conversation hung suspended until the two younger women returned, and after that Will found himself uttering inanities in response to Amelia's commonplace revelations about the hyacinths she had begun forcing in the conservatory. He was so grateful to her for taking up the burden of conversation that he found himself agreeing that he had always found blue hyacinths to possess a stronger scent than pink or white—something to which he had never paid the slightest attention. He wondered if that were true, and wondered whether he was absolutely certain of the difference between a hyacinth and a narcissus, another flower she indicated an interest in cultivating. He also found himself wishing that war would break out so he would have good reason to flee the premises.

At last the ladies departed, the port was passed among the gentlemen, and after one drink for courtesy's sake the Earl excused himself to deal with some pressing matter or other. Ronald simply got up and left, without the bother of saying anything to his brother or their guest.

Davy swirled the sweet wine around the bottom of his glass. "It's just as well I am not much of a drinking man," he said thoughtfully. "I'm sorry, Will. Shall we join the ladies?"

"I suppose we must," Will said.

But the ladies were equally distressed over the widow's outburst, and Lady Eugenie appeared to be experiencing a

return of the sore throat she'd been suffering a few days earlier. Will thought the girl must really be feeling unwell, since
she made no objection when Lady Anne chivvied her off to
bed.

After a little while, Amelia and Jane also excused themselves and went to their rooms. The gentlemen rose as they
exited, and Davy turned to Will. "Would you enjoy a game
of chess or some cards?"

"If it would please you, certainly," Will said. "But I
would be just as happy to retire for the evening."

"A pretty family gathering I have invited you to witness!" Davy's face was as downcast as Will had ever seen it.

"I do believe Lady Virginia might be a little unbalanced
in her grief," he answered, "but your brother was deliberately
baiting her. I like your sister Amelia very well, she is so
much like you. And your other sisters are doing their best in
very trying circumstances. This situation cannot be easy for
any of your family."

"Except for Ronald," Davy said bitterly. "He relishes it.
Will, if you would rather not endure this wrangle, I would
not be offended if you were to go to an inn, or back to Tavistock, or even to Kit's place in London. I hate to inflict this
upon you."

It was good that they had been constrained in expressing
their affection by years on a ship, where there was virtually
no privacy. The practice of self-control was almost instinc-
tive, in both speech and action. "Of course I'll go, if you
wish it. But only if you truly want me to—if you would prefer to be private with your family."

"You are closer than family." Davy rubbed his hands
over his face. "God, Will, without you, I'd be lost."

Will wanted very badly to touch him, but knew that he
would be lost if he did. Of all times and places, this was one
where Davy needed him to be strong. Perhaps, after the
house was quiet, they might steal a few moments together in
the dressing room. "Then I'll stay. No distempered in-laws
will make me haul down my colors."

Davy gave him a weary, lopsided smile. "Let's go upstairs."

The fire was small but comforting, and they lingered before it until the maid had come to run the warming-pans between the sheets. They put out their candles, changed into nightshirts, and retreated to the sanctuary of the dressing room.

They hardly spoke. There was nothing to say, really, and it was safer to keep quiet, alert for any sound out in the hall. But even without the pleasure of sex, there was an inexpressible comfort in holding Davy against him, feeling the warmth of his body through the two thin layers of nightclothes. If only they had been two half-pay sailors, forced by necessity to share a bed...but at least they did have this place to be together, for a little while.

And for how much longer? Matters here would come to a crisis; that must happen. And matters in the larger world were moving toward that, too. At some point, a few weeks or a few months, the war would explode again and he would be called away.

Could he go?

He remembered what life had been like, in those weeks while Davy was lying convalescent in Kingston. He'd been a splendid officer then, daring beyond all reason. It was easy to risk your life when you truly did not care if you ever saw another sunrise. If Davy had died, he would been not only indifferent to death, but actively seeking it. There were worse ways to die than going out in a blaze of glory.

But not now, not while he had something so precious here in his arms. He held Davy close, reveling in the warmth of him. If only they could...

Davy raised his face from Will's shoulder, and brushed his lips against Will's. "Don't mean to tease," he said softly.

"I know."

A kiss was all they dared. For now, it was enough.

Chapter 9

The next day brought a small surprise; the Vicar came to call, and David Archer was made to feel his age. He blinked when "Reverend Newkirk" was announced at the door of the drawing room, where he and Will were idly conversing with Amelia and Jane. He looked at the Reverend, and looked again. "Peter Newkirk! Is that you?"

"Archer! Yes, I had heard you were visiting, of course." He paid his respects to the ladies, then said, "How have you been, my dear fellow?"

"Well enough. And may I present Captain Marshall, my friend and shipmate? Will, this is my distant cousin Peter Newkirk—one-time chief instigator of mischief when we were schoolboys—he was a year ahead of me—and now Vicar. How he managed it, I shall never know."

As Newkirk and Will shook hands, the Vicar said, "A love of Latin was the start of it, Archer. As to the position, the Earl kindly gave me the living after my predecessor went to his reward. I'm undeserving, of course, but I have been assured by my teachers that a little sin in one's youth is indispensable for a man of the cloth, as a man who has never sinned has no true understanding of human frailty."

"A sensible philosophy, sir," Will said. "I'm pleased to make your acquaintance."

"What brings you here today?" David asked.

"Your brother's widow wished to speak to me," Newkirk said. "If I can be of any comfort to her, I shall be most happy to oblige."

"Thank you so much for coming," Amelia said, joining them. "I can take you up to her now, if you wish."

"Yes, thank you."

He followed her out, but Amelia was back, alone, in only a few minutes. "Davy, would you come with me, please?"

"Of course," he said, following her out to the hall. "What is it?"

"Virginia's back on her hobby-horse again," his sister said grimly. "She's telling the poor Vicar that he must order Ronald to confess and repent and if Ronald refuses, his guilt should be denounced from the pulpit. I don't think Peter has ever run into this sort of crisis before, poor man. He looks quite distraught."

"It didn't take her long," David said as they hurried up the stairs.

"No, I think she must have been fretting over this all night. She asked Father to send for the Vicar first thing this morning."

"Where is Father?"

"Closeted with Ronald, the estate books, and Thomas Legge. I should prefer not to interrupt them unless it's absolutely necessary."

"If for no other reason than to deny Ronald the pleasure of knowing he goaded Virginia into creating another scene."

"Yes, exactly. I sent her maid out to fetch some tea as soon as she started carrying on, but the Lord only knows what she may have been saying before I arrived."

That was all the family needed—rumor of murder among the servants. "I don't imagine there's much chance of stopping the gossip now, after that outburst at dinner. But I'll do what I can."

"If you go back downstairs before I do, please ask Jane to look in on Genie and see if she is feeling any better."

"And not listening at the keyhole?"

"I hope not—and I hope this racket does not carry into Mother's room!"

He could hear his sister-in-law's voice raised even before

Amelia opened the door, but the diatribe paused for a moment when he entered the hot, stuffy room. Propped up in bed with a coverlet smoothed across her mountainous figure, Virginia pinned him with a glance. "David! You know what has happened here. *You* know!" Her face was flushed and damp; the force of her anger and frustration hit him like a cannon recoil. "Tell this man he *must* be the instrument of God's truth and God's vengeance!"

"Yes, certainly I will," David said, keeping his voice even. "But really, Virginia, you yourself must keep calm for the baby's sake. I can tell Reverend Newkirk all about it downstairs, so you will not be further distressed."

She sighed, falling back against the pillows. "You are a true brother. You and your friend will have to take my part—"

He could not let her start on that again. "Yes, we'll deal with everything," he said. "Did you wish to pray with the Vicar, before he goes?"

"Praying is useless," she said, starting up again. "*Useless!* I have prayed myself hoarse. Now is the time for action!"

"Yes, of course. Rest assured I shall do everything necessary." He glanced at Peter and nodded toward the door, which popped open to admit a flustered maid carrying a tea tray.

After assuring Virginia that he would pray over the matter, poor Newkirk took a hasty leave. "Thank you for coming, sir," Amelia said at the doorway. "I will stay with her for a little while. I believe the doctor left a cordial for her to drink."

"She needs something stronger than a cordial!" Newkirk declared once the door was closed. "Archer, I conducted your brother's funeral and condoled with your parents, but the Lady Virginia was prostrate and I had no speech with her until today. Is there—*could* there be—any truth to that outrageous claim?"

David was unable to answer. The mirror that had just

been held up to him showed a very disturbing image; he wondered if his own suspicions sounded as insane as Virginia's accusations. This was no time to speak of them, at any rate. "I don't see how there could be," he said carefully. "The coroner ruled my brother's death accidental, and to the best of our knowledge, Ronald was in London at the time."

"She said that your brother Ronald gave her reason to believe that he had been here in secret—that he had indeed killed Lord Mark. Has he said anything of the sort to anyone else? Do you—" He broke off as another maid came down the hall with a tea tray, and disappeared into the Countess' chambers.

"I know nothing of that, but Lady Virginia did not become agitated until Ronald returned a few days ago. My father has said that he was in London, and so we all believe. I do think Ronald was always envious of Mark's position, and Virginia was aware of his feelings, but envy is not uncommon in a younger son—and while envy might be a powerful motive, murder is hardly inevitable."

Newkirk nodded. "And yet jealousy so often leads to violence. I shall be glad when I've added a few years to my own understanding. I must speak with the Earl, but his own experience is so far beyond my own..."

"I agree, you should see him, but my father is closeted with my brother and our man of business at the moment; I would rather not interrupt them unless you are in a hurry. As to your experience—you'll add the years soon enough, and I know you have the advantage of my father when it comes to theology. He must surely agree with you that Virginia's behavior is outside the bounds of reason. Would you care for tea and some refreshments? I think Mr. Legge will be leaving fairly soon. And in the meantime, perhaps we had better send for the doctor."

"I agree. Such agitation cannot be good for either Lady Virginia or her child."

David deposited Newkirk in the drawing room and drew Jane aside to convey Amelia's message. She volunteered to send a servant off for tea and cakes, and David saw to it that a messenger was sent to find the doctor. By the time Dr. Fiske arrived, the tea had been consumed, the business meeting adjourned, and Mr. Legge was taking his departure. Ronald, thankfully, made himself scarce—where he went, David neither knew nor cared.

While Amelia escorted the doctor up to Virginia's room, David took Newkirk to see the Earl, then rejoined Will in the drawing room, where his friend was alone, ensconced in one of a pair of wing-chairs and perusing an old edition of the *Naval Gazette*.

"I don't believe I've seen so much bustle here since we arrived," Will said. "Is there anything I can do to help?"

David dropped into the other chair. "Not unless you can persuade my sister-in-law that her cause is *not* best served by accusing Ronald of fratricide, at the top of her lungs, to anyone who will listen."

"Oh, dear."

"You have a gift for understatement," David said wryly. "It was Newkirk's suggestion that we call Dr. Fiske, and I only hope he has some sort of medicine to help settle her nerves. I'd best stay on hand in case of further alarms, but if you'd like to retreat to your room I wouldn't blame you. I'll join you there as soon as the dust settles."

"And leave you in the lurch?"

"There's no telling what mood my father will be in after Newkirk talks to him, and there's still the doctor's report after that. Father can growl at me if he likes." He shrugged. "My father is accustomed to order in his household. He has little tolerance of irregular behavior and histrionics, still less in the presence of a guest."

"I'll get out from underfoot, then. But do let me know if you need me."

David smiled wearily. "Always—but in reserve, for now."

Will gave his arm a sympathetic squeeze and took his leave.

David was pleased to have the less onerous chore of thanking the Vicar and escorting him to the door while Amelia saw Dr. Fiske to the Earl's study and stayed on hand for the doctor's report. She was shooed away when Fiske was invited to stay for a drink, and joined her brother in the drawing room.

"What news?" David asked her. "And how are you bearing up?"

"Oh, I'll do. Virginia seems to be well enough, physically. The doctor said she should be given chamomile tea and her forehead bathed with lavender water. He does not wish her given more laudanum than is already in her cordial, as he thinks it might not be good for the baby—he said he was averse to risking the child's health just to keep the mother quiet. Father agreed."

"Well, that makes sense, I suppose," David said. "But it's going to be lively around here until that child is born."

"Perhaps not. Dr. Fiske did order Virginia to stay quietly in her room, and we are under no circumstances to allow Ronald anywhere near her."

"Also sensible—whether or not he believes her accusations. The Vicar said something interesting, Lia. He said Virginia claimed that Ronald led her to believe he did kill Mark. Were you with them at the time?"

"No. How strange! I wonder when he might have done that?"

"I've no idea. If he meant to discredit her suspicions, that would be a clever way to go about it—admit that he'd done it, so quietly that no one else heard, so all her accusations would sound more and more unbalanced."

"That would be incredibly cruel, Davy."

"Of course it would—but so is murder cruel. And where has our heir-apparent gone, do you know?"

"Off to visit friends," she said. "He may not be back until late, or even until tomorrow. I don't suppose you could call up a press-gang and have him quietly spirited away—for even a little while?"

He smiled without humor. "Don't tempt me. If the war were on, and we were in Portsmouth, I think it might be managed. And I'd do my best to get him on a ship bound for Australia. Or perhaps New Zealand—I hear the cannibals there are particularly fierce."

⚓ ⚓ ⚓

Will sat by the fire with his *Gazette*, reading once more the letter sent in by his former commanding officer concerning an action in which he and Davy had taken part. As usual, Captain Smith downplayed his own heroism and lavishly praised officers and crew. That had been the last action they had seen in *Calypso,* that best of all frigates. It had been less than two years since they had all been transferred to another ship, but it seemed like an age long past.

How easy life had been then—even in the middle of a war, even with the necessity of keeping their love concealed from everyone. It had been so much simpler before the fear bored its way into his soul. He'd been able to fight with Davy at his side, trusting their luck to keep them safe. He had known what to do. He'd had a job, responsibilities, respect.

Here? Grenbrook Manor was *terra incognita* and he was out of his element, completely shorn of responsibility and authority. All he could do was follow Davy's lead, but Davy seemed hamstrung by his family's expectations. And there appeared to be no way they could prove that Ronald Archer had done murder, if indeed he had. The coroner had ruled, the body was buried, and Will saw no further avenue for investigation. They were at an impasse.

He leaned back and closed his eyes for a moment, starting awake at a touch on his shoulder. It was Davy, looking weary and annoyed. Will guessed he would love to be back on the *Calypso* himself, with a gun crew awaiting his command. "You look as though you've had one visitor too many," he said.

"No, just one case of hysterics too many. Virginia went

off again and the doctor did have to give her a dose of laudanum before he left, though he hadn't intended to."

"What possible good does she imagine she's doing?"

Davy held up both hands, forestalling discussion. "I think she's lost to rational thought, Will, and dealing with her obsession is beyond me. Even if she's correct in her suspicions, and you know I share them, she's only making things worse for everyone. I mean to go out for a ride and clear my own head. If I don't spend some time away from all this, I may run amok myself."

The suggestion made Will feel a hundred pounds lighter. "I hope you will not object to my company?"

"I depend upon it. Are you feeling adventurous enough to ride horseback in the dark?"

"Even that," Will said. "So long as you give me that mild-mannered creature who refrained from throwing me during our first encounter."

Davy laughed. "Let's have a ride down to the village, then. I'm told the current batch of ale at the Bull is particularly good. Not that it matters. I'd drink cold tea from an old boot if it would get me out of here."

The sky was not quite dark when they set out, and Will found himself less apprehensive in the saddle, more able to appreciate his surroundings—the deepening blue of the sky, the tracery of branches dead-black against that background, the scent of warming earth under the chill that fell on the land after the sun went down.

"It's a pretty night, isn't it?" Davy said beside him. "At times like this, I find myself wishing for the impossible— that the Peace would last— Oh, I know," he added before Will could voice his doubts on that score. "That will never happen, unless Bonaparte were to die suddenly. Without his bloody-minded ambition, I think the rest of them might find a way to end it."

"But what then?" Will could scarcely imagine a life that didn't involve war or expectation of war. "I could live well enough on half-pay, but what would I do?"

"Oh, there will be other fights, count on it. India, Africa, South America...I'm not serious, Will, I am only dreaming. We could buy a little sloop, something small enough that we'd need no crew, and sail away together," Davy's voice grew wistful. "We might spend a summer visiting the Channel Islands—drop anchor at night, furl the sails, and sleep in until the sun woke us—and take our own time going up on deck."

Will had a brief, lovely memory of Davy and a hammock, their last Christmas aboard the *Mermaid*. "It's a good dream. Perhaps someday we shall."

"Perhaps." Davy fell silent, and they rode quietly for awhile, the moon bright at three-quarters, the stars and planets becoming visible one by one.

It was a fine dream, but entirely impractical. Davy came from a class that could contemplate leisure, but Will himself had never thought of a life outside the Navy. When the war resumed, his best hope would be for command of a small vessel of some sort. He could do that. He could do it well. But he found himself no longer able to wish whole-heartedly for that day to come. He might be a better officer, knowing that David Archer was safe ashore—but he could not imagine how he'd find the strength to walk away from him. A pretty dilemma, and all his own, and he saw no resolution for it.

The road wound around moon-silvered fields, then came out suddenly before a small cluster of buildings, a two-story inn across from a stable, and a blacksmith shop next to that, with a few cottages between the businesses. "We have reached the metropolis," Davy announced. "Let's get the horses inside the stable and ourselves outside a drink."

Will's horse followed Davy's. That had been the easiest lesson in horsemanship—that most horses would follow another, so there was no need to steer if you had a more experienced rider to take the lead. He was learning, slowly; he even managed to dismount without incident. Davy knew the hostler—Davy apparently knew everyone—and once again Will had the opportunity to express his admiration for Lieutenant Archer's seamanship and bravery, confirming the local opinion that for all his having his nose in a book, there was nothing shy about Master David!

"You are beloved of your countrymen," he said when they escaped into the cool evening. "I had not expected you to find such a warm reception, from the things you've told me about your home."

"I'm surprised myself," Davy admitted. "It may be that so many young men leave and never return, they rejoice in any familiar face."

"No one came home?"

"Oh, a few have—some from the Army, a handful who went to the coast to join the Sea Fencibles. But not many."

"Would the soldiers have been from your brother's regiment?"

"Some may have been. I believe I could find out. And I see where this inquiry is heading." He stopped at the door to the inn and said quietly, "We'd best mind our tongues inside. Then again—perhaps a careful word might bring us information."

Will nodded. "Lead on."

A warm gust of air washed over them when Davy swung open the door, carrying on it a wave of odors—beer, pipe-smoke, and the sweat of hard-working men. Lacking only the scent of a ship's timbers and salt air, it was not so different from the usual below-decks fug. Will counted eight tables, half of them empty, and no more than eight or nine men present. In such a small village, Will guessed that most of the residents would be home with their families at this hour.

Again, he was struck by the warmth with which the men greeted Davy. Congratulations on his rank, condolences for his loss—all were given with the greatest respect, making it clear that Lieutenant Archer was held in high regard. And Davy immediately increased that regard by buying a round for all present.

"A toast—to my brother's memory," Davy said, and the

high spirits of the room suddenly stilled. "To my brother Mark," he repeated in the quiet. "May he rest in peace."

"And long life and health to His Lordship," someone added, drawing a murmur of approval. Will raised his own tankard, and followed Davy's lead to a table against the far wall.

"It's a shame neither Ronald nor I were able to be on hand for the funeral," Davy said. "It does seem strange that he'd have been unable to get here from London. But since he arrived after we did—"

The arrival of two mugs of ale stopped his speech, and he raised his hand slightly in a small gesture to stop Will's reply.

"Compliments of the house, gentlemen," the serving girl said. At a closer look, Will realized she was not so young as she had first seemed; her brown hair was contained only by a kerchief, but her dark eyes had a hard look to them. "Was you speaking of your brother, sir?"

"You've sharp ears, Kittie," Davy said. "But it's nothing that concerns you."

"That's as may be," she said, tossing her head. "And maybe not. And maybe," she lowered her voice, "may be I could tell you something as would make you think otherwise about when your brother came riding back. But as it doesn't concern me, I'll say no more, young sir." With another flounce, she departed, her grand exit marred by a patron who called for her to refill his tankard.

"Saucy baggage," Will observed.

"More trouble than she's worth," Davy said. Keeping an eye on her until she vanished into the kitchen, he added quietly, "The last thing we needed is gossip in the village, and this particular girl has a tongue that wags without discretion or sense. If she weren't the landlord's daughter, she'd have been turned off years ago."

Matching his tone, Will said, "But what she suggested...do you suppose Ronald might really have returned earlier, and kept himself out of sight?"

"That would answer many of our questions," Davy replied. "But, much as I would like to believe it, it's not likely he could stay out of sight. The villagers know all of us too well. If he had been here, someone ought to have seen him."

Will nodded toward the kitchen. "Perhaps someone did. Would she lie for him?"

Davy laughed humorlessly. "Would she? She has. I'll tell you about it on the way home."

They spent an hour or so sipping ale while Davy told sea stories and listened to news about the local farmers. When their mugs were empty and a couple of the other men had gone on their way, they took their leave and went to retrieve their horses. The night had gone chill, but the moon and stars were brighter now in the cold clear air, and the road ahead was easy to see.

"So tell me about this Jezebel," Will said, once they were clear of the village.

"I believe she's afflicted with ambition far above her abilities," Davy said. "The summer before I went to sea, Ronald decided to gain a bit of glory at my expense, so he bribed her to tell some cock-and-bull story that I'd made unwelcome advances toward her dainty self."

"What?"

"Truly! It's not that I hadn't observed and admired her 'attributes,' but I certainly hadn't done any more than that. She's a couple of years older—quite a difference to a fifteen-year-old boy—and she'd hinted that she might be willing to make a man of me."

"I trust your instincts held you back."

"Yes, I developed a fair sense of self-preservation early on. And the lie backfired on them both because Mother had sent me off on an errand that afternoon and I was incontrovertibly elsewhere."

"You're joking."

"Not a bit. And when it turned out that I'd spent half the day listening to the Vicar rehearse his next sermon—"

"Your mother made you do that? Whatever –"

"No, no, just happenstance. The Vicar's wife was ill—the Vicar we had when I was a child, not Peter Newkirk. My mother sent me over with a jar of calf's-foot jelly and the old fellow trapped me into listening to his pearls of theological wisdom. I knew that if I skipped out he'd only inflict it on his wife, and she was already feeling poorly, which was why Mother sent the jelly in the first place, so I flung myself into the breach." He shrugged. "He was a good old fellow, really. Why not humor him?"

"But the accusation...?" Will persisted.

"Oh, Kittie claimed she was only teasing because I was such a sobersides. In fact she was getting her revenge because I hadn't accepted her indelicate advances. If Ronald had not put it into her head, I expect she'd have thought of it sooner or later. She's determined to get her hooks into some poor sod, and I think she honestly believed she could drag me to the altar. I should have let her try, really. It would have been a treat to see my father give her a broadside."

"So as a witness, she would be unconvincing?"

"Worse than useless—positively damaging. I expect her to run off to Ronald and warn him we're discussing his itinerary. That might prove interesting..." He thought back carefully. "Nothing we said since we entered should have led her to believe we were discussing incriminating circumstances. But if he's worried about whether he's left any traces of an earlier arrival, it might make him uneasy."

"The play's the thing," Will said, pleased with his Shakespearean reference.

"He's not king, thank God—and I doubt if he has a conscience."

"But how do you suppose she would have seen him, and no one else be any the wiser?"

"I don't know. The family always lived above the inn, but her mother's been dead for years, there are no brothers or sisters still at home, and I believe the only other woman in the house is her grandmother, who's deaf as a post. Kittie would be just the sort to play at intrigue without any notion of what she might be getting into. Whether she's one of Ronald's lightskirts is anyone's guess...but she is ambitious. She could have married any number of local men, but she seems to think she can do better."

"She could hardly imagine your brother would marry her!"

"No one with any sense would imagine it, but she hasn't any sense at all. I could see him hinting that he might, to gain her assistance. And I can imagine her going along with it because she'd enjoy being privy to a secret, and she might think she could use that to pry an offer out of him."

"Do you think she would be susceptible to bribery—from us, I mean?"

"There's a notion. Even if she were not a credible witness, we might get some useful tidbits. Or we might get a bundle of lies. There's no way of knowing."

"Then we shall have to visit that charming spot again, and soon."

"I'm afraid so. But not tomorrow, if you please. The ale was good, but for now I've had my fill of Kittie's posturing."

They rode slowly along the road, the starlight brighter now that it was full dark. Davy dropped back a pace or two, and Will knew he was watching his own uneasy balance in the saddle. "What's amiss with your seat?" Davy finally asked.

"Does it show?" Will sighed. "The right stirrup seems a little longer than the other, but I daresay it's really my leg that's shorter."

"Raise up and put your weight on both legs equally," Davy suggested. "See if it doesn't shift a bit. And next time, we'll make certain everything's adjusted properly before we start off."

Will stood in the stirrups, then settled back down. "It's no problem, really. It seemed fine when we rode out."

"Straps can stretch, or the girth might not be quite as tight—or it might be a little tighter, if the hostler adjusted it. A horse is a lot like a ship, Will. Even if you do everything properly, they'll still surprise you sometimes."

"I am still waiting to feel as easy up here as I do on the quarterdeck," Will said as they rounded a tree-lined bend. "Though it's not—" He sensed rather than saw a wisp of something approaching his face, like a strand of cobweb, and reached to brush it away—and his hand touched cord.

He reacted before he quite knew what he was doing, yanking back on the reins with his left hand and wheeling about. "Stop!"

Davy had checked his mount already. "What is it?"

"Unless you have monstrous huge spiders here who don't mind the cold—" He caught the line that stretched across the path, and gave it a sharp tug. It was strong cord and tied to something solid, but Will was strong, too, and angry. The cord snapped free from one tree in the line of them that ran along the right side of the road, between them and the open fields. He handed the loose end over to Davy.

"Just at the height of a rider," Davy said. "If we'd been going at any pace, it could have caught us both."

"No danger of that with me in the lead," Will said.

"It's no joke, Will. If he'd strung it lower to catch the horses..." Davy leaned back, looking along the road they'd covered, then squinted into the thicket at their left. It was so dark on this bit of the road that he followed the movements mostly by sound. "Do you hear anything?" he breathed.

It was a time of year when there were few night sounds—the hoot of an occasional owl, the skitter of small things that lived in last fall's dead leaves. But at this moment there was no sound. Nothing at all. Will shook his head.

"Nor I." Davy dropped down out of the saddle for an instant and was back up just as quickly, something in his hand. "No jokes, Will. Stay on that horse no matter what, and follow me."

Chapter 10

W ithout another word, Davy drew back his arm and let fly with whatever clod he'd picked up from the trail, sent it crashing into the roadway a dozen yards ahead. Will thought he heard a faint rustle in the underbrush on their left, but didn't have time to be certain; Davy turned his horse at right angles to the path, tugging at the bridle of Will's mount as he went by, leading him directly between the trees and out into the open fields.

Then they were away, their breaths visible in the frosty moonlight. Will had learned enough to stay on a cantering horse, and though he didn't like it much, he managed for a quarter of an hour, until Davy brought them down to a brisk walk and dropped back so they could ride side by side.

"Where are we now?" Will asked.

"Heading directly home. The road wanders around past cottages and barns. This is faster, and if anyone comes after us, we'll be able to see him."

"Were you expecting an ambush?"

"No. And that was interesting, was it not? A line at the height of the chest—the upper chest. If we'd been trotting, it could have swept you out of the saddle, or torn your throat if we'd been going faster. If we had been riding abreast—"

He didn't need to explain further. If either of them had been knocked to the ground, injured or not, they would have been vulnerable to attack. "I should have brought my pistol."

"I did," Davy said. "And out here, I could at least make out a proper target. But I don't think we have reason to fear an open attack when we have the chance to defend ourselves. We're out of range of even the finest rifle now. "

"That was a cavalry trick, wasn't it?" Will asked.

"Used against cavalry, yes. Not as dangerous to the horses as a line stretched lower down. But an injury to a horse would show, and could not be credited to a stray branch across the path. If it had caught you across the chest—"

"I'd have been on the ground, no question. And you as well, if you weren't able to get out of the way in time."

"Or if I didn't ride right over you. It's a damned good thing you saw that line."

Will shrugged. "I was riding so slowly I'd have seen a thread."

"Nonetheless," Davy was sounding more his usual cheery self, "since we were so disobliging as to keep the odds two to one, I expect we're past the risk, at least for this evening."

"Shall we go back tomorrow and look around?" Will suggested. "I wonder whether there might not have been more than one line across the road. That's what I'd have done—set a second trap further on, to stop anyone who might ride ahead to get help."

"If there was another, I'm sure it will be gone before we reach home."

The heat rising from his horse kept Will's legs warm, but a chill touched the back of his neck. "We were easy targets for a moment there," he said. "Both of us."

"Easy, but not dead-certain—he couldn't know whether we might return fire." Davy snorted. "Or who knows? That might have been meant as a warning. It's just his sort of melodrama."

"I wish we'd gone after him," Will said. "Caught him red-handed."

"So do I, but with only one pistol between the two of us? If that ambush was serious, he might have had two pistols, or even more. Or he might have claimed he was only playing a trick on you, the way a seaman would hoax a landlubber."

"Not much of a joke."

"No," Davy said, "But very much his style. And if we were found shot on the road—or never found at all—you can be sure Ronald would have an alibi—one that might be provided by Kittie herself."

A thought occurred to Will. "It has been a damp week, and I'm sure the ground is muddy. Davy—didn't you said your brother Mark's valet is seeing to Ronald's clothing?"

"Muddy boots! Yes, I can ask James if he noticed anything amiss. He'll tell me—and he would keep quiet about my asking, too."

"That would still not prove anything, would it?"

"No—just circumstantial evidence. But that trap did prove one thing, Will."

"What's that?"

"Someone is afraid we'll learn something in the village. That means there must be something to learn."

They rode on awhile in silence, and before very long Will saw a lantern in the distance. Davy's horse began to move faster, heading for its stable. Will felt his horse change gait, but somehow it was easier to stay aboard this time.

"Almost there," Davy said. "By the way, congratulations. You're posting."

⚓ ⚓ ⚓

Nothing happened the next day, and David Archer was just as well pleased with the quiet. He was in favor of any day that passed without another outburst from Virginia. He did not know if it was Ronald's absence or Dr. Fisk's medicine that kept her quiescent, nor did he care.

He and Will rode for an hour or so in the morning with Amelia and Jane, back to the site of what could not quite be called an ambush. As David had predicted, there was no sign of the cord that had been stretched across the road, and a nearby patch of muddy, trampled brush could have been the tracks of one man or several—or a couple of deer bedding down for the night.

They called the matter hopeless and spent a peaceful afternoon indoors, searching the shelves of the library for a copy of *Tristam Shandy,* which Amelia had begun reading after Christmas. She could remember that she had found it amusing, but not where she had last set it down. The book turned up at last unaccountably sandwiched between some bound volumes of a ladies' journal, and Jane suggested that they might take turns reading aloud to one another. The Archers, having had Shakespeare read to them from childhood by their mother, thought it a grand idea.

Will declined to read aloud, and after a few chapters of the rambling, idiosyncratic narrative he was frowning, obviously perplexed at the lack of a coherent storyline. David, familiar with the book and knowing that Will's love of order would never be satisfied by this tale, finally took pity on him and asked if he would be willing to read a report from the *Naval Gazette* instead—a low trick, but it worked. Will was happy to oblige and the ladies were willing to listen. It might not have been the liveliest way David had ever passed a long, wet afternoon, but he found a quiet, sociable interlude a welcome change.

On the disappointing side, Ronald stayed with whomever he had been visiting until just before dark, and when he returned his boots showed a fresh polish, no doubt applied by a friend's servant or someone at an inn a bit more distant than the village.

"Do you think it would be worth riding out to see if we might learn where he stayed?" Will asked, as they dressed for supper.

"Perhaps, if we had any notion of what direction he'd gone. It's not really proper for him to go jaunting about the countryside, not with the family so recently in mourning—in fact, that's why I would rather not do so myself."

"Do you suppose he stayed at an inn somewhere?"

"That's my guess, and I can understand how he might want to have a little time to himself, away from my father's supervision. But Ronald does have friends in the area, and I expect those friends are the sort who would hardly think twice at his presence, proper or not. It's a pity we don't have a Bow Street Runner to do the investigation. If we began sniffing around on his trail ourselves, we'd be bound to raise suspicion."

"It's my guess we already have," Will said. "At least, if your guess about that trap was correct. Or do you think that might have been simple malice?"

"It could be, easily." He sat down before the fire, suddenly weary of the whole affair. "I begin to wonder if there are any answers to be found, Will. I look at Virginia and her absolute, irrational certainty, and I wonder if my own dislike of my brother is not leading me to create monsters lurking under the bed, as a child might do."

Will stood close, resting a hand on his shoulder. "If you had said that yesterday, I would have agreed with you. But it was no imaginary monster on the path last night. And try as I might, I cannot imagine who else would have set that trap— or for what reason."

"But that's what makes me wonder, Will. What *reason* was there to that? Simple harassment? Was it merely to inconvenience us, or would we have been set upon and murdered if it had succeeded?"

Will sat across from him. "I had been wondering about that myself. Perhaps he—I suppose we may as well hypothesize that our villain is Ronald—believes that such persecution will send you packing."

"If that's the case, he does not know me at all."

Will smiled. "But is that such a surprise? He does *not* know you—certainly not as the man you have become. And I doubt that he ever took the time to become acquainted with you, even as a child."

David nodded slowly. "True. And as a child—oh, Will, what I'd have given to have a friend like you, back then!— all I did was avoid him, and spend as much time as I could with Amelia. It galls me to think that he might believe I could be frightened into running away, but as you say, that is quite possible."

"I hope that's his reasoning," Will said. "Because the other possibility is worse, and it has nothing to do with what we might learn from that barmaid."

"What's that?"

"Your sister said that Ronald has been informed that you will stand as guardian to the younger ladies of the household, in the event of your father's death." Will shook his head, as though unwilling to put the thought to words. "Davy, what if he decided to make certain you would not be around to fulfill that responsibility?"

David took a breath to scoff, then met Will's sober eyes, and closed his mouth. It was a suggestion he could not dismiss. "That," he said at last, "that would go beyond all reason. One death could appear accidental. A second? That would be—"

"Perhaps a third," Will said. "I think that someone in your family must write to your brother's commanding officer, and see what details may be discovered about the death of Ronald's wife."

David shook his head. "Ronald is utterly selfish and he can be cruel," he said, "but I have never known him to be so single-minded as to be stupid. Ordinarily, he would have set himself to charm you, and make me appear insignificant."

"He may have had sense enough to realize such a task would be impossible."

"It's true, you showed no awe of his elevated status. Ronald prefers sycophants to equals. But to deal with all one's problems by killing off those who seem to be in the way...That might work once or twice, but it could not be sustained."

"Not under ordinary circumstances, no," Will said, "but your brother has been to war. And what is war, in its basest sense, but killing those who oppose you? You and I have known men like Captain Smith, who kill when duty requires it but stop when the enemy lowers his flag. But we've also seen those who start out mean and develop a taste for death, like a herd-dog who begins hunting sheep. Remember Simpson, that foremast jack Captain Smith hanged after he murdered a whore in Portugal? That woman's life meant nothing to him—he strangled her in cold blood."

David nodded. A dozen childhood memories assailed him—toys stolen or broken, animals tormented, beatings that Ronald carefully concealed from their parents and governess—and worse at school, when he had a clique of followers to support him. "And you think my brother may be such a one."

"I think he may be." Will's voice was gentle. "But only because you have been telling me he is ever since you first mentioned him. And I have seen enough now to believe that you may be right."

⚓ ⚓ ⚓

They were given a day's respite after what David was thinking of as the alarums and confusion. Virginia kept to her room. Unfortunately, so did the Countess. David was puzzled at his mother's refusal to stir from her boudoir. He knew that Will was probably right, and the loss of her eldest son had been a devastating blow, but this apathy was unlike her—even when she was ill, she was more inclined to fuss over everyone else than to let anyone care for her.

"Just an hour downstairs, Mama," he encouraged. "We would all take heart if you would only come down and spend some time with the family."

"Not yet, my dear," she said placidly. "Anne is more than capable of acting as hostess, and I know Amelia has the household well in hand." She pulled her blankets up a little closer to her chin. "Is Captain Marshall being looked after?"

"Yes, Mama."

"Well, then, since he is nearly family, there's no need to worry yourself."

And that was that. David kissed her cheek and left, feeling that she had gone off somewhere just out of reach.

The Earl was taking most of his meals with his wife. Ronald was in and out during the day, but not present in the dining room, either; he generally had breakfast sent up to his room instead of spending time at table with his family, then vanished until the household had gone to bed. At least, David thought, with their parents tucked away there was no need for any of them to pretend they enjoyed Ronald's company, though Anne did voice a complaint that he might at least attempt to give the appearance that he had an interest in his own family. Amelia replied tartly that she preferred honest disinterest, and the matter dropped.

They had no significant news from the outside world, either from Sir Percy or the slightly delayed paper from London. Everyone knew Bonaparte was preparing for war, but the peace dragged on. And the weather helped no one's mood. An occasional hour of wintry sunlight was invariably followed by clouds and mist, and sometimes rain. David cudgeled his brain for anything more that they might investigate, but as Will said, short of asking Ronald questions that he would surely refuse to answer—and betraying their suspicions in the process—they could do nothing more than wait for him to betray himself in some way.

He wished he had some idea of the form that action might take.

⚓ ⚓ ⚓

Things were not going according to plan. The fools were supposed to stay at the house, not go snooping around in the village. That stupid beer-hauling bitch—talking to them! Sound carried a long way at night, and there was no doubt her name was mentioned. And she would be open to bribery, without a doubt. She would sell anything for the right price, especially if it made her the center of attention. She must be dealt with.

But there was another danger even more pressing, one that must be seen to immediately. Time was short, and all one's plans might be sent to perdition by a single stroke of

*bad luck. Better to make certain that demented harpy was
silenced before her drug-fueled prophecy came to pass.*

And then ...then one would have power, money, and absolute control.

No reason to wait any longer.
Tonight.

Chapter 11

"Davy, get up!"

The voice beside his ear was quiet but urgent. Despite it being pitch-dark in the bedroom, David knew it was Will shaking his shoulder. He dragged himself out of the soundest sleep he'd had since returning home, and pushed himself up. "What's wrong? What time is it?"

"A little past four. Out in the hall—come quick!"

He snatched up his dressing-gown and followed, though Will moved too fast for him to keep up, and by the time he was out in the hall Will was nowhere to be seen. As he peered around, blinking, David saw Amelia's door open on the other side of the gallery. She poked her head out, shielding a candle with one hand. The flickering light and deep shadows made her look like something from a dream. "Davy, what is it?"

"Down here!" Will called softly. "She is still breathing, but do we dare move her?"

David followed the sound of Will's voice to the stairway, and Amelia came behind him with the candle "Who is it?" he asked, awake enough to realize that this was no dream. "What's wrong?"

"It's Lady Virginia. I think she must have fallen."

As the light fell across the figure sprawled near the balustrade, halfway down the stairs, David saw that Will was correct. "But how could she get out here? Why would she leave her room? Where's her maid?"

"Get Kirby," Amelia suggested, bringing the light closer.

"Allow me to sit beside her, Captain. Would you get me a glass of water, please?"

David took a candle from one of the sconces at the top of the stair, and lit it from his sister's taper.

She caught at his arm as he leaned close. "Davy, if anyone asks, let them think that I first discovered her."

"Very well, but why?"

"If this was not an accident, then someone pushed her—and it would be better if there were no hint that either of you were involved. I can honestly say I saw you looking out in the hall, and we can both say we thought we heard something."

"You're right," he said. "Good thinking. Will?"

"I'll do as you think best." Will followed him up the stairs. "Would water from my room be acceptable?"

"As well as any, I suppose. I'll get Kirby, then see what happened to Virginia's maid. She should know better than to let her go stumbling around in the dark!"

He and Will parted at the top of the stair, and he went to summon his mother's unflappable maid. He had barely scratched at the door when it opened, and Kirby stood there holding a candlestick. "Master David, what is that commotion?"

"Is my mother awake?"

When Kirby shook her head, he said, "Good," and drew her out into the hall, explaining the situation in as few words as possible. "Please go help my sister—I'll see what's become of Lady Virginia's maid."

"Margaret is devoted to her ladyship," Kirby said. "She would surely have kept her from wandering about!"

"So I should have thought," David said.

And so she might have, if she had been awake. Lady Virginia's maid, Margaret, was sitting in a straight chair in the private parlor, just outside her mistress' room, with a small lamp burning on the table beside her, and a half-darned sock on the floor beneath the chair. She ought to have heard and seen what happened. Indeed, it seemed impossible that

Virginia could have walked past her without being noticed, even though Margaret was dead to the world, for her feet were extended partway across the path to her ladyship's bedroom.

David cleared his throat, called the young woman's name, and finally took hold of one shoulder and shook her.

She groaned and sat upright. "Yes, sir?"

"Are you unwell?" he asked.

"No, sir!" She scrambled to her feet and attempted a curtsey, but her knees failed and she dropped back into the chair. "Yes, sir. Sorry, sir."

David had not paid much notice to Virginia's maid—he had never seen her before this visit—but when he'd been in her room earlier, while the Vicar was there, she had seemed perfectly alert and well-behaved. He was certain his sister-in-law would not tolerate a tippler, and the maid did not seem drunk, nor was there any smell of spirits. He could detect no guile in her pale, anxious face, only confusion.

Once she knew what had happened, she would be in a panic over what must appear to be dereliction of duty. The real crisis was out in the hall, but Will, Amelia, and Kirby were equal to dealing with whatever might be required out there. David thought he might learn more if he asked his questions now, before Margaret knew what had transpired.

He pulled up a footstool and sat upon it, bringing himself closer to her eye level. "Margaret, when I entered, you seemed to be asleep. What is the last thing you remember?"

"Lord, sir, I must have been asleep. Lady Anne sent me off to rest for awhile this afternoon, but I've been with my lady all through the nights. Even if I rest my eyes I listen, and if she moves I jump right up...but my head aches so!" She touched her left temple and winced.

He brought the lamp close enough to look, and saw a lump forming on the side of her face, vanishing into the hairline. "You've had a nasty wallop there—it's starting to bruise. Do you remember what happened?"

"No, sir, nothing. Might be I fell and hit my head, but

then how would I come to be sitting here?"

"I couldn't say," he responded. He couldn't say, but he could guess—the maid had been dozing, understandably enough, and a quick blow to the head had insured that she would not awaken until it was much too late. "You must summon your courage, Margaret. There has been an accident. I'm afraid Lady Virginia has taken a fall down the stairs."

It was his turn to wince when she let out a wail of dismay. She jumped up; David caught her before she pitched onto her face. She pulled fretfully away from his support and stumbled two steps to the bedroom doorway, where she could see for herself that the bed was empty. "Oh, *no!*"

Then she fainted.

He groaned and bent to heave her back into the chair, wondering what to do next. Wake the Earl, that was certain—if the activity the hall hadn't already done the job.

But when he got back to the staircase, he saw no sign of his father. There were servants aplenty on the stair, though. Under the combined supervision of Leland, Kirby, and Amelia, Virginia was being lifted onto a sling of blankets. Amelia had a few quiet words with the butler, and then joined David. "She's breathing, but unevenly," his sister said. "Her pulse is weak, and I could not wake her. Nor could Kirby. They're going to put her back in her bed—I've no idea what else we can do."

"Has someone gone for the doctor?" he asked, as the awkward procession struggled up the stairs and headed for Virginia's room.

"Yes, Leland sent a boy out to the stables, to take the gig and fetch Dr. Fiske. That poor man! He must sometimes wish he had become a scholar, or studied for the ministry."

"Perhaps we ought to send for the Vicar, too," David said. "Just in case."

Will, a mere spectator, sidled over. "What of the maid?"

"She had been knocked unconscious, and it took some doing to wake her up."

"Knocked unconscious?" he echoed incredulously. "By Lady Virginia?"

"I expect that is what we're intended to believe. Amelia, did Ronald ever come home, do you know?"

"He did not," she said. "According to Leland, he is once more off visiting friends."

"How convenient." And how singularly inappropriate, with the family so recently bereaved. A sudden suspicion struck him. "You had better tell Kirby not to try waking Margaret, she fainted again when I told her what happened. Will, come with me, please!"

He strode down the hall to the room that had been Mark's and was now infested by Ronald. He knocked, just in case his brother had returned unannounced, then turned the knob and entered.

"What are you looking for?" Will asked.

"I'm not sure. More of my unsubstantiated suspicions, I'm afraid. I find it curious that every time someone in the family dies, Ronald seems to be elsewhere. I wish I'd had the wit to realize that Virginia and her baby were bound to be his next target."

"Not necessarily," Will said. "All he needed to do was wait until the child was born. If it should be a girl—"

"And if not? I think even Ronald might hesitate to murder a baby, and he'd have known that a new heir would be guarded so closely he would have no chance. I'd have camped out at her doorstep myself. But to give Virginia a shove down the stairs..."

The candle's light showed nothing, and he felt foolish. What had he expected, a list of fell deeds to be done pinned to the mantle with a dagger? He moved to the window, hoping the doctor would at least have dry weather for his early journey, but there were raindrops on the mullioned panes.

And, oddly, raindrops on the windowsill as well. Not many, just a few half-dried spots of water, as though someone had opened the window briefly, not long ago. That was also peculiar. Since no one would be sleeping in this room, the servants would have had no reason to enter—nor would they have opened a window on such a wet, cold night.

Will saw the spots too, and raised the candle higher. "Is that window broken?"

"No..." David ran a hand along the edge of the window frame, up to the latch. "But it's not latched, Will! Look!" He pushed the window open a crack, leaning out a little. As he'd remembered, the ivy grew thick and tough along this side of the building, the vines heavier than halyards.

"Easy enough to climb up or down," Will said.

"And easy to leave the window unlatched, if the night is not windy. Those vines are strong as any rigging."

"Is that the voice of experience?"

"Of course. I did my share of night-climbing as a boy, and I'm sure Ronald did, too. He was often out when the household went to bed and back in bed the next morning. I want to find out where he was supposed to have stayed tonight...though I daren't make it a direct question, or he may guess that we know he came home to visit."

Will ran a finger along the damp sill, then dried it with the sleeve of his nightshirt and pushed the window open again until some random drops spattered on the stone. "We should see how long it takes for this to dry," he said, "and we will have a notion of how long ago he was here."

"I wonder if he will have the nerve to come back in the morning," David said. "By the way, Will, you were the first to find Virginia—what woke you?"

"I must have been dreaming—nothing I remember—and there was something in my dream about a door closing. I heard it quite distinctly; it woke me. I should have just gone back to sleep, but ..." He shrugged. "I had the conviction that the sound had been real, so I got up to look in the hall. I heard the sound of movement from the stair, found that someone was lying there, and came to wake you."

"You must have heard the closing of this door. We should ask Amelia if she heard it, too. But for now, I think it's time to wake my father. And as with the doctor's last visit, I think it would be best if you take yourself discreetly away for now."

"I hate leaving you to face all this," Will said.

"And I would love to let you have the honors!" David replied, attempting to lighten the mood. "But you might as well take the chance to get dressed. I have a feeling it's going to be a long day."

⚓ ⚓ ⚓

In any case, it was a long half-hour before the Earl was up and about and convinced that his offspring had taken all the correct actions without his supervision. As they settled around the table in the little sitting-room between Amelia and Jane's bedrooms, he could do nothing but yawn and complain about the cause of his surprising absence during the crisis.

On Fiske's orders, he had taken a dose of laudanum himself upon retiring, and had slept through everything, much to his own disgust. "I should have known better. 'You need your rest,' he said." He snorted. "I'm asleep for no more than six hours and that woman decides to go roaming and endanger her child!"

"I'm sure that wasn't her intention, Papa," Amelia said wryly. Exactly the right tone, David thought—at least for Amelia it was.

The Earl snorted once more. "Walking in her sleep, I suppose. You haven't bothered your mother about this, I hope!"

"No, sir," David answered. "Kirby heard us in the hall and came out to help, but Mother was asleep when she left and still sleeping when she went back. Anne is awake and sitting with Virginia, Captain Marshall is getting dressed—"

"As is Jane," Amelia put in. "Genie is still in bed. I hope she sleeps as late as she usually does."

Their father nodded. "I want no mention of this to your mother until after Fiske has seen Virginia. There's no need to cause her unnecessary distress."

That had been David's thought as well, but he had known suggesting it would only irritate his father. "Yes, sir. The boy went off over an hour ago, so if Dr. Fiske is at home they should be here before much longer."

"Good." The Earl yawned hugely, covering it with one hand. "Damn that quack's potion! I thought tea would do something to dispel it, but it's useless."

David caught his sister's eye, and she spoke up. "Papa, would you like to lie down until the doctor arrives, and give the medicine time to wear off?"

"No, I would not!" he said, but the last word vanished in another yawn. "But I had better, I suppose." He stood up, not quite as steady on his feet as David would have wished. "You may as well see him in and explain the situation; I would only be repeating what you've told me. But I want to talk with him before he leaves. Laudanum, indeed! I'm not in my dotage just yet!"

Amelia went with him, disguising her solicitude with questions about what to ask the doctor. David decided to watch rather than help and risk irritating his father again. He was more concerned than he liked to admit over his parent's uncharacteristic docility. It was foolish to worry; he knew that. The Earl seldom took any sleeping draught other than his customary port or brandy, he was nearing seventy, and the past few weeks had been difficult ones. The dose of laudanum had obviously knocked him out, proving Dr. Fiske's diagnosis of fatigue although his patient would not admit it. But the shape he was in, even a man as stubborn as the Earl might concede to lying down as a graceful alternative to falling flat on his face.

All that granted, it was still distressing to see the man who had been as strong and immovable as Gibraltar suddenly agree to go back to his bedchamber while there was a crisis in his house. It was wrong, unnatural.

No. It was the most natural thing in the world. It was the way of things that the older generation would step back so that the next, younger and stronger, could shoulder the burdens. But, God in Heaven, there could not be a worse time, with the responsibility falling in one direction and the power in another.

David picked up his teacup and drained it, in agreement for once with his father—the tea did nothing to make him feel more alert or rested. He might as well go get into his own clothes, and see whether Will had sat down for a moment and gone back to sleep. Poor Will. David almost hoped he was catching forty winks.

He also hoped that Dr. Fiske arrived before Ronald came sauntering back, feigning innocence and full of false solicitude, or someone else might go tumbling down those damned stairs.

⚓ ⚓ ⚓

Daybreak was near by the time the doctor arrived, a wet, grey dawn appropriate to the occasion. "Where is the lady?" Dr Fiske demanded, pausing in the doorway only long enough for Leland to take the rain-soaked coat from his shoulders

"This way, sir." David was no more willing than the physician to stand on ceremony and wait for Leland to lead the way. He didn't much like Virginia, never had, but this ...

"Your boy didn't say anything but 'she's dying,'" Fiske said. "What's happened?"

"She took a bad fall down the staircase. No one has any idea why she might have been wandering around in the dead of night. Her maid has a bruise on her temple, and when I found her she was hard to waken."

"Do you think her ladyship struck her own maid?"

"I could not say, sir, and I would not attempt to guess why she would do so."

"The question ought to be *how* she could have done it. Did she take her cordial at bedtime?"

"Yes, sir, my sister Amelia watched her drink it."

"It would take a great deal of resolve to overpower that medication. Was she in an hysterical state?"

"According to her maid, no. But I imagine that in her state of mind, anything might be possible. She has been unconscious since we found her a little over two hours ago. My sister says she muttered briefly, after she was put to bed, and her breathing has grown harsh this past half-hour. But ...well, sir, you were here not long ago. She had remained uneasy in her mind on the matter of my brother's death, full of fears and accusations."

"Yes, yes. Were there any visible injuries? The child...?"

David could only shrug, and then they were at the bedroom door, where a knot of anxious servants melted away at the advent of the physician. Kirby opened the door and led them through the sitting room. As they entered the bedroom, Margaret left off bathing her mistress' forehead and turned back the counterpane.

Fiske took hold of Virginia's lax wrist. After a few seconds he glared at the hapless maid. "When did she stop breathing?"

"She —" The woman bent closer, and let out a shriek. "Oh, my dear Lord! No! Just this moment, it must be, oh, dear heaven! She turned away when I touched her just a moment ago—" She took a couple of quick, squeaky breaths and turned frantically to Amelia, standing at the far side of the bed. "You saw, my lady?"

"Yes," Amelia said, her face white but composed. "Just as you entered, I believe. A few harsh breaths...then stillness."

Fiske took a small disk from his pocket and polished it on his sleeve. A mirror, David saw. A chip of silvered glass that stayed bright and undimmed by breath when he held it up to the woman's silent lips. "I'm sorry," the doctor said. "I am too late."

And then, in the deathly quiet of the room, they saw a small movement under the coverlet stretched over Virginia's belly. David cringed inwardly. The baby, so near to term, would die slowly, suffocated. Another death on the household.

"Go get a basin of hot water," Fiske told the maid. "Go. Now. And you, Lady Amelia." He cut David and Will out with a look. "Not you two." He folded back the covers, set his black bag down on the spotless counterpane and unbuckled it. "Navy, you said?"

Will swallowed. "Yes."

"Seen some bloodshed?"

"More than I care to remember," Will said. "What are you—"

"Up on your Shakespeare?"

"Julius Caesar?" David guessed. "Do you think we can save him?" Out of the corner of his eye, he saw his sister pull the door shut behind her.

"We might," Fiske said. "Due in two weeks' time. If we're quick about it…" He selected a small, sharp instrument from the case and sliced ruthlessly through the soft wool of Virginia's nightdress. "Hold that shawl ready. You— Marshall? Stir up the fire, we'll need to keep the child warm." Probing carefully with his left hand—"Ah, there you are, you rascal, stay there…" he raised the scalpel once more and brought it down, and David had to turn his head away.

She should have screamed. Any sailor under the knife would have. More than the cloudless mirror or her marble pallor, that unearthly silence convinced David that his sister-in-law was indeed dead. Not all the blood he'd seen shed in battle could have prepared him for the sight of the gruesome birth, but he managed to keep hold of his nerves as well as the squirming infant that Fiske deposited on the delicate woolen shawl draped over his shaking hands.

David swallowed his gorge. He'd seen calves born, and horses, and that one summer Freya had delivered her pups right in the nursery…they'd looked very much like this, but smaller. It was just a baby, he told himself, just a baby…and it wasn't breathing. "Oh my God."

"Steady there," the doctor said. "We must unwrap the little chap—Oh, pardon me, the young lady." He peeled off the caul and cleared the child's wrinkled face, pushing gently on her belly. With a great whoop, the tiny chest expanded and color rushed into the wizened body. A thin wail wavered in the air, and Fiske grinned foolishly. "The finest sound in the world. There, there, my dear, your uncle David will look after you."

He wrapped the ends of the shawl around the baby and pushed her toward David. "Hold her there while I deal with the cord." Once again, David looked away. In a moment the doctor said, "Take her into the sitting room and keep her warm by the fire. I need to tidy up here, before that maid comes back in and starts howling like a banshee. I've already spoken to Mrs. Jordan, in the village—wet-nurse—in case she might be needed. You'd best send someone for her—tell her to come quick as the Lord will let her."

David nodded numbly, and took the baby over near the hearth, finding a strange comfort in the jerky, involuntary movements of its arms and legs. He sat down in the low chair near the warmth, and realized his knees were shaking. After a moment he felt Will move closer to stand beside him, hovering, one hand on his shoulder. "A little girl," Will said under his breath.

"Yes. A little girl." His eyes went unbidden to the doctor, who was hastily repairing the damage to the body. A little girl. Not a son who would avenge his father. Not a new heir. A helpless baby girl who would be no threat at all, to anyone.

A child now orphaned, and to no purpose.

Chapter 12

"Shall I make myself discreetly invisible?" Will asked.

"If you like. In fact, you might go downstairs and see if there's any sign of breakfast. I'll be down when the doctor's finished. That girl should bring up the water soon, and I imagine Amelia will rally the troops to do whatever is needed. Ask whoever's serving to make up a pot of coffee for the doctor, would you? I know he'll need to speak to my father before he leaves."

Relief was not long in coming. Even before Margaret managed to find a basin of hot water, Amelia returned. Anticipating what they would need, she had gone to fetch their old Nurse, whose face lit up at the sight of Mark's newest and last child, one small bright spot to end a long and very dark night. David was happy to hand the baby into Nurse's arms, relieved to have someone far more qualified to care for her.

"Boy or girl?" Amelia murmured, standing close.

"Girl."

"Ah," she said, a world of meaning in the syllable.

"Yes, and safer for it," he said as he made use of the washbasin. "But only for the present. What remains to be done?" David had been worried that his sister might be too shaken by this latest catastrophe to carry on, but she seemed to be in much the same state he was—numb, the way men could get after the cannon had been battering them for hours with waves of sound and concussion. Too numb to feel, but not quite too numb to function.

"I need to sit down and make a list," she said, smothering a yawn. "I cannot seem to keep a thought in my head. I spoke to Father. I think Mama will give Kirby instructions about what to do about ..." She glanced at the bedroom door, and her composure wavered a little. "There's no end to it, is there? How much longer will this go on?"

"I don't know." He gave her a hug. "Poor old thing, why don't you run downstairs now? I sent Will off to find some breakfast, and you deserve it as much as he. Or would you like me to have something sent up to your room?"

"I should like to go down for breakfast, I think. But first I will go and wash my face and see if Jane is awake."

"She slept through all this?"

"Yes. It would have been cruel to wake her. She stayed with her own mother through her last illness, and it was a difficult death. I know she would have sat with me, but since she and Virginia were never close, I thought it best to let her sleep."

"Was Virginia ever close to any of you?" he asked.

"She and Mary got on very well," Amelia said. "We were all on reasonably good terms, but Jane and Genie and I did mean to go and live with Mother at the Dower House when Mark inherited."

"I wouldn't have wanted to live with her, either," he said.

Amelia smiled sadly. "It's true Virginia could be difficult, but I pitied her. I think if she had ever been able to give Mark a son, she might have been more assured and less fretful."

David thought it more likely that she would have become insufferable if that were the case, but Amelia generally viewed people less cynically than he did himself. "Since we'll never know, there's no harm in hoping you were right," he said. "Go along, then. I'll see you downstairs."

He felt he ought to stay until Dr. Fiske had completed his examination of the body, but the doctor said he required no assistance for that task and David kept catching himself dozing off. He finally decided that there would be no harm in a walk down the hall, so he excused himself and stepped out of the suite. The rest of the household was up and about, and the Earl, who had apparently slept long enough to shake off his fatigue, was pacing the hall outside Virginia's suite when his son emerged.

"Amelia told me," he said without preamble. "Did Virginia ever wake and explain what she was doing out in the hall?"

"No, sir. She passed away without saying a word. Does Mother know?"

"Yes. Took it well. She said that at least Virginia is at peace now."

"I hope so." His mother's view was at least preferable to the notion of Virginia's angry spirit storming through the halls—though if she could be persuaded to haunt Ronald, that might be worth seeing.

"I wanted to name the child after your mother," his father said abruptly. "She says we should name her Michaela, after Fiske. That seems fair enough—he did save her life."

"Dr. Fiske certainly deserves the honor," David said. He felt he ought to suggest consultation with Virginia's family, but decided there was nothing to be gained by it. The baby would most likely remain here at Grenbrook, in any case. This had been her father's home. She would be the apple of everyone's eye, and unlikely to object to any name her grandparents chose to give her. "What of Mark's other daughters?" he asked.

"They've never liked it here, and I don't want to bring them out from London under the circumstances. That Stafford woman dotes on those girls, so I think it's best they stay with her for now. I hope she wants to keep them with her in London until she can marry 'em off. I expect she will if I pay for their keep!"

David blinked. He had not considered Mark's three elder daughters, and he pitied them, but he hoped his father was right about their Grandmother Stafford. "And the new baby?"

"Even if I were fool enough to pack a newborn off to London, your mother isn't! I need to send word about the funeral, of course, but I shall let her decide whether the girls need to attend. Since Virginia meant to have the child christened here, I mean to prevent those Staffords from giving her one of those insipid milksop names that she saddled the first three with. Didn't do them any good that I ever saw."

Patience, Prudence, and Verity would probably not appreciate their grandfather's assessment, but David was inclined to agree. He was able to avoid any comment on the matter, because Dr. Fiske appeared and asked for a word with the Earl. David waited only long enough to see if his presence was required, then went off downstairs to find Will and a large quantity of coffee.

⚓ ⚓ ⚓

As usual, Grenbrook's staff saw to it that breakfast was everything one might desire, even if one had awakened to a shocking tragedy at an ungodly hour. Will was halfway through a large plate of eggs and ham when Davy made his way downstairs, followed shortly after by Lady Amelia and Jane Winston. They were seated in a smaller salon a little way from the main dining room, and there was a dearth of conversation among them after an announcement from Amelia that Anne was having breakfast in her mother's rooms, and Eugenia was fretting because Nurse would not let her come near the new baby until she was absolutely free of what had developed into a bad cold. "I hope she is well soon. Not that Nurse needs any help, but Genie could do her white-work there, and have something happy to distract her."

As they sat there eating quietly, Will thought how much the situation felt like the first break after a battle, after the decks had been cleared and the bodies counted.

Finally Amelia stirred. "I wonder if there must be an inquest on Virginia's accident. I hope not."

"It's required in cases of sudden or violent death," Davy said. "This was certainly sudden. But I think the chance of it being ruled accidental is very good. The medication would have disturbed her balance and her judgment, and she showed no sign of being suicidal. Quite the opposite, in fact."

"I only hope the jury does not hold poor Margaret responsible," Jane said.

Davy shook his head. "She had been doing some mending—I saw it on the floor beside her chair. To use the lamp's light, she'd have turned away from the bedroom door, and it's obvious she was knocked unconscious. She hadn't any reason to injure herself, and I doubt she had the guile."

It seemed to Will that Davy was avoiding any mention of their suspicions. He knew that Amelia was aware of them, but perhaps there was some reason for not involving Jane. "I'd guess Margaret was asleep at the time," he said, and both ladies nodded agreement.

"Very likely," Davy said. "What else would—" He stopped, listening, and Will heard the sound of raised voices coming down the hall. Ronald had apparently returned, his father had met him on the way in, and from the sound of it neither of them was aware that anyone else was near enough to hear them.

The Earl was not modulating his voice. "Heir or not, you are under my roof and I demand an explanation of where you have been!"

"I was out with friends. Why? Is there anything going on in the house that required my presence?"

"Your brother's wife fell down the stairs while you were out!"

"She would hardly need my assistance to do that." Ronald sounded bored. "She is well, I trust?"

"She is dead, damn you! And I have had all I am going to stand of your gadding about the county while the household is in mourning! Are your friends unwilling to respect our bereavement, that they invite you to stay out until all hours when you should be here at home?"

"I have not asked them, and I am very grateful that they

refrain from ever mentioning the proprieties."

"I want their names. I'll have none of them in this house again, not while I live."

"Surely you don't imagine—" As they passed the closed doors and continued on down the hall, their voices became muffled, and then stopped abruptly.

"They've gone into Father's office," Amelia said. "I do hope he had something to eat before Ronald came in."

"I saw one of the maids bringing a tray when he went off with Dr. Fiske," Davy replied. "But that is a good question, if he can get an answer to it. Where has Ronald been keeping himself? Unless things have changed a great deal since I was last home, most of our neighbors would observe the proprieties to the letter. If he's been out cocking or playing cards, I think he would have to go pretty far afield."

"I have no idea where he might have gone," Jane answered, eyes on the teacup she had barely touched. "I know of a few gentlemen who avoid his company, but none who seek it."

"Might there be..." Amelia glanced at Will, then said carefully, "a woman? I hesitate to say a *lady*...and should probably not say even that."

Davy met Will's eyes. "It's possible," he said. "In fact, I might almost say very likely."

"Yes," Will agreed, "but how are we to find out? If your father is angry that one of his sons has been riding around the countryside instead of staying at home where he belongs...I could go, I expect, but I don't know anyone."

"No, Will, I think we may do it together, and with Father's blessing. Mrs. Jordan is already here to care for the baby, and it was good of her to come at such an hour. I'm sure we could get away to take a gift to her family."

"Not only could you, Mama has spoken to me about that very thing," Amelia said. "She wishes to send Mr. Jordan a basket of food and perhaps a bottle of wine, since his wife will be staying here."

"Doesn't he have family right there in the village—a sister, if I remember?"

"Of course—and she'll be glad of the provisions, if she's caring for Mr. Jordan and their little boy."

Davy shrugged with a slight smile. "You see, Will? We shall observe the proprieties and see if we cannot observe something else as well. I must go and see my mother in any case; I'm sure she will give me my orders."

"Finish your breakfast first," was his sister's practical advice.

"And before we go anywhere," Will said, "I think we ought to nip outside and check the ground beneath a certain window. Can we do that without being observed?"

"Oh, certainly," David said. "We might be seen by some of the servants, but not by my brother. There are French windows in the next room. We don't generally use them at this time of the year, but they open on the same side of the house as Ronald's room. So long as he remains with Father in the office across the hall, he cannot see us."

"I'll stay here," Jane offered. "If I hear them coming out, I can wave my handkerchief in that window—"

David nodded. "A bit melodramatic, but it will serve. Come, Will!"

"I'm coming too," Amelia said, following along. "If we should need to tell Father about this, the more witnesses the better."

They made a hasty exit through the French windows and hurried along the side of the house to see what they could find while Jane remained with her tea in the breakfast room, handkerchief at the ready.

"At least these are very old slippers," Amelia said, gamely treading the spongy wet grass. "And thank goodness the rain has stopped!"

The rain had soaked the flower beds all around the base of the building, but the earth directly below the window in question had been churned up beyond what any ground-skeeper would do at this time of year.

"Look," Will said. "That proves it." He pointed to the

mark of a boot-heel, the edges slightly melted from the rain but clear enough to be certain that it wasn't anything other than the spot where someone had dropped down from the ropy strands of ivy.

David frowned upward, noticing an uneven outward bulge in the vegetation. "And I'd say the vines are pulled away from the wall—there, just below the window, and again a few feet lower, over to the left. You wouldn't notice it unless you were looking, but see the difference between those places and the growth under the other windows?"

"Yes," Amelia said, pulling the shawl she wore more closely around her. "I agree, I congratulate you on your perspicacity, and I am going back indoors before I freeze through!"

Will apologized profusely and doffed his uniform coat in what David thought was a true Sir Walter Raleigh manner—though he refrained from saying so. As he settled the coat around Amelia's shoulders, Will asked hesitantly, "My lady, it seemed to me that you did not wish to discuss the particulars of our suspicion in Miss Winston's presence. Is she trustworthy?"

"Oh, heavens, yes!" she replied. "But I do appreciate your discretion. I said nothing to her out of consideration, not distrust. Jane is afraid of Ronald, and Virginia's accident has terrified her. Her home life was..." she stopped, biting her lip.

David knew the reason for his sister's reticence. "Jane's father is a bully, Will, as his father was before him, and I would not be surprised to learn that his wife's death was more the result of an 'accident' like Virginia's than any illness."

Amelia nodded. "It was. There's a taint of violence in the men in Mama's family. The women either became bitter, like Grandmother Winston, or died young, like Jane's mother. Mark was like Father—he might roar, but he would cut off his own hand before he would ever strike a woman."

"Mama said something to that effect once," David said as

they reached the steps to the French windows. "I had caught another dressing-down and was complaining about how cruel Father was, and she said he was the gentlest man she'd ever known. And he always has been, to her and you girls."

She nodded. "Yes. And she adores him for that. I only wish he'd been able to see that you had more of her sensibility and less of his own force."

"Oh, I've learned to be fierce," he said. "Out of necessity. But I'm still a bookish ninny who would not trade Shakespeare for the finest pack of foxhounds ever whelped. If we go out to the Jordans' later, would you and Jane like to come along as Mama's representatives, and get out of the house for a while?"

"That would be lovely," she said, handing Will back his coat. She bent to pull off her slippers and made a face. "As I thought, soaked through. Let us go rescue Jane and report to our mother for marching orders!"

⚓ ⚓ ⚓

As the morning wore on the weather improved, and by the time the four of them set off for the village, the sun had put in an appearance. Once again, they took both gig and saddle horses, though this time Will and Davy were both on horseback while the ladies drove. Although he knew he was never likely to ride to hounds—at least, not if he could avoid it—Will found that he was no longer convinced that he was going to fall off at any moment. He happened to glance up and see Davy observing him, and their eyes met in one of those moments where no words were needed. He said them anyway: "You are an excellent teacher, Mr. Archer!"

"It only needed time, Will. Anyone who can balance on a yardarm can balance on a horse."

The Jordan cottage was empty but the smithy was next door, and Mr. Jordan was busily making repairs to some iron tool whose purpose Will neither knew nor wanted to learn. Jordan insisted that the gift was unnecessary but accepted it with profuse thanks, and offered his sympathy for their loss along with congratulations for the new arrival. Davy and Lady Amelia said all that was necessary and they left the smithy in a pleasanter mood than they had known for several days.

That lasted only a few minutes. They had handed the ladies back into the gig and were about to remount when the proprietor of the Bull and Sheaf approached them. He looked troubled, and after offering his own sympathies he said, "Lieutenant Archer, I know it's unlikely, but might any of you ladies and gentlemen have heard anything about what's become of my daughter Kittie?"

"What do you mean, Mr. Carter? What's become of her? Is she missing?"

"Aye, sir, she is, and I'm about worried sick! I was away yesterday evening, delivering a keg of beer to a farm out toward Tavistock—Oxman's, it was, and after I'd tapped the keg, George offered me a bed for the night. That's nothing new, I figured Kittie could close up and put my old mother to bed all right—which she did—but when I got back early this next morning expecting to find her up and about, all I found was me Mam shouting for her breakfast."

Jane made a small distressed sound and Amelia wordlessly took her hand.

"She didn't know where your daughter had gone?" Davy asked.

"Sir, she hadn't heard a blessed thing. No surprise, that, she don't hear anything unless you stand a foot from her and shout—but neither has anyone else, nor has anyone seen Kittie since the place closed last night! It's true she's always saying she'll run away to London, but her clothes are still in her room and there's nothing missing from the house or the bar, and the cash-box is where it's always been, and nothing missing there either. I'm that worried—"

"And I can't blame you," Davy said. "I wish we could help you, but we've not seen her either, not since the night we were here."

"Might she have gone to visit a friend?" Amelia asked.

"Leavin' her old gran alone? No, my lady. Kittie's a flighty girl, and I guess that's my fault, havin' her help me in the business, and with my wife gone, but she wouldn't leave the old lady to get her own breakfast. Nor is there anyone in walking distance that she might have gone to see."

"I'm sorry," Davy said. "I've been away from home for some years now, but if I can be of help...What of my brother's hounds? Might they be pressed into service?"

"Aye, that's what I've been thinking," Carter said. "Old Ralph Rolle, he's got a dog he swears by, found his grandson what had wandered off. Ralph said he'd come by and see if his Gyp can find any trail. She can't have gone very far, I'll swear to that. There's nothing but the mail coach comes through here, and that's not due until this afternoon—and I was here when it went through yesterday, and I know Kittie was right there in my house when it passed."

Davy nodded and clapped him on the shoulder. "I'll tell my father what's happened and see what he thinks best. I hope she shows up safe and sound, and this turns out to be some misunderstanding."

"Thank'ee, sir. I do hope you're right."

Will felt sick. He had a feeling that Carter was never going to see his daughter again, and even if the girl had been the duplicitous vixen Davy had described, she was more foolish than evil. She might have deserved a comeuppance, but it was more likely that what she got was the promise of a trip to London and a quick, violent death.

Davy had performed his duties magnificently, showing nothing more than anyone might reasonably expect—surprise, concern, and a note of distress. But on the way back, he rode close enough to Will to mutter, "You're right, Will. It's like a dog killing sheep...he's got the taste for blood and there's no telling where it's going to end if we don't put a stop to it."

Chapter 13

B ut they did nothing about it that day. The Earl and Countess were involved in arrangements for Virginia's funeral and presumably the inquest, though his father did not mention that and David preferred not to ask. Ronald sulked in his room for awhile and then went out, saying he was going to take a walk. He was, Amelia had learned, under orders not to leave the grounds, but there was no reason to expect he would obey.

After tea, Anne surveyed the faces assembled around the table. "I know you are both of you adults," she said to her younger sister and brother, "but if you were still children I should advise you two to go upstairs to your rooms and take a nap—and I would say the same to Captain Marshall too, if he has been up since four in the morning and running errands for us half the afternoon."

David Archer found the thought of his comfortable bed a very lovely thing. Anne might be overly inclined to play First Lieutenant to the Countess, but in this case he could only say, "Thank you. It has been a very long day. Will, I intend to heed my sister's advice, and if you are wise I think you'll do the same."

"So long I am called back on-duty if needed, I think I shall. Thank you, my lady."

"Your presence has been a comfort to all of us, sir," Anne said. "My mother told me as much a little while ago, and reminded me to look after you."

Will shrugged. "If I've been of any help in return for

your kindness and hospitality, I'm glad of it. Until later, my lady."

Amelia rose too, and the three of them excused themselves. They were too weary even for conversation as they mounted the staircase, but once the door of his room was closed and he was alone with Will, David felt the weight of it all descend upon him. He sat heavily in one of the chairs near the window. What was he going to do? What *could* he do? There was plenty of circumstantial evidence, but nothing that could be presented as absolute proof.

"It was kind of your sister to give us an excuse to get away," Will said, drawing near. "I don't believe I have the fortitude for light conversation with Lady Eugenie."

"You needn't worry. She's still coughing and confined to bed, and once she's set free she'll go straight to the nursery—she's mad to see the new baby. You are no longer the most interesting person in her life, and you certainly deserve a little peace and quiet."

"As do you." Will sat in the other chair and yawned. "But you look more ready for a fight than for sleep."

"If only that were true. I'm not ready, Will, not at all. We must act, and soon, but he has left no witnesses who might implicate him. And who remains, now, to stand in the way of his ambition? My father, myself—"

"And I," Will said. "If it comes to that, in any way I can. But we might as well begin in an orderly manner. Your brother the honorary Viscount has as yet no alibi of any kind that has been confirmed. His own word...Well, your father might believe it, but I think the law would require a little more than that. If he's left no witnesses against him, he has yet to mention any who might substantiate his story."

It was good to know that Will was solidly on his side, at last. "I wonder where Ronald would say he was last night. And even more, I wonder what it would take to persuade my father to insist that Ronald prove his whereabouts, either last night or when Mark died."

"Perhaps he did—last night's, at any rate."

"I doubt it. You heard how Ronald deflected his questions. And even if he did insist, if Ronald were to lie, how would he know? Would my father even attempt to find out if his answer were true? To test an alibi requires an admission of doubt, and he has never been willing to do that—not to his children. I almost believe he would rather not know."

Leaning close, voice low, Will said, "Davy, your father may be dedicated to his family, but he does not seem willing to be deceived. At some point he must begin to wonder about these strange absences and accidents. I have been thinking— what if I were to take myself off your hands and find lodgings elsewhere, so that I might travel around to inns and make inquiries?"

David caught his hand. "Please don't, Will. With you here, I have one very able man I can depend upon. And you may call me foolish, but I do not care for the notion of you riding around alone in unfamiliar territory—especially not on a hired horse!"

Will looked relieved. "Very well. I doubt I'd have much success, and I would not be pleased to leave you alone, either. Now, sir, may I act as valet and help you off with your attire?"

Fatigued as he was, David had to smile. "I think not, Captain. But let us step into the dressing-room for a moment and hang our coats upon the rack in that useful chamber."

"And perform any other actions that may seem necessary?"

He was longing to be held, if only for a moment, and Will looked as if he had that very thing in mind. "Indeed, you may, sir."

⚓ ⚓ ⚓

Two days passed, wholly consumed by sad necessities. The Coroner convened a jury, which ruled that Lady Virginia Archer had died of misadventure. When her body was released for burial, she was laid to rest alongside her husband in the family plot. The Countess joined her husband for the funeral ceremony, but she and her youngest daughter were afterward escorted back to the house by her youngest son and his fellow officer, both of them somber and correct in dress uniform with black armbands, while the rest of the family remained for the burial.

In the ordinary way of things, the event would have been the talk of the village, but the tragedy at the Manor was eclipsed by one nearer their own lives. Old Ralph's dog Gyp found Kittie Carter out on the edge of the moor, dead, at the bottom of a pit that had probably been a well at some time in the dim past. She had been there at least a day and her neck was broken; that was all Dr. Fiske was prepared to say until the Coroner convened yet another inquest.

Friends who lived in the area came to Grenbrook after the funeral to offer their condolences, but it seemed to David that few of them thought it necessary or considerate to stay very long. The weather might have helped to keep the ordeal short; it was cold and wet, and given the fact that most of them had been there only a month before to bury Mark, there was really very little more anyone could say.

After a slow evening and a somber supper of cold meats, after all the guests had gone, no one seemed inclined to conversation. David had been happy to see their well-meaning neighbors leave as quickly as courtesy would allow. There had been a few people present he would have liked to spend more time with, but he had precious little energy to spare for idle conversation. He knew that matters must reach a crisis soon. It might be weeks or months before the Peace of Amiens was broken, but it might be only a matter of days—and though he did not intend to return to the Service, he had very little faith in his own ability to solve this tangle without Will here beside him.

The family made an early night of it, and even Will, after a quick embrace in their little sanctuary, went off to bed and to sleep.

David lay awake for a long time. What were they going to do? What was *he* going to do—about Will, about Amelia and the other girls? How long was it going to be before an attempt was made on the Earl himself? He thought his father safe enough while he and Will were there, but they had all thought Virginia safe enough, there in her own room, watched by her maid.

Tomorrow, he would have to speak to Amelia about setting up some kind of watch. She would know which of the servants would be subtle enough to keep a discreet eye on the Earl without his knowledge. That should be possible; most of them were wary of Ronald anyway.

But that was only a stopgap, not a solution. He had to find a way to prove that Virginia had not accidentally fallen down those stairs. And Kitty Carter...perhaps someone in the village had seen something that might help. There had to be something.

He should think about watching his own back, too. But not tonight. He was too weary to even consider that.

It was a relief to pull up the covers, extinguish the candle, and dismiss his overwhelming worries into the night's darkness.

⚓ ⚓ ⚓

The following morning, Will had a question of his own. As they sat in their dressing gowns near the fire, sipping chocolate, he said, too quietly to be heard by anyone in the hall, "Davy, what do you believe happened to your brother Mark? I have a notion, but you have never said precisely what you suspect."

"Why do you ask?"

"Because that might give us another direction in which to look. I gather you think he was shot from a distance, and the murderer used a second shot, from your brother's own gun, to camouflage the fatal wound."

David considered the description. "Yes. That's it precisely. The first shot from hiding, probably the gazebo where we found the gunpowder. He might have stalked Mark from the cover of the woods, or simply waited there for a time."

"But how did he know when to wait, and where? I have been turning that over in my mind, and it seems strange that anyone might lurk in such a remote area. He might have had to come back every day for weeks, and eventually someone would surely have noticed."

"Oh, that's no mystery. Mark had a few places that he particularly liked to hunt. The fishing pool was one of them—it's open water, so game naturally goes there. And at that time of year, the very end of hunting season, if the weather was not completely foul, Mark would be out with a gun. He had his little ways—it always pleased him to put food on the table through his own efforts. A fowl from the barnyard was my father's beneficence; a pheasant brought down by his own skill was Mark's accomplishment—*his* contribution to the family."

Will nodded. "So the killer knew that the time was right, and a few days' surveillance was likely to bring him there."

"Yes—and you've help me understand why I was suspicious from the start. No one would know all those things but a member of this household, and *cui bono?*"

"I wish that got us any closer to proving any of it," Will said.

"I wish we had been here."

"Just as well we were not. I wouldn't wish either of us under suspicion!"

"No, but if I'd been able to see the body—" A wave of grief swept over him, and David suddenly found his vision blurred by tears. "Sorry—sorry to be so foolish. It's just struck me, Will. Until now, my brother's death has not felt real. But I just now realized I'll truly never see him again."

"I felt that way when my father died," Will said. "Most of the time it was not quite real, then without warning it was too real to bear. It will pass, in time."

"But there's no time for sorrow now," David said impatiently, wiping his face. "I'll mourn later. What I was thinking was that if I'd been able to see his clothing, I might have noticed if anything was wrong, whether there were powder burns—there should have been—or any other sign that things were not as they seemed."

"There was an inquest…"

"And an obvious verdict. He was out alone; no one in the household bore him any malice. With everything to live for and a child on the way, possibly a son at last, it could not have been suicide. A freak accident would be the simplest way to explain it. No one would look for evidence of the murder of a man who had no enemies and nothing in his pockets to steal."

Will nodded. Then he asked, "Who prepared the body?"

"I don't know. My mother would. Amelia might know, too, but I'd rather not cause either of them any further grief. But I think there's someone besides my mother who'd have the answer."

⚓ ⚓ ⚓

"Master Da—I mean, Lieutenant Archer. What may I do for you, sir?"

He smiled. "You needn't cosset my vanity, Kirby. Is my mother awake?"

With a glance at the bedroom door, the maid answered, "I'm sorry, sir, but she's been sound asleep for a good while now, and may rest until dinnertime."

"I thought she might be sleeping." He moved into the room anyway, keeping his voice low. "I should prefer not to distress her, but there was something I wished to know. On the day my brother died, after the doctor left…can you tell me what happened that day?"

"What do you mean, sir?" The considering look she gave him made David think she had some suspicion of his purpose. Kirby had known David Archer since he was born. She had begun at Grenbrook as an ordinary housemaid, been pressed into service when his mother's maid and many of the other servants had been laid low with influenza, and had shown a talent for the work as well as a level head. Now in her forties, Kirby ranked with Leland and Mrs. Hubbard in the top echelon of importance among the servants. Lady Grenbrook relied on Kirby, and had never uttered a word of complaint about her.

"I know that when someone dies, the women of the household...prepare the body for burial." This was harder to speak of than he had expected. No doubt it had been harder still for those who'd had the doing of it. "Do you know who performed that last service for my brother?"

"Well, I did, sir, most of it. Your lady mother meant to— she did for your brother George, who was taken when he was only two, and she meant to send her other boy along with her own hands."

David knew of George, but that lost brother had been born and died several years before Amelia came along. He had never really thought about what that loss had meant to his mother. "She's game clear through."

"Aye, sir, but this time, it was more than her heart could bear. We'd only begun when she was overcome and had to sit down where she could not see...it was hard, sir, her oldest son and all. Two of the other maids helped me, and once we had him washed and a bandage wrapped round those horrible wounds..." She looked away and swallowed.

"Do you have any spirits in the room, Kirby?" he asked. "It might do you good—"

"There's only sherry, sir, but I'm all right. I've not much more to tell you. We bandaged Lord Mark up and got him into his Sunday best, and then the men came and carried him out to the parlor."

"Did you examine his clothing?" David saw the sherry and glasses, on a low table near the bedroom door, and decided that if she did not need medicinal assistance, he did. But he poured some for her anyway, and she did not refuse a second time.

"Bless you, sir, what was there to see? He'd bled something terrible, poor man, and his coat all over holes from the shot. I never looked any closer than I had to. We only wanted to be done with it and lay him to rest."

Well, that was really no more than he should have expected. "What of Dr. Fiske? Did he examine the body before you washed it?"

Kirby shook her head. "That I do not know. I was with her ladyship when Dr. Fiske was here. Death by misadventure was what the coroner said, and the doctor testified that he'd died of a—well, you know all that, sir."

"Yes." He sighed. It had only been a slim chance, at best. "So his clothes...were they burned, then?"

Kirby glanced at the door, and lowered her voice even further. "No, sir. I should have done that, I know, but your lady mother ...she would not have it. I can't say why she would do such a thing—she's never asked to see them since—but she told me to put them aside and keep them safe, and so I did."

⚓ ⚓ ⚓

"She had them stowed away, Will," he said, pushing the door of his room shut with one elbow. "I told her not to let anyone know we'd had that little talk, for her own safety. I must get these back to her as soon as possible."

"At least there's nothing remarkable about you visiting your mother," Will said, "and I can act as lookout when you return them. Is it safe to inspect the things here?"

"I saw no one in the hall just now," David said. "I think we must trust our luck. But in your room, if you don't mind—and let us lock the door."

He had not expected the smell of battle here in the peaceful countryside, but as he unwrapped the old sheet Kirby had used to cover the bundle he recognized the rank scent of it. He spread the sheet out on the writing desk near the window in case any dried crusts fell off the clothing, as they were likely to, and separated the stiff, wrinkled garments. The breeches were horribly bloodstained but undamaged. The rust-colored shirt, once clean white linen, was in shreds.

"They must have had to cut it off him," Will said, grimacing. "What of the coat?"

That, too, was stiff with blood, the front of it so perforated that it seemed about to fall to pieces. David laid it out on the table as carefully as he could. A fowling piece fired at close range would do that, he supposed—and he could see that there were powder burns, as one might expect from so near a blast.

Will knew what that meant, too. "So the gun did discharge point-blank, not from any distance."

"Apparently not." David closed his eyes. Will said nothing, but he hardly needed to. Whatever he might believe, or wish to believe, this damage told the story clearly enough. The gun had gone off somehow, killing Mark, just as everyone had said all along. "Very well, then. I still hate to see Ronald as heir, and I still want to know where he was the night Virginia fell, but I'm glad to see this. Bad enough to lose one brother without knowing the other murdered him." He folded the upper half of the coat over, and froze.

There, in the very center of the back, was a hole.

A bullet hole. Not a rip made in falling, not a tear from a stray bit of shot. A round, neat hole, the sort that looked so insignificant until you looked on the other side of the body to find the exit wound.

Mark had been killed by a bullet in the back. David Archer looked up, and met Will Marshall's eyes.

"Davy," Will said in the stunned silence, "Forgive me for ever doubting you."

"It's proof to you," David said, "and to me too. But it will never be sufficient for my father."

"Would it be sufficient for the Coroner?"

"Go to him, over my father's head?"

"If we must."

"Let me think on that, Will. Please. I am not certain I could take that step."

Will started to say something, but only shook his head. "Wrap those back up, then, and be certain Kirby hides them well—and warn her that her life might depend on keeping them secret. We must wait and see what develops."

Chapter 14

The next development, damning evidence that Will thought ought to be sufficient for even a Grand Jury, arrived in the mail the following afternoon. Sir Percy had paid a king's ransom to send a copy of the current *Naval Gazette,* and enclosed within it was the answer to a question Will had known must eventually be asked.

"Inquiries reveal that the officer in question was released from duty on 15th December in order to travel to his family home in Devon. There is no indication of his presence at his lodgings in London from that date to the present. His horse was taken from its usual livery stable, also on that date, and has not yet been returned.

It has been suggested by two fellow officers that this gentleman retired to the country to gather resources to deal with debts of honor, and there is no suggestion that he was expected to fail in this purpose. No attempt has been made, at this point, to confirm or deny this rumor.

This is all the information available with a discreet preliminary investigation. Please advise if more detail is required."

"Dear God," said Lady Amelia, holding the sheet of parchment as though she expected it to turn into a serpent.

"So you wrote to Sir Percy after all," Davy said. "And I presume you did it immediately after we both explained to you why we could not make such an inquiry."

He did not sound as angry as Will had expected. "Yes, I did. I apologize to you both, but it seemed to me that until we had either confirmed or disproved the claim that he had been in London, we had nothing on which to base any hypothesis."

"If Father should find out..." Lady Amelia said. "How could we ever explain?"

"Your brother Mark is dead," Will said bluntly, "and now so is his wife. A young woman from the village vanished from her home and was found, also apparently dead from a fall, after she hinted to us that she knew Ronald had been back here sooner than he claimed to be. I hate to state the obvious, my lady, but at some point your father will have to find out about this. He must be informed that his son's alibi is nothing more than a fabrication."

"He's right, Amelia," Davy said. "Ronald's lie must be challenged. It will upset Father, without a doubt, but—for heaven's sake, if Ronald is determined to become Earl as fast as he possibly can, Father himself is the next target. I believe he is safe while Will and I are here, but I could be mistaken. We must tell Father. If we had done something sooner, Virginia might still be alive."

She worried her lower lip. "Yes, I know, but the inquiry itself will create suspicion!"

Will shook his head. "My lady, Sir Percy is acquainted with men who deal with military intelligence. A discreet investigation such as this would have meant sending a clerk to check on the records of leave granted to men in your brother's regiment, nothing more. In peacetime, there is no reason men should not be given leave at Christmas, and no surprise at all that an officer should ask for a list of those who are away on leave. And I am equally certain no eyebrows would be raised if a fellow soldier were to stop at your brother's lodgings, or his livery stable, and ask if Major Archer had returned from visiting his family. There is nothing in this letter that would have raised the slightest question in anyone's mind. It is all harmless outside the context of your eldest brother's death."

"That's true," Davy said. "But now that we have this information, what do we do with it if Father refuses to act? Amelia's right, Will—he is hardly likely to be grateful to learn that Ronald's been lying to him. He'll be mad as fire that this inquiry was made, no matter how discreetly. But he *is* the magistrate, as well as head of the family. He must be told."

"Who'll bell the cat?" Amelia asked. "Which of us should be chosen to be the sacrificial victim?"

Davy smiled slightly. "It must be me," he said. "Will can't; I think he should be nearby, to vouch for Sir Percy's discretion if Father should ask, but it would be impossible for Will to admit to having shown such presumption. I must take responsibility for the inquiry if we're not to see him thrown right out of the house." He raised a hand to stop Will's protest. "No, Will, you were right. I should have done it in the first place. I should have written Sir Percy the moment I heard that alibi, because I never believed it for a moment. I must do this myself." He turned to his sister. "And I think you had better be close at hand, too, Lia, because if you're present Father might be able to restrain himself from murdering the two of us."

⚓ ⚓ ⚓

There was a term for this sort of mission in the Army: forlorn hope. When a wall had to be breached, they asked for volunteers, and anyone who survived usually got a particularly fine reward, easy to offer because there were so seldom any survivors. The point of such an attack was to create a breach in the enemy defenses, no matter what the cost.

Of course, in the Navy they never bothered to ask for volunteers. *We few, we happy few...* David Archer knocked on the door of his father's study. When he heard, "Come in!" he pushed the heavy door open and stepped into the lion's den.

"What is it?"

David took a breath, released it, and spoke as calmly as he could, wasting no time in preliminaries. "Father, I have reason to believe that Ronald had a hand in Virginia's accident. I have also received word, from a highly-placed source in the military, that Ronald was given leave to come home at Christmas and that he apparently did leave London in plenty of time to arrive long before he made his appearance."

He put the paper down on the desk, facing away from himself, and watched as his father quickly read it through.

For a moment there was nothing but silence. Then, "You sent a letter questioning your brother's word? You *dared?*"

The words fell like heated shot in the quiet of the study, with the same devastating effect as that evil missile. David had not faced his father's fury since that long-ago day when he'd left the family home to join the Navy, but it had lost none of its scorching heat. "Someone had to, sir. I cannot help that the answer was one we might not have wished to hear."

"And just what do you expect me to do with this...scurrilous rumor?"

"Not rumor, sir. Reliable information, from a completely discreet and well-placed source within His Majesty's intelligence service. This is as sound as any briefing sent to the King himself."

"Your brother's whereabouts are *no concern of yours!*"

The fury hit him full force, but there was something behind it, and David was shocked to realize what it was. His father was afraid. The anger was real, but it was a screen concealing fear. "On the contrary, sir, they most certainly are. I was taught, from as far back as I can remember, that justice is every man's responsibility. I was taught that when any man conceals the truth for personal gain, he shares in the guilt of the offense."

"This is not—"

David plowed ahead. "I was taught that *by my father,* sir. Have the rules of justice changed so much since I was a child, that evidence suggesting murder may be ignored?"

"Silence!"

David took a deep breath, feeling as though he'd just lit the fuse that would set fire to all his bridges, and tried to speak in a normal tone. "Father, did you know that the window in Ronald's room had been left unlocked the night Virginia died? That there was water on the windowsill, and footprints on the ground beneath?"

"And you chose not to tell me?"

"At first there was no time, and afterward..." He shrugged. "Would you have listened?"

"To such a tale? No, I would not."

"Not even if Amelia could swear to you that she also saw the footprints? There may still be traces beneath the window, if you want to look for yourself. Captain Marshall saw them too, though since you do not know him as I do, you cannot know that he would never falsify—"

"You have discussed our personal affairs with a stranger?"

There it was again, that fear, even louder than the anger this time. "I have discussed them with the one person in this house, apart from my sister, whom I knew to be intelligent, wholly discreet, and willing to deal with me as a rational adult."

"Why are you trying to paint your brother as a murderer?"

"Sir, why are you trying to absolve him? I am trying to find out the truth of my brother's death, and the death of his wife, and an attempt to destroy the child who might have been his heir—*your* heir. Virginia's maid was knocked unconscious with a single well-placed blow. Can you not see how ludicrous it is to imagine a woman dosed with sedatives, who had been accustomed to sleeping heavily through the night, suddenly running amok and attacking her own maid?"

His father waved a dismissive hand. "She had gone mad."

"She knew a hawk from a handsaw, Father, and she was too drugged to get out of bed—the doctor told me as much.

But there's more. We now know that Ronald vanished from London in the middle of December, and the innkeeper's daughter down at the Bull hinted to me that she had seen him during the time he claimed to be with his regiment. And now *she's* dead—after vanishing on the same night that Virginia died, a night when Ronald was out of the house—and he refuses to tell anyone where he was, or produce any witness to vouch for him. Has he ever given you any accounting of his whereabouts?"

He might as well consider the question rhetorical; his father's glare said he wasn't getting an answer. He forged ahead. "I suppose there might be some other explanation of their deaths, and Mark's, that has nothing at all to do with Ronald, but all three within a month's time seems to me to push coincidence to the very limit of credibility—and it makes me fear for your safety."

The Earl was slowly shaking his head, and David knew that he had failed. Worse, he'd shown his hand and gained nothing by it. Should he mention the bullet hole in Mark's coat? No; that could only mean trouble for Kirby, and perhaps destruction of the evidence that would be needed for an exhumation order. He knew, now, that he was going to see this to the bitter end, even if it meant taking that evidence to London, to the Temple Bar. He was going to see Mark's murderer brought to justice.

"You traitor," his father said in a low voice full of revulsion. "You vile, unnatural creature. If I did not know your mother so well, I would say you are no son of mine."

"Say it if you like," David said with a recklessness born of despair. "That's how you've always treated me, anyway. But before you denounce me, sir, tell me one thing. Tell me what happened to Ronald's wife Lenore!"

He waited to a count of five; he could have counted to five thousand and received the same response. He left the room quickly but with as much dignity as he could muster, closing the door rather than slamming it. He shook his head as he passed the breakfast room where Will and Amelia hovered just inside the doorway, his footsteps picking up speed as he went up the stair and down the hall. They swiftly followed him upstairs and into his room, a serious social gaffe on Amelia's part, but one that mattered little to them at the moment.

"Did you hear any of that debacle?" he asked.

"A bellow or two, at the very start," Amelia said. "Nothing more. Why did you not call us in?"

"It would have done no good, and only been more trouble for you. He may ask you about the footprints beneath the ivy, if he stops fuming long enough to consider what I've said. I don't expect he will, though."

"He disregarded the evidence?" Will asked.

"Will, the only thing he cared about was that I had dared to question Ronald's precious alibi. I kept your name out of the matter, except as someone with whom I'd discussed the evidence, and as witness to the footmarks beneath the window."

"And the coat—"

"I never mentioned that. We may need it later. But his reaction was exactly what I'd expected—he'll prevent a scandal if it kills him. He is furious that I doubted Ronald's alibi or spoke about any of this to you, and he seems determined to believe that Virginia, in the last stages of pregnancy and with a dose of laudanum in her that would tranquilize an ox, got up and brained her maid before flinging herself down the stair!"

His tongue seemed to be running miles ahead of his thoughts, probably the result of having had to hold it for the past couple of weeks. "I think I'd better tell Tobias to bring down our sea-chests and start packing them. As soon as His Lordship gets over being speechless with rage, he's likely to order us out of the house and abjure me to darken his door no more."

"Oh, Davy," Amelia said.

"Yes, and I apologize to you especially—he'll probably have Beauchamp back here in a flash and add yet another codicil to his will casting me out into the coldest ring of Hell."

"And what will happen should we leave?" Will asked. "We cannot. In all conscience, we cannot leave, not now."

"You may not have a choice," Amelia said. "Davy, can you teach me how to use a pistol?"

"I can and will," he answered. "But not well enough to keep you safe. I suppose I could call Ronald out. That'd be a pretty problem, wouldn't it, no matter which way it fell out."

Will shook his head. "Not worth the risk to you. If it comes to that, I'll challenge him. Yes, and I'll tell your father who wrote that letter, too. But I think we have one more angle of attack. Think, Davy. We have evidence enough to take this over your father's head, but there is another person who might be interested in hearing what we know about your brother Ronald."

"Yes, I know. The Coroner. But I cannot take that route unless there is absolutely no other choice. I cannot and will not do that to the rest of my family."

"That was not the man I had in mind," Will said.

"Who, then?"

"Your brother Ronald."

"What?"

Will shrugged. "As I see it, that's our only chance."

"What do you mean? Are you saying we should try to convince him that the evidence against him is so overwhelming his only hope is to abdicate or confess? He'd never do it, Will. He's too full of himself—and he knows he's left no witnesses."

"You have the word of unimpeachable witnesses that he was on leave well before Christmas, and had claimed to be going home. You have my word—which should be worth something—that the barmaid hinted he'd been in the neighborhood long before he showed himself here. And you have physical evidence enough to warrant an exhumation."

David knew that, but was suddenly reluctant. "Evidence I daren't use, not right now. Will, my mother has been through too much already—and so has my father, though he'd never admit to feeling the strain."

"I must agree with my brother on this," Amelia said. "We could never force our parents to dig Mark up again, after—" She stopped suddenly, and pressed her hands tightly against her face. After a moment she said, "I cannot even speak of it...think of it. No."

Will watched her with sympathy, but shook his head. "I understand how you must feel, even though I believe it might be necessary. But what I had in mind was nothing like that. Davy, would you say your brother is a vain man?"

"Yes, of course."

"That was my impression as well. Think of this: he has accomplished his life's ambition. He has cleared a path to title and fortune, eliminated everyone who stood in his way...and he dares not tell a soul. I think he would love to boast of what he's done, so long as he felt sure he would never be held accountable."

"That's possible," David admitted. "Still—"

"He underestimates you. What if you were to goad him into admitting his guilt, under circumstances that would let him feel certain he could do so—alone, just the two of you—so that it would be your word against his if you were to accuse him to anyone else?"

"But that would be useless," Amelia objected. "It would be just that—his word alone—and Father would side with Ronald to avoid a scandal. What good would a confession to Davy do, other than make him the next target?"

"Quite a lot, perhaps...if someone else were to overhear the conversation. Ourselves, for instance—then we could testify in support.." His eyes met David's. "Though it would be better still if we were able to enlist a disinterested third party such as Dr. Fiske, or the Vicar."

"Not Peter Newkirk," David said. "He's dependent on my father for the living. He might do it, if he had only himself to consider, but he mentioned to me that his wife has just given him a son. I'd hate to set his conscience against his sense of duty to his own family."

Will nodded. "Very well, then. What about the doctor?"

"If we can find him and bring him here without anyone the wiser? Possibly. But how? No, I think your idea might work—and damn me if I don't want to see if I can get him to admit it—but I do not see how we'll get an objective witness."

"Perhaps Jane?" Amelia suggested.

"No. She's known to dislike Ronald, she is your dear friend and people would, I am certain, believe she would lie to support you—" He saw her brows draw together and said hastily, "No, Lia, I don't believe she would, not in something this serious—but more to the point, she's as dependent on Father as Newkirk is. Perhaps if Gilliam were at home, or if you could persuade Anne—but I don't see how Anne could keep still if she heard us arguing. Who does that leave? Mama and Genie, and I'd never expose either of them to anything like that. It would be bad enough for them to hear third-hand."

"The one who needs to hear it is Father," Amelia said. "He must face the truth."

"Don't waste your time trying to convince him," David advised her. "He'll have none of it."

"It will be bad enough for everyone in your family," Will said soberly. "The only good that can possibly come out of this is that your family—particularly your father—will be will be safe. How long do you think he'll live if Ronald grows impatient for the position to which he considers himself entitled?"

Amelia said nothing. David said, "Not long. The first chance he has to arrange an accident, once you and I have left the place."

"That's how I see it," Will said. "If you undertake to pry a confession out of your brother and succeed, we shall be honor-bound to act. If you choose not to try, he has won."

"And if I try and fail?"

"There is still the Coroner. We can turn what evidence we have over to the Crown and hope that justice will prevail. But I am certain you would succeed. He's not afraid of you, Davy—and he should be."

Chapter 15

T he Earl of Grenbrook ran his estate in an orderly way, and that sense of order extended to the arrangement of his home. His own office adjoined a small library where his personal reference books and the records of the estate were kept, some of them dating back more than a century. On the other side of that library was another room that he had set aside as Mark's office.

David Archer stood at the far end of the hall, as tense as the moment before an enemy ship came into range. The door latches were in good working order; he had checked them the night before and knew that Will and Amelia could pass silently from his father's office and into the library, where they would be able to overhear what occurred in the other room. Will had wondered if he should be armed; David had advised against it, but he now wondered if he'd been foolish to do so.

He really didn't have much faith in their plan. But he had nothing better to offer, and he knew that as soon as the Earl found a way to remove him and Will from the house without upsetting his wife, they would have lost the last chance to settle this without dragging the family into the harsh light of scandal.

At least Ronald had been intrigued enough—or perhaps nervous enough—to agree to this meeting. Perhaps he was not as confident as he seemed.

It was time to stop stalling. He had to keep the hall clear for a few moments, in case Ronald looked out to be sure they were alone. Will and Amelia would not make their move until he'd been inside for a full minute.

It took all his resolution to make his feet move down the hall, but as he laid his hand upon the doorknob, he was pleased that it did not tremble.

"Good afternoon, Ronald."

"It is indeed." Ronald sat in his elder brother's chair as though it had always been his by right. "All the questions are settled at last. What was it you wanted to tell me, little brother?"

"That you have not been nearly as clever as you think."

"Oh, but I have." He waved a hand at the well-furnished room. "I have been playing the good boy for days now, listening to endless drivel about crop rotation and the bloodlines of cattle, being drilled on the names and occupations of a herd of faceless peasants. I ought to be congratulated."

"You ought to be arrested," David said, enjoying the startled look that erased Ronald's smirk. "I know you killed Mark. I know where, and I know how."

Ronald managed a convincing laugh. "That's nonsense." He rose suddenly and darted first to the door of the library, then to the hall door. "Alone? You're braver than I thought." Returning to his chair, he leaned back a little. "And more stupid."

"You were seen in the village shortly before Mark's death—long before you officially arrived home."

"So you say. I'd love to see you prove it. In any case, there were plenty of people in the village before his death. Are they all murderers?"

Will and Amelia should be in the next room by now. David heard nothing, but he knew he could rely upon them. "Did any of the others hope to gain what you did? Did anyone else lie to conceal his presence? You chose your accomplice unwisely, though. She could not resist bragging to me that she had seen you here before you made yourself known. You were a little tardy there, Ronald. How was it you let her live so long?"

"If we were speaking hypothetically—"

"Which we are not—"

"Isn't it obvious? The opportunity to dispense with that risk could only occur when her father was away for the night. But really, is it so surprising that I would take my time in returning to this stifling den of respectability?" He shook his head. "Sorry, little brother. Prior to announcing my presence, I took a few days to visit an old acquaintance who was inclined to be obliging, for a price. And while I'd prefer not to flaunt my conquests in the bosom of my family, I think you overreach yourself in concluding that I'm guilty of fratricide."

David refused to be drawn in to the response. "You and your 'acquaintance'—though I hardly think you brought her along—left a spill of gunpowder in the gazebo near the site where Mark was killed."

Ronald snorted. "Is that all? If you hope to convince Father that I've done the heinous deed by showing him a pinch of powder and claiming it's mine, what makes you think he would ever believe you?"

"The attempted ambush when Captain Marshall and I rode back from the village, perhaps. Your boots were beautifully shined when you finally came home, but there were deep scratches beneath the polish. Poor James was beside himself trying to imagine how you did such damage. But we know, don't we?"

With a lazy smile, Ronald said, "*I* know. You can only conjecture."

"And that long absence between the time of Mark's death and your appearance here, following your lie about your whereabouts? We can prove that your commanding officer gave you leave to come home, and no matter how fond you were of your paramour, you might have at least gone to the funeral. Where were you then?"

"Ah, that. I was so crushed by the news that I drank myself insensible, and was too ashamed to show my face the next day."

It was like trying to make a dent in a bowl of water. For every accusation, Ronald had a plausible answer. David began to despair that he'd ever get an honest response. "Is it worth it, Ronald? Four lives gone, one of them your own brother—and for what?"

"For money and power, of course—the money, mainly. What else is there?"

"Quite a lot—but you've never been aware of anything else, have you?"

He laughed again. "You are a pathetic little worm, David. You always have been—and now you've added lying to your sins, as I'm sure our father will inform you if you should be stupid enough to tell him these stories."

Ronald sounded so sure of himself that David wondered for a moment if he actually believed what he was saying. "Lying? Why would I lie about such things?"

"No doubt for the same reason you claim I murdered Mark." At David's genuine puzzlement, he went on, "because then you would be the heir—"

Oh, no. David went numb and cold. *He's right. My God, he's right.*

He hardly heard Ronald rattle on, "And a hero besides. You've apparently had a taste of that, and I'm sure you like it better than being the runt of the litter. But you've no reason to think Pater would believe you—" he stopped, staring at David, and laughed again. "You told him, didn't you? You little fool! Did you think it would do you any good?"

David shrugged, letting his brother mistake the reason for his stunned silence. He took a breath and said, "Not really. I had hoped.... But I've decided that if he's fool enough to take your word—"

"Of course he is. Respectability must triumph at all costs. How could you make such a shocking accusation? Our father would strike you down rather than let you utter it in public— even if he knew it to be true. 'Don't you know what that would do to your mother?'"

That last was delivered in such perfect imitation of the

Earl's tones that David wanted to smash his fist into his brother's smug grin. But he mastered the anger, dropped his eyes, let his shoulders slump. "There is that, isn't there? The suspicion is too terrible to entertain. And I expect a good appearance matters more than the truth."

"Of course it does. Hasn't it always?"

"And you've always been such a plausible liar, haven't you, Ronald? But tell me, brother dear—just between us, since I've no hope of ever proving it—*did* you kill Mark?"

The smirk broadened, and with a thrill of horror David saw the conscienceless killer look out of his brother's eyes. "Just between us, Davy-my-boy? Yes, I did. It was so surprisingly easy, I wish I'd done it years ago. What's more, if you don't go back to your nice little ship, go back to sea and stay there...I'll kill you, too."

"That is *enough!*"

The door from the library slammed open, and the Earl of Grenbrook strode into the room, his face suffused with fury and his eyes fixed on the face of his son and heir. Will and Amelia hovered in the doorway behind him, clearly uncertain of their next move.

The Earl spared a glance for his youngest son, who stood frozen in astonishment. But all he had to say was, "Out." As Ronald made to follow, he said, *"Sit."*

David left the room as quickly as he could, and the library door slammed behind him as Amelia rushed into his arms. A key turned in the lock.

"Oh, Davy, you did it—thank God! But, dear heaven, how horrible. I never wanted to believe it!"

David patted his sister's shoulder absently, meeting Will's eyes. "Neither did I," he said. "Neither did I." And it was the truth; he had not wanted to believe it, even though he had known for certain, known from the start. "Lia, how on earth did you convince him?"

"I didn't have to convince him," she said. "I only asked him to come with us. He had been outside early this morning, Davy, looking at the garden bed beneath the ivy. I asked him to give me five minutes, in Mark's memory. He said he would humor me, but I believe he had been thinking about what you told him yesterday."

"What now?" Will asked, pragmatic as ever.

David tried to think over the sound of violent argument that filtered through the heavy door. "The hallway," he said. "Even if he's locked that door, a servant might pass Mark's study. We should keep this private, if we can."

"Private?" Will said as they crossed through the library and out into the hall. "Davy, it's murder. How can you keep something like murder *private?*"

Will's voice was low and David appreciated it, but he did not want to voice the half-formed fear that filled his mind. He pushed it away with words. "He will not turn a blind eye to this, Will. He loved Mark—more than Ronald, certainly more than me. The family's future was my father's whole purpose, and Mark was that future."

"But to conceal—"

"He will not conceal it." Amelia had gone pale. Her voice was quiet, almost a whisper. "He could not."

Meeting her eyes, David saw that her mind was running in the same direction as his own. He turned to Will. "There will be no question of that. My father is the local magistrate, remember. He would not conceal such a crime, no matter who committed it."

The argument in the study had subsided, the voices lowered to a murmur.

"I think..." David spoke more to his sister than to Will. "I think that he might give Ronald the chance to sign a confession and flee the country before he takes action. A murderer cannot inherit a title, but to have him seized and bound over by his own family...the scandal would be terrible, and I do not know if Mother would survive the ordeal. His greatest purpose will be to protect her."

Amelia nodded mutely.

Will edged toward the door, trying to hear what was going on. "Is it safe to leave him in there, alone with your brother? What's one more murder to—"

A pistol cracked behind the locked door. One shot. The suddenness of it made David jump, but it did not surprise him. "Did Father have a gun?" he asked Amelia.

Her face was white. "Yes. A duelling pistol."

"I wish I had one," Will said. "I'll wager your brother was armed, as well. Why should he balk at one more life?" He moved toward the door as a key turned in the lock, unobtrusively putting himself first in the line of fire.

But, as David expected, it was his father who opened the door, his face an unhealthy shade of red, but set like stone. "Damned disobedient brats!" he said. "I told you to leave!"

"Yes, sir," David answered without moving.

The old man's stare bored into his soul, drawing the moment out until David wanted to turn and walk away— away from this house, away from all of it. But he knew he could not leave. Not now. Not ever. And his father knew it, too.

"I'm sorry," David said. *Sorry I had to show you what Ronald was, sorry Mark is dead, sorry I'm not the heir you wanted. We're stuck with each other now, like it or not.*

"Don't be," his father said. "You did your duty." A spasm of pain crossed his face, and he caught at the doorframe. "Get your sister out of here. Not a sight for—"

He clutched at the air with a low moan, and pitched forward. Will helped David break his fall and lower him to the ground as Amelia screamed, "Papa!" and dropped to her knees.

The Earl was conscious, breathing heavily. He appeared puzzled. Amelia was near tears. "Papa, please, speak to me!"

David heard footsteps coming down the hall. "Will—" But Will had already taken the key out of the office door, locking it again from the hall side. "Thank you! Lia, stay here." He pushed to his feet and ran toward the footsteps, which proved to belong to the butler, who was followed by one of the maids. "Leland, my father has collapsed. I fear it may be his heart. You must send for the doctor immediately."

"Yes, Lieutenant."

Good man, he didn't stop to ask unnecessary questions. "Susan—" He thought it was Susan; she nodded, at any rate—"go fetch two of the footmen. My father has suffered some sort of attack and must be taken to his room immediately."

That attended to, he returned to the crisis. His father was still lying on the floor but was attempting to rise, against Amelia's objections. She'd loosened his neckcloth; trust her to do the sensible thing! Will was kneeling beside them both, unobtrusively checking the Earl's pulse.

David dropped to his knees and took his father's other hand. It was clammy. "Father. We've sent for the doctor. You must stay quiet."

Amelia had regained control of herself. "What shall I do, Davy?"

"Find one of the maids, have her make certain that Father's bed is ready. Then see to it that no one—absolutely no one—disturbs Mother until I have had the chance to speak to her."

"I left Jane with Mother," Amelia said. "I can tell her to say that she's to be left alone, on Father's orders. No one will question that."

"Yes. Good. Be as quick as you may. If we are not here when you return, go to Father's room. I've sent for servants to carry him to bed."

"Bed!" his father muttered. "Can't go to—" He grimaced.

"Lie still, you old fool!" David heard himself snap. "I don't want to tell my mother she's lost another son *and* her husband! I'll see to the rest of it—*trust* me, for once in your life!" He took off his own coat, and put it over his father. "Will—the key?"

Will handed it over without a word. He took it, let himself into the study, and locked the door behind him. The room reeked of gunpowder and blood, the close quarters making the odors more intense than a gundeck after a battle. Ronald sat sprawled in his father's chair, collapsed upon the desk, a pistol in his hand and his brains all over the back of the chair. There was a letter, unblotted, on the desk before him. And there was a leather sack, heavy when David lifted it. It was full of gold sovereigns.

He picked up the letter.

I, Ronald Milton Archer, confess that I shot my brother Mark in order to take his place as my father's heir. I am sorry to have brought this shame upon my family. I beg forgiveness in God's sight.

It was signed. And David could see what had happened as clearly as if he'd been present. The Earl had dictated that letter, holding out the gold and a chance for escape as an inducement—Ronald would never have cared about shaming anyone else. And the prayer for absolution...that, too, would have been his father's doing. Ronald had written this confession, probably at gunpoint, expecting to be given money and the chance of flight.

And then his father shot him dead.

David was certain of that, for two reasons. First off, the gun in his brother's lax hand was his father's duelling pistol. If Ronald had been armed, he'd have held his father off at gunpoint or even shot him, taken the money, and run. But the clincher was that there were no powder burns on Ronald's face or clothing. The shot had to have come from at least a foot away. As magistrate, of course, the Earl could have seen to it that that any contradictory evidence was suppressed. This was outside the letter of the law, well beyond a magistrate's authority, but it could broadly be seen as within the spirit of British justice. The murderer had been apprehended... and justice had been done.

Very well. This would do, at least for now. David blotted the letter, stowed it in his coat pocket, and went back out into the hall just in time to meet Susan and two footmen trotting down the hall a makeshift stretcher. Amelia was at their heels.

He drew her and Will aside, out of earshot, as the servants began tending to their fallen lord. "Father arranged the scene to make it look as though Ronald committed suicide. If we can lay that to his gambling problems, rather than Mark's death, there need never be a whisper of murder. Lia, you go with Father—I'll tell Leland about Ronald. Do not tell Mother, or anyone else, anything about this for now."

"Not even Jane?"

"Can you trust her?"

"Absolutely."

"Very well—but if she's watching Mother I doubt you'll have a chance to speak to her in private before we get things settled. Just stay with Father until Dr. Fiske arrives. If the doctor should ask you what happened, try to let Father explain, if he's able, so we will have some notion of his intentions. Tell Fiske that you saw Father collapse, I told you Ronald was shot...try to seem confused."

She attempted a smile. "I shan't have to try."

He thought back to the mess in the study. "One other thing—send Susan to Mother's room, tell her to send Kirby down here. And have Kirby bring a blanket, sponge, and a basin of water."

He took a moment to take his father's hand again, as the footmen settled him onto the stretcher. "Father? I've been in the study, and I understand what happened. Everything. I shall attend to it. Do you understand?"

The Earl's head lolled to one side; he grimaced. "Good boy. Sorry...sorry I misjudged you. I'm not usually so wrong!"

David could have dealt with anger; an apology from the man who never apologized was more than he could bear. Fighting back tears, he bent and kissed his father's forehead. "Stay with us, you stubborn old mule!"

He took Will into the study, locking the door behind them, and explained the situation. Will agreed that the looming gambling scandal ought to be sufficient cause for suicide. "In fact, Davy, you might say you had spoken to him about it. I have the letter from Sir Percy as evidence, should anyone ask."

"Dr. Fiske and my father are old friends. If he lives, I think he may tell the doctor at least some of the truth—if he has not guessed it himself. If Father dies..." He closed his eyes and took a deep breath as the weight of that possibility pressed down on him. "If he does, we'll have to make the best of it. Fiske is no fool—it wouldn't surprise me if he guesses what's happened. If he suspects that Ronald had something to do with Virginia's death, this—" he gestured at the desk— "should settle the matter. But we must muddle the trail. A man about to shoot himself would not have needed money."

He picked up the sack of coins and hid it away at the back of a bottom drawer, closed the ink-bottle, wiped the pen dry and put it in its holder. The proximity of Ronald's motionless body made his skin crawl; he had an uneasy sense that his brother would suddenly rear back, the lax fingers stiffen into reaching claws...he gritted his teeth and pushed away the fanciful notions, forcing his own reluctant hands to perform the actions.

Will watched solemnly. "What can I do to help?"

Grateful for the distraction, David said, "Will, look at this tableau. Do you see anything to suggest that this might have been anything other than self-slaughter?"

"Only the powder burns. The lack of them, I should say."

"Yes—but you notice that because we were looking for them earlier. There's nothing we can do about that now."

Will glanced at the note. "This is clear evidence of suicide. Do you mean to destroy it?"

"No. My father had something in mind, and we might need it as evidence, but it would be better if we can avoid the mention of murder..." He considered the scene for a long moment, then decided that he was only making things worse. "Will, I am trying too hard to be clever. I think it's best to simply clean this room. In fact, I'm going to have it as tidy as possible before the doctor arrives."

Will bit his lip, then nodded. "Yes. Why should you not? To leave things as they are might suggest that you found something amiss—that you expected official inquiry. You have the note, that surely explains everything. Why would you *not* restore order?"

His words lifted a weight from David's conscience. "Thank you. I've sent for Kirby because I need someone trustworthy to help with this, but I don't mean to say anything in her presence that she could not repeat, under oath, to a coroner. And in any case, we could hardly keep things as they are until an inquest is called. That will be a day or two, at least."

Will nodded, and started at a tap on the door behind him. David turned the key and held it open just wide enough to see that his mother's maid had followed instructions to the letter. "Thank you for coming, Kirby. Did my sister explain what had happened?"

"No, sir, only that there'd been a terrible accident, and your father's been taken ill."

"It's worse than that, I'm afraid. Far worse. I sent for you because I know you will do everything possible to help me and protect my mother."

"Of course, Master David."

He had to admire the way she was pointedly *not* trying to peer past him. "There has been another tragedy. My brother Ronald is dead—"

Kirby's hand flew to her mouth. "No! Oh, my poor lady!"

"—and something about his death distressed my father so very badly that he fell to the ground before our eyes. He is resting in his room now, and we have sent for the doctor. I know that it is beneath your position to help with housework—I cannot in all fairness *require* it of you—but I do ask you to help me make my brother's body presentable for the doctor. There will be gossip in the servants' hall, I know—"

She set her jaw. "Not if *I* have ought to say about it!"

"Exactly. I knew we could depend on you. If you would pass me that blanket, Captain Marshall and I will arrange things to spare you as much distress as possible."

She handed it over, two blankets, in fact, and, for some reason, a roll of bandage. "Is—is there much blood, sir?" she asked.

He was momentarily taken aback. "On the desk...and on the chair. Why do you ask?"

"Well, it is *not* my duty to deal with such things, sir, in the ordinary way, but since Lady Virginia's accident some of the younger maids are nervy. If you mean to keep this as quiet as may be, I had better fetch Mr. Leland. Between the two of us, we can do what needs to be done."

"Thank you," he said. "I think that would be best." He relieved her of the sponge and basin, and locked the door again. "I tremble to think what would become of this family without our people," he said.

"She reminds me of Barrow," Will said. "Where would either of us have been without him to teach us the ropes? Davy, I—I know it is little enough, but would you like me to shift the body?"

"It'll take both of us," David said grimly.

It did, and he was glad of the second blanket, though they found the simplest thing to do was to roll the chair away from the desk and over to one side, and simply slide the body out of it. David avoided looking at his brother's face, but even so it was a relief to finally pull the blanket over that bloody ruin.

He stood, and his eyes met Will's. And then the reality of his situation hit him full force. There would be no little house in London, or Portsmouth, or anywhere else. He was no longer a younger son with a modest competence, free to live where and as he chose. He was Viscount Archer now, the heir of Grenbrook, a man with responsibilities he had not chosen and did not want. He felt a little numb.

"Thank God that's over," Will said.

"I only wish it were. Will, what is to become of us now?"

With a crooked smile, Will said, "I suppose I shall have to call you 'my lord.' And it's funny, but I don't believe I shall mind at all."

He held out his hand, and David seized it like a lifeline. "God, Will—" Both doors were locked, the curtains drawn; he pulled Will close and took the chance of a kiss, letting the comfort of that contact block out all else. He let it draw out as long as he could; no telling when they'd have another opportunity. Then he buried his face in his lover's shoulder and held on for dear life, until he felt his panicked heartbeat slow back to normal.

And then he did his duty. He unlocked the door, admitted the servants, saw to the disposition of his brother's body and the restoration of order in his family's home.

Chapter 16

The next few hours went by in a blur. Dr. Fiske arrived and attended the Earl, giving his opinion that his patient had suffered a heart attack but seemed to be recovering, and in no immediate danger. The Earl, conscious but very weak, told Fiske that Ronald had admitted to pushing his sister-in-law down the stair, and had been given the choice of arrest or suicide. The doctor made a brief inspection of the body—in fact, he lifted the blanket, nodded, and put it back—and agreed that Ronald had died as the result of a gunshot wound to the head, no doubt the result of the accidental discharge of his pistol. He agreed to have a word with the coroner so the family would not have to endure the disgrace of suicide heaped on their other sorrows.

Still wrapped in a mental fog, David found himself outside the door of his mother's room. He'd thought he dreaded confronting Ronald, but this...was there any gentle way he could break such news?

Kirby admitted him with a nod. "She's awake, my lord."

"Thank you." *My lord," she said. To me. Good God, it's real, isn't it?* He took a deep breath and passed through the pleasant sitting room, into the warmth of the bedroom where his mother sat propped up against a mountain of pillows. Her color was good, at any rate. He bent and kissed her cheek. "Mama."

"Oh, my dear son." There was more strength in her hand than he had expected. "I had expected your father. Where is he?"

"He is doing well." There, whatever else, he would not have her fearing the worst. "Mama, he had a very disturbing conversation with Ronald earlier this afternoon, and ...it appears that Ronald shot himself, either during that time, or immediately after it." He could see dread on her face, so he said quickly, "Dr. Fiske thinks Papa has had a heart attack— not a severe one, thank God. He is resting now, and the doctor believes he will recover."

"I must go to him," she said, throwing back the bed-clothes. "Call Kirby."

"But, Mama—"

He had expected frailty and shock. He got, "Son, do as I tell you. I have loved your father for over forty years and if he is ill, my place is beside him. He has enough on his shoulders, I must let him know that he needn't worry about me."

He put out a hand, but as far as he could tell, she was in no more distress than he was himself. Possibly less. "Are you...are you strong enough?"

"Now that I will not have to accuse one of my sons of murdering his brother? Oh, yes, dear, I will do perfectly well. She raised her voice. "Kirby! My dressing gown, please."

He froze, transfixed by her words. "You knew?"

Kirby popped in at the doorway. "Yes, my lady?"

"I must go see my husband, and do not waste time telling me I cannot. My dressing gown and slippers, if you please!" When the maid disappeared, she said, "Yes, dear. When we were seeing to Mark's...final arrangements, I saw that he had been shot from behind. And I thought of poor Lenore, how we never did learn what precisely had become of her, and how evasive Ronald was when I asked him about her death. I knew, then, but I could not bring myself to tell your father."

A sharp laugh forced itself out. "You might have told me!"

"Oh, dear, I could not do that, either. Your father might have thought that you were attempting to accuse your brother for your own benefit. I know that you could not do such a thing, but he has never seen you in your true light."

He could hardly argue with her. He'd said as much to Will, more than once. "What did you mean to do, ma'am? I know you could not have let it pass!"

She shook her head, the ribbons on her cap fluttering. "I—at first, I was horrified. I could not think! If Virginia's child had been a boy, I should have had to tell my darling everything, so he might keep the baby safe. I believe I was hoping that Ronald might ..." She faltered, but dabbed at her eyes and went on, "might show some sign of remorse, and confess what he had done. When he only grew more complacent, I knew I would have to speak, but—oh, Davy, I hope you never see a child of your own body sink so far into evil, and be faced with the choice of exposing him or—"

She began to cry, then, and he was almost relieved to see it. Having carried that same burden himself, he marveled that she had only taken to her bed. Her own son, who had once been a baby as small and helpless as that newborn child in the nursery...He took a step closer and put his arms around her, worried by how small she was, how seemingly fragile. "It will be all right now, Mama. I promise."

Kirby appeared at the door, the dressing gown in her arms. She met his eye and made a discreet withdrawal, returning in a few minutes when the Countess had got herself back under control. "Here you are, my lady. Dr. Fiske says his lordship's not to be fussed over, so you must put on a brave face for his sake. If you please, I have a cold compress here, with a few drops of lavender-water, and if you will let me just put it on your eyelids for a moment..."

"I can see you are in better hands than mine," David said, and withdrew.

⚓ ⚓ ⚓

He sat at the desk that had been his brother's, wondering how he was ever going to grow into the job. At least he need not take on the whole sprawling mass of it immediately, that was a small mercy, but he had to start shouldering some of the burden straightaway. He must learn what to do as fast as he was able. He didn't know how much time he had to do that, either. The tragedies of the past month had pared years off his father's life, and probably his mother's, as well.

It hasn't done much for mine, either, come to that.

How was he to carry on? He could keep Will here for a little while—tell his mother that Commander Marshall had no kith nor kin to go to, and that would be all she needed to know. His father might grumble—to him, of course, and no one else—but David could say that Will's pride had led him to offer to pay his board, and that would serve to goad the Earl's own pride into a declaration that no guest at *his* home would be expected to pay as though Grenbrook were some sort of lodging-house. No, he could keep Will close for awhile...until war resumed, or he grew restless, or Sir Percy came up with some other clandestine assignment.

And after that—what then? Become the Lord of the Manor, and wait for an occasional letter from his old friend and former shipmate, and pray that he would see him once more, if duty ever brought him into Plymouth?

No more shore leave together. No little house in Portsmouth. No Will in his arms or bed, or even in a carriage. Never again.

He buried his face in his hands, wishing there were some way he might pass this burden on to someone else. But there was no one. Only himself, the least promising twig on the Archer tree, left to sustain and protect the family.

A gentle tap at the door interrupted his somber reflections. Hoping it was Will, he called, "Come in."

Amelia peeked tentatively around the door. "Am I disturbing you?"

"Oh, not at all. Come in. I appreciate the interruption." As she quietly closed the door behind her, he gestured at the pile of agricultural books and notes arranged neatly on the desk. "I was just wishing that little Michaela had been little Mark. I'd have made a better guardian than a Viscount. Lia, how am I going to manage all this?"

She dropped a quick kiss on his cheek before choosing the chair nearest his own. "I know you can do it, my dear. I only wish you did not *have* to do it, that you could be free to go back to sea with Captain Marshall. I know you would much rather be with him."

"Oh, don't distress yourself over that." He hesitated, wondering how much he could tell her. "I might not have stayed at sea even if Mark were still alive. Will and I have grown close, over the years, and when I was wounded, he—" No, best not to follow that path any further. "That is, before I knew whether I would even recover enough to go back to sea, I began to consider whether that was how I wanted to spend my life—and probably end my life. I'm not a cat, with nine of them to risk, and a naval career was never my ambition. You remember why I ran off to sea in the first place."

"I do." She smiled. "And I always thought it a great pity that you could not have stayed behind to hear Father boast about your gumption. He was proud that you had the character to want to do right by the girl, even if you hadn't the sense to realize such an alliance was impossible, and that you weren't going to settle for being anyone's baby brother, not even if it meant you had to start as an over-aged midshipman."

"I wish he'd found it in him to say that to me," David said. "Though Uncle Jack did pass on the money he sent for my kit. That rather surprised me."

"Father always was harder on you boys than he wanted to be, I think. He felt he had to be stern to make you strong. And the longer he went on that way, it seemed the more difficult it was for him to give you any encouragement."

"It worked, I suppose," he said. "It worked very well, in Mark's case."

"He does care about our happiness, Davy. Look at how he gave Mark the Four-Acre to experiment with, and gave Anne his blessing even though he had reservations about

Clive. Or the way he's given his word that I will be able to be a spinster if I choose." She glanced over. "You will honor that, too, I hope?"

"Oh, for heaven's sake, Lia, of course I will, though I think you are perfectly silly in believing you must settle for that. Still, if there's no man who takes your fancy, I would never press you to marry just to get you off my hands. If you like, you can have the house in London that Grandmother left me. I shall probably beg you to stay here and act as hostess someday, after Mother is gone. The most unnerving aspect of this whole change in my status is that I must now consider what I shall do about providing an heir, when the very last thing I want is—"

"A wife," she finished. "Because there is someone you love more."

He felt the tingle of danger, staring at his sister as he tried to imagine why in the world she had said such a thing. "What do you mean?" he asked carefully.

"Oh, Davy, my dear, please don't look so stony-faced!" She sprang up, and went to the door, leaning out to peer down the hall in either direction. "Yes, we are perfectly alone." She closed the door and returned, pulling her chair very close, taking his hand. "I may be mistaken, and if so, I do beg your pardon. But it is clear to me that you love Captain Marshall a great deal, and unless I am much mistaken, his feelings for you are the same."

She did not say that in an accusing way. She said it as though she approved, as though it were perfectly acceptable. Had the tragedies of the past weeks unhinged her reason?

"What can I say to that, Lia?" he asked helplessly. "'Yes' would condemn me before God and man, and put his life at risk as well. 'No' would…" He shook his head. "I'll not lie to you. I cannot answer at all."

"You need not. And please, do not think I accuse you!" She folded her hands in her lap, and studied her fingers. "I am doing this all wrong, Davy. I had hoped to suggest an answer for us both."

"What do you mean?"

She kept her eyes down. "I speak of such feelings—and yes, I know they are forbidden, but that does not stop them, and not all the Bibles in the world will convince me they are evil—because that is the reason I do not wish to marry. I wish to live quietly with Jane because I love her and she loves me. Once we are well into our thirties we shall be just another pair of old maids—"

"You *what?*" he demanded. "Amelia, how could—what—how—?"

She blushed bright pink but met his eyes squarely. "I wish you would not ask such questions unless you are *certain* you are willing to hear the answers!"

"No, no!" he said hastily. "I assure you, I do not, but..." He shook his head, not only taken flat aback but dismasted as well. "And I thought this situation was already too complicated for me to handle!"

"Well, you needn't do anything if you would rather not," she said. "But it did occur to me that when you are head of the family—and I hope that day is many years in the future—we might all live together very comfortably and discreetly. No one would think ill if Captain Marshall were to visit us when he was not at sea. He does seem to love the Navy, but you really cannot leave us for such a perilous career."

He was so far past nonplussed that he hardly knew what to say. "And what does Jane think of this proposal?" he asked finally.

"She thought it would be lovely if I were to marry Captain Marshall and she could marry you," Amelia said. "For appearance, mainly, but also to make us one family. I did point out that we might have mistaken your friendship with him, and even if we had not, either of you might have plans to marry someone else altogether. And she was afraid that you might think her ambitious."

"Ambitious?"

"To be Countess, of course," she said. "Surely you

realize that you *will* be expected to marry."

"Yes," he said, not bothering to hide his irritation. "I do realize that. Father has already pointed out that it was a damned good thing—pardon the language, it was his, not mine—that I hadn't tied myself to that damned actress when I was too damned young and stupid to think about my responsibility to The Family."

She smiled, obviously recognizing the paternal style. "I thought he might have said something. I am sorry, Davy. Truly, I am. I used to envy your freedom to run off to sea, but we're none of us free, are we?"

"Oh, we're better off than most," he said. "And I must not feel sorry for myself just because I have choices to make that most men would give their right arms for. After all, I suppose I *could* abandon my responsibilities and go off to sea—or to London, or anywhere else." He shrugged. "But I can't, you know. Even if I didn't care twopence for any of you—and I do—the title would just follow me around like an albatross, and land on me sooner or later."

"I'm sure Mr. Coleridge would be amazed to hear his poem used in such a context."

"Well, follow me around like the Ancient Mariner, then. I sympathize with the old fellow—this is partly my own doing."

"It was not—no more than it was mine. How could either of us allow Ronald to profit from murdering our brother? How long do you think it would have been before Father had an 'accident' of some sort?"

Put that way, he was able to accept her absolution. "I know."

"Well then, what do you think of the idea?" she persisted. "I know it is unusual, but just consider our sister Mary. She wed Lord Crandall for rank and fortune, and made no secret of her ambition. He married her for her beauty and charm. If there is no great love between them, they are at least satisfied with the arrangement, and their children seem happy."

"She is fond of him, I think," Davy said, though he'd said much the same to Will long ago about Mary's businesslike arrangement.

"And I think you and Jane are fond of one another. Friendship is a good basis for a marriage, is it not? For that matter, if things had been otherwise, I would have looked favorably upon Captain Marshall."

"And he on you, I think— Oh, this is absurd, Lia. We could never make such an arrangement work."

"Why not?" she asked.

He started to reply, but was unable to form a rebuttal. Her suggestion was, in fact, the first glimpse he had of a future that might include Will in a socially acceptable way, even if he were not willing to leave the sea and make his home in Devonshire. As long as they were building castles in the air, why not build a grand one? What if Will were to be given some sort of assignment that would allow him to stay in England—a position in the Admiralty, for instance? That wouldn't hold the glory or chance of prize-money that he would get from regular service in the Navy, but if he were to marry Amelia, her marriage portion added to his prize money would provide a comfortable living. He would not need to buy a place for himself, either. This house was easily large enough for them all, particularly since there was likely to be a dearth of offspring.

Will would never consider such a thing, of course. Not only was Will averse to life ashore, he could be amazingly stubborn, and David had long suspected that he was actually afraid of women.

But Will did like Amelia, at least. That might be a start.

"I'll speak to him," he said.

Chapter 17

"If this is a joke," Marshall said, "I don't think much of it." He had thought that Davy merely wanted to get out of the house for awhile, when he suggested that they take a ride together, and he was happy to oblige. The day was overcast, but the sun was doing its best to break through the clouds. They had ridden to one of those lovely quiet places Amelia had mentioned, a narrow stream where they dismounted and sat on a few tumbled stones, watching the water run. Will had been content—until he was faced with this absurd proposition.

"You know I would never joke of such a thing, Will. But this could solve so many of our problems."

"And create far more, I think!"

"How so? It would mean that this could be your home, too. You would not even have to go back to sea, if you chose to stay."

"A year ago, you were urging me to go back to sea." Will smiled at the memory, bittersweet though it was—he and Davy huddled together under the covers at Kit's estate in Jamaica, waiting for the dawn that might part them forever. "You spoke of duty, and how I was needed."

"Perhaps I've grown more selfish—or less willing to see you sacrificed. I suppose you will be needed. And, Will, if—no, *when* the call comes, I expect you will answer it."

"It's all I know how to do." As the words left his mouth, he realized how true that was, and how much it meant to him—that there was something he could do, and do well.

Davy raised an eyebrow. "Are you speaking of the Navy, or commanding a ship?"

"They're one and the same."

Davy reached across the chasm that had opened between them—only a foot or so between them, but it seemed like miles—and put his hand on Will's. "No, they're not, not really. England is an island. All things come and go by water. What matters, I think, is where your ambition truly lies. I have a cousin whose family owns a fleet. If what you want is a ship, I know one could be found."

"A merchantman?"

Davy smiled. "Well, yes—and your face tells me that you do *not* consider that the same thing."

"I had never considered it at all. But would that not make me a hired hand, and 'in trade,' and less than a gentleman?"

"If you were the owner, or even part owner—no, hear me out, Will—a man who owns his ship can do as he likes with it, so long as you don't mean to start smuggling."

"I could never afford to run a ship."

"*You* could not. *We* could, together. This estate has interest in some of the major trading companies. If you were to use some of your prize-money to buy interest in a ship, no one save our man of business need know what the division of shares might be."

Will saw the problem with that immediately. "I have no head for business, either. Nor any experience—"

Davy waved a hand impatiently. "Nor any need—what do you think a man of business is for? But if you must, go back to the Navy, or something like it. We might see if Sir Percy has enough influence to get you a post with the Sea Fencibles."

"He couldn't possibly. They were disbanded."

"They'll be re-formed quickly enough when the war resumes. Can you think of a better job for someone with intelligence experience than as a spy-catcher, intercepting smuggled gold and information? You would be the ideal man for a command in that service, and if you were stationed near Plymouth—"

"Impossible!"

"Will, I don't mean to cause you distress. I am only try-ing to discover some way that we may at least see one an-other from time to time. God knows I did my best, but you set me ashore—" He raised a hand, forestalling Will's pro-test. "I do not blame you, I should probably feel the same in your place. In any case, my duty lies here now. I could not go with you now, even if you would have me."

Will cursed his own weakness. "It's not that I don't want you—"

"I know, Will." Davy held Will's eyes in that contact more intimate than a kiss, then looked away. "I know. And yet here we are, where neither of us wants to be."

He released Will's hand, stood and walked to the edge of the water. "Perhaps I'm only playing make-believe in think-ing there is any hope for us at all. I look out at this land, this beautiful place, and I see an army of people, all counting on me to care for them. More than that—they count on me to marry and raise a child who will see to it that the place is looked after when I'm gone. There is an *oblige* that goes with *noblesse*, when all's said and done."

"Other officers leave their wives to manage," Will said. "Look at Lady Pellew. Sir Edward has no qualms—"

"That situation is entirely different," Davy replied. "My mother would never attempt to take the reins here, even if she were able. And no matter how fond he may be of Amelia, there is no way my father would allow his daughter to step into his shoes in managing the estate, even though I am sure she could do it. But you forget our original dilemma. As I said long ago, if I were to stay in the Navy it would only be if I were to serve with you. Are you saying that you have had a change of heart on that subject?"

Will shook his head. "I wish that I could, but even so—"

"Yes. Even so, everything has changed. I care about my home. I care, despite myself. I had not expected to feel such an obligation, but even before I suspected Ronald, the thought of watching him loot Grenbrook to support his own vices...I thank God we were able to stop him. I'll never be the man Mark was, but I mean to do my best."

"I know you will," Will said. It should have been easy to be angry with Davy for his ridiculous proposition, but he found it impossible. With their dream of a life together already foundered, it was no surprise that his lover might snatch at this improbable scheme. "It's simply...Davy, I know you used to joke about my marrying your sister, but—I think she likes me, but I know she does not love me. Why in the world would she even suggest such a thing?"

"Because she has no real desire for a husband," Davy said.

Will blinked stupidly. "Would you care to explain what you mean by that?"

"Will, I would like to. In fact, that is why I brought you out here, away from everyone. I must ask you not to shout, or get excited." He came back, sat close, and lowered his voice. "Please try to be calm."

"I am— " He caught himself and took a deep breath. "Very well. I am calm."

"You're not, but thank you for making the effort. Now, do you remember how Barrow discerned the precise nature of our friendship, and decided to keep it secret out of regard for us?"

"Yes. What has that—"

"It's much the same thing. Amelia has also discerned—"

"Oh, no," Will said. "Your sister? Davy, what would a maiden lady know about—"

"Love?" Davy's smile was ironic. "Will, she *is* my sister. Until I met you, she was the one person in the world with whom I could be myself, though of course I never told her of all the years I was smitten with you. She and I were speaking of the changes in my situation, particularly the fact that I am now expected to marry and beget an heir—something I recall you once urged me to do, in no uncertain terms."

"Yes, but—"

"She suggested that we might all help one another. You

could marry her with no obligation to give her a child, though that is something you might both reconsider at some point; it would not distress me in the least. I could marry Cousin Jane, and provided we were all extremely discreet—"

"Davy, that might do very well for us, but it hardly seems fair to the ladies. And what's so funny?"

Davy's eyes were dancing. "My dear Captain Marshall, the ladies have their own arrangement. Why do you think they wished to set up a spinster establishment together?"

That was a notion that Will's mind could not encompass. He could feel his ears turning red.

"Try not to dwell on it," Davy advised kindly. "I hardly imagine they reflect too much on the particulars of what we do when we are private together. At least, I hope to God they don't!"

Will closed his eyes. It didn't help. But since he knew next to nothing about women, his imagination soon ran blessedly dry.

"Will?" Davy prodded his shoulder. "Speak to me, sir!"

"I would if I could think of anything to say. It sounds mad."

Davy smiled, relaxing a little. "It does, I agree. And there's the matter of an heir, which Jane is apparently willing to provide if I wish—and Lord knows, she'd have the worst of the bargain. I am...undecided on that aspect of the question. But that isn't a dire necessity, since we'd also have the unentailed property. Even if Grenbrook were to go to some cousin or other, the ladies would be left with a handsome living after you and I are gone. Assuming we go first, of course."

"It all seems rather cold-blooded," Will said. "Less so, perhaps, than if you were to marry some stranger for the sake of an heir—"

"Not cold-blooded at all," Davy objected. "If you want *sangfroid* at its chilliest, look at Ronald's alliance with poor Lenore. He married her to get his hands on her inheritance, and, I'm certain, did away with her as soon as possible after her grandparents died. This would be a matter of four people who care about one another forming a family for mutual support and protection. When you look at it, Will, isn't that what a family is meant to be?"

Will felt backed into a corner. "Mr. Archer, I hardly know these ladies! I met them barely a fortnight ago, and you are suggesting that I—"

That, finally, stopped Davy's campaign. His face fell. "My God, you're right. I apologize, Will. I've known them all my life, and I feel I've known you at least that long, so it seemed...Forgive me. Let us speak no more of it."

"I am not refusing to consider the idea," Will amended. "Rationally, I can see the merit in it. But your sister may change her mind. She is young, after all—"

"She's twenty-four," Davy said. "She had three seasons in the London marriage marts, gracefully declined several offers, and so far as I can tell, is entirely sure in her mind regarding what she wants. And I don't mind saying I was never so surprised in my life as when she told me what that is! But I can understand her feelings, because it's so very close to what I want myself. And I believe that together we might accomplish it."

Will refused to be distracted. "I would be a terrible husband."

"But an excellent friend—which, I believe, is all she would ask you to be."

"That, I might manage." It seemed Davy had all the answers. Why was he being so contrary? Will didn't know many women, but he had to admire Lady Amelia, even if it was due mostly to her close resemblance to her brother. But he didn't want to hope. He was, he realized, afraid to hope. "Must we decide immediately?"

"Of course not. We've had three deaths in the family in the space of a month, and an engagement or wedding anytime soon would be completely out of the question. People are bound to talk, and I expect they will look at the manner of Ronald's death and draw their own conclusions. No, the last thing we want to do is call attention to our activities."

Will relaxed a little.

"The only thing I must do, for now," Davy said, "is avoid a fatal accident. In six months or so, I might start hinting that Jane and I are considering an alliance. It would be better to wait awhile longer before you and Amelia made any serious decision, though I admit the idea of a double wedding, with all of us together at the altar, has a certain appeal."

Will was about to make a sarcastic retort, but something in that image resonated in his soul. "If we have time to consider our course..."

"Yes, so long as you manage to stay alive! In a way, this situation suits me very well—I can resign my commission for the same reason Mark did a few years back, and leave no one wondering if I've lost my nerve. And it's no deception. I *am* urgently needed here at home. I know nothing about how to run this place—and that's not the only thing I need to learn. I'm nowhere near ready to step into my father's shoes."

Will had the sense of Davy drawing away, as the land did when one set sail. He wanted to reach out and seize him, but knew that would make no difference. "You'll be in Parliament one day," he said quietly.

Davy grimaced. "Yet another reason I hope my father recovers completely and has a long, full life. I hate politics. But yes, that's very likely. And it's why I pray you will not desert me."

"But...from the sound of it, you'll have a wife, if you want one."

"In name only. That's all many men have, I suppose. But after what you and I have had together, that is not enough."

"Davy—it's everything I had hoped for, for you. Even better than I'd dared imagine—"

"Damn it, Will! Stop imagining my life for me! What makes you think that's what *I* had hoped for? For God's sake, I don't want a title. I don't want a wife." He looked up, his eyes pleading. "I want *you.* I need one person strong enough to hold fast when the world goes mad. Even if you were only home once in a long while, even if the Navy has first claim on you...if you were married to my sister, you would legally be a part of my family. If you left the Navy, you would have a home. If you were hurt, we could care for you. If you—" he looked away. "If you were killed, at least I would *know*."

He let out a deep breath. "My apologies. I am verging on the maudlin. No doubt if you went out in a blaze of glory I would hear, eventually, in any case." He got up, wandered a few steps away, then turned. "It's your decision, Will," he said. "It always has been. I realize that any choice will be difficult for you, but—" he spread his hands, palms up. "I have no choices left me. What do you want?"

"What?"

"What do *you* want for us, Will? What do you want for *yourself?*"

The question stopped him dead. Since he had joined the Navy, what he wanted had been what he supposed anyone would want—promotion, prize money, recognition in the *Naval Gazette*. Did not every midshipman dream of the day he might make Post Captain, with his foot securely on the ladder of promotion to Admiral?

Back in Jamaica, all that had turned to ashes. He had been ready to throw it all over for Davy, for a life shuttling petty cargo among the islands. He had more options now, all of them better—and one of them included staying in the Navy, on that clear path to Post Captain. He had only one more step to go.

"Will?"

"I—I'm sorry. I had never considered that."

Davy laughed aloud and sat down, shaking his head. "Oh, Will. I might have known. Try considering that, if you please. Imagine your life, ten years from now. What might it be like, if all goes well? What would you hope for it to be? Is there a place in it for me?"

"Of course!" Will said without thinking—but that was

the only thing that came easily. What would he do if he left the Navy, came ashore for good? He knew nothing of farming, and there seemed no place for him in the running of an estate such as this. But he could run a ship, and he knew that a merchant captain might do very well for himself.

If he stayed in the Navy, at least for a time, that would be easiest of all. He would have no say in where he was sent, might well wind up on the other side of the world and be gone for years. He might never return. Since there was no one else who had a claim on his affection, what would he risk, really, by going along with this mad scheme?

He looked up and saw that Davy was watching him once again, his eyes the blue-grey of wind and water. That beautiful face, unswerving loyalty...and a body that loved fully, a heart that would not permit love to be sullied with shame. David Archer had become part of his life, the center of his very existence.

Will had held command for a short while without his love beside him. He could do it again, if he had to. But for how long? How long before his soul withered away under that terrible solitude? He craved the company of his fellow man less than most, but he knew that he had changed from the boy he had once been, an ambitious midshipman who wanted his own ship more than anything and had no close connections.

He had one now. This love had come to him through a most extraordinary set of circumstances that would never occur again...nor would he wish for anything like it with anyone else. "I don't mean to be such a trial," he said at last.

"Nor do I. I do not want to lose you, but if you want your freedom, I cannot hold you."

"*No.* No, the last thing I want is to be free of you. But I must have some purpose—I cannot hang on your sleeve here, any more than you could hang about in Portsmouth waiting for me."

"Be honest, then—what better arrangement could we have? You've found you can't run a ship with me standing beside you like a walking target."

"More like my heart in the open, an easy target risk for any stray shot—"

Davy smiled crookedly. "Oh, Will...that bad?"

He shrugged. "Yes. I'm sorry."

"There's no need for apology now. Fate seems to have made the decision for both of us, given me a better task than hanging in limbo for months on end, waiting for you to spend a few hours ashore. I had dreaded that prospect—but I have a man's work now, real responsibilities. I shall miss the freedom, but I think I'll be better for having the place to care for while you're gone. For you, it would be no worse than it is for any officer who leaves his sweetheart ashore and sails off to battle. You know I will always be here when you return. If you still want me."

"I know. And I do want you, Davy. Of course I do."

"Then we will find a little time to be together. We will make the time. No matter how much I might be needed here on the estate, a few days now and then would hardly matter. If I knew your ship was due in Portsmouth, I'd hand the whole circus over to our manager and hie myself off to Pompey. And we'd take the long road home, Will—in a closed carriage."

It might work. It just might. And the image of a double wedding...the two of them standing up together before God and man, even if they were camouflaged by a pair of brides, struck a chord deep in his heart. Almost against his better judgment, Will said, "Perhaps we might attempt an engagement, and see how we fare."

Davy's face lit up, and Will added, before he was tempted to do something foolish, "A very *long* engagement."

"We need to discuss this in more detail," Davy said. "Privately. Captain Marshall, I must travel to London to resign my commission. Would you do me the honor of accompanying me?"

~End~

About the Author

Lee Rowan has been writing since childhood, but professionally only since spring of 2006, with the publication of her Eppie-winning novel, *Ransom*. She is a lady of a certain age, old enough to know better but young enough to do it anyway. A confirmed bookaholic with a wife of many years, she is kept in line by a cadre of cats and a dog who gets her away from the computer and out of the house at least once a day.

LaVergne, TN USA
17 March 2011
220564LV00001B/81/P